Other works by Robin Merrill

Romantic Suspense

Some Like It Red Hot

Red Hot August Night (forthcoming)

Mystery Suspense

"Fast Pace", *Medley of Murder,* Red Coyote Press

"Coffee Break", *Map of Murder,* Red Coyote Press

Far Flung Places (forthcoming)

Sci-Fi/Paranormal Suspense

Awakening the Senses (forthcoming)

To Queen Bee
Enjoy life - It's Hot!
Robin Merrill
Tucson 2-21-09

Some Like it Red Hot

Robin Merrill

ISBN 978-0-9774306-4-2
LCCN 2007943179

Published by Acacia Publishing, Inc.
Phoenix, Arizona
www.acaciapublishing.com

Printed in the United States of America

Cover Design by Kelly Isola

Dedication

Arwyn Sophia Kuhr
January 17, 2007

Sidney Leigh Lyman
November 10, 2006

Live Strong

Theories pass. The frog remains.
Jean Rostand

Acknowledgements

Finding people to thank for their help and support is not difficult. They are legion. Family, friends, writing buddies who have launched similar dreams on the treacherous voyage to publication. Others who contributed along the way. Finding the right words to say to these people, however, is not so quick and easy, for I would have literally failed without each one.

Yet I don't think they realize how much I needed them. Their encouragement that my work merited the struggle and sacrifice to persevere. Their help and support as I absorbed the skills to navigate the course. Their honesty in sharing their own stories, and their excitement in awaiting mine.

In particular, I thank my daughters Llewellyn and Dharma—all my family, truly, especially Nancy—writers Susan Budavari, Merle Mccann and many others, editors Donna Hanna and Carmen Uquidi-Pratt. Long-time friends Marilyn Lemons, Karen Utt, Jeff and Diane Nayer, the Musker family, and those newer, Pat and Diane Lyman, the Kuhrs—especially my son-in-law Frank—and a slew of others old and new who deserve mention but that would take a book in itself. Thanks to RHS queens Barb, Janet, and Terri for their wonderful help, also my publisher, Karen Gray.

I'm deeply appreciative of the Red Hat ladies and RV people I've interviewed whose stories directly inspired scenes and characters in this book. If it isn't criminal, it probably began with one of their stories.

Most of all, thanks to all of you who read my work. I hope you have as much fun in the reading as I have in the writing. If you want more information, or have a story to tell me, visit my site at www.robin-merrill.com.

Robin Merrill

Chapter 1

"You were real lucky, Lotsi," John, the mechanic, told me as he cleaned his greasy hands on a faded red cloth. "The damage could've been a lot worse." We stood together beside my thirty-six foot RV in the crowded shop stall, examining the stripped down wheel well. Dual wheels and their components lay stacked to one side.

John explained the mysteries of hubs, axles and bearings while I stood simmering in the Las Vegas heat, stinking of fire retardant and burnt oil. My fifty-eight year old brain still hadn't recovered from the shock of seeing my home hooked behind Big Daddy, the giant truck that towed me into town, and I struggled to make sense of John's explanation.

I do mean struggled. Could anything be more boring than axel assemblies? Nothing came to mind. Yet now that I lived in a collection of such mechanical parts, understanding the greasy world of my motorhome seemed necessary. So I bucked up, studied the dissected axle, and listened harder to my instructor. My sexy, intriguing instructor.

"See this discoloration?" John said as he pointed to an area on the axle.

Squinting, I noted the delicate mottled shades of blue and purple on the textured surface and some irreverent part of me thought it would make an interesting 3-D wall hanging, matted in that lovely blue.

"Took a lot of heat to do that," he said, "but even worse is the galling. That's the warping and pitting right here on the metal surface. See that?" His finger traced over the damaged area, right where the intriguing pattern was heaviest.

"Seized bearings can do this much damage, but another few yards, a few seconds, and that there axle wouldn't have just blued, you'da had a fire, for sure. Even if you'd saved your RV, there'd be a new hub, maybe the whole axle, new tires. Serious bucks. As it is, we can repair the galling and replace the bearings, run you about $2,700, maybe $2,900."

At first I felt lucky, damn lucky, then sticker shock hit and I blinked away fun images of wall hangings. "Yikes! How, ah, how long do you think the repairs will take?"

"Well now, that's the other thing." John threw the rag on the tool bench behind us, cocked his hip and settled his hands on each hipbone, accenting his superior body.

I'd noticed that body right off. He was a good-looking man, younger than I was—all the good ones were now days—but not by too much. Nothing wrong with a younger man when you're just looking, right?

That's all I've been doing for a lot of years. Just looking.

So look I did. His uniform helped. The trim fitting dark work pants, showing his male assets and a few grease stains. The tan shirt, with a logo and his name conveniently displayed, stretched across his muscled chest. The bit of tattoo I could see on his bicep below the rolled up sleeve gave my eyes an excuse to linger. Just looking.

"We order parts today," John said, getting me back on track with my wheel bearings and not my libido, "it'll take three or four days to get them, another day or two on the rack. If we can't smooth the galling, that's a different ballgame. New axle. Add a week or so, another couple grand. You got a place to stay?"

"Yes, I do. I'm meeting some friends at the RV Park over by Boulder Station. I'll stay with them."

Then I thought about what this stay in the shop meant. Oh, god. The sick feeling that had festered in my gut for several hours tightened into a painful knot. Homeless. I was now officially homeless. A turtle without its shell.

I pressed a fist against my stomach. The next two weeks were supposed to be a welcome respite, a buffer between the labor dispute that ended my career and the coming awkward reunion with my daughter and granddaughter. I needed this time with my friend Gwen Evans and her husband Shay to recover from months of stress and uncertainty, to gain some emotional stability before tackling my family.

Now it seemed Murphy's Law had caught up with me, and things had indeed gone wrong. Again. Yes, it could have been worse. But I had a terrible feeling Murphy wasn't done with me yet.

Earlier this afternoon, before Murphy came to call, I'd been in my motorhome approaching Las Vegas, happily messing with the radio. I had the radio buttons nailed, one of the few gadgets I'd figured out in the RVs cockpit. That's what the salesman called it. The cockpit.

Granted, there were enough gauges and dials and buttons and switches to rival an airplane, but the lumbering gas-driven Rexall sure didn't give me that thrill of flying low I had cruising in my Acura RL. Well, the one I used to own.

Four days of satellite music were enough. One station after another ended up sounding like TV dinners—more of the same old thing. Like the last ten years of my life.

I switched from satellite to FM, ran up and down the band searching for a decent Las Vegas station with a strong signal. Not much happening. According to the GPS display, I was eighty miles out, heading in on I-15 in a roundabout route from Seattle through Salt Lake City.

At least *I* thought it was roundabout. The GPS program thought it was the best way to get from my former home in Emerald City to Sin City, the fantasy world of gamblers and conventioneers. I'm not a gambler, but a few years ago, I'd joined over 5,500 women decked out in purple and red for an annual Red Hot Ladies Club convention in Las Vegas, so I'd already experienced the fantasy.

Having a good time wasn't all the RHLC meant to me, though. It'd helped me realize I'd become intimidated at being an older woman in our culture, especially in the business world. Yes, I'd fought my way up the corporate ladder to upper management. Now that I approached sixty, my company wanted to trade me in for two thirty-something guys. I almost let them get away with it, until I remember what a fellow Red Hot Lady said and decided by God I wasn't dead, I wasn't dumb, and I sure as hell wasn't done with them yet. Not by a long shot.

So I'd launched a counteroffensive, and now I was a victor of sorts, taking the scenic route into Las Vegas, still trying to find a radio station.

Seventy miles out. A swing in the road caused the GPS map to shift, or maybe it was time for one of the odd rearrangements it did occasionally. I glared at the little black screen stuck to the huge RV front window. At least it didn't yak at me.

I've resisted using a GPS for years now. All those buttons to push and instructions to read and maps with arrows going this way and that to follow and display bars to keep track of and somehow I am supposed to watch the road and negotiate traffic at the same time? Yeah, right.

That's when The Voice announces, "You have missed the turn. Recalibrating route."

Part of me longs for the good old days when I threw a tent and a box of camping junk in the car and my daughter

Kaitlynn and I took off for the mountains. Then the fifty-eight-year-old part of me considers the queen-sized bed, refrigerator, air conditioning, stove, lights, bathroom—yeah, I'm spoiled. Now days I leave camping in the rough to the younger set.

However, high tech camping comes with high tech work. There's the blasted GPS, the remote rear camera, hydraulic levelers, water tanks, sewer hookups and dumps, and the satellite TV antenna. As for me, I'm still working on driving into cramped gas stations and backing into tiny spaces at RV Parks.

Jeez, what is with the reception around here? Surely, I was close enough by now to...ah ha! There it is. The beat catches hold in an explosion of sound as the lyrics expose the newsroom boys' lust for dirty laundry.

Who is that singer? Funny how I can sing the words, lift them straight from some deep recess in my memory bank, but the name of the guy eludes me. Does the mind store names and tunes in different places? This is driving me nuts. I listen to the voice, that distinctive voice. I know that voice. That's...that's...Don Henley!

I smiled, stoked with triumph.

The tunes just kept coming. It'd been ages since I was cruising like this. Years sloughed off in jagged bits of shell. Outside are miles of the same sort of rock, sand, scrub, and bare hills I'd been driving through for hours on end. Inside, I'm walking with Billy Joel along his river of dreams, and my dreams soar right along with that snappy rhythm.

Thank you God for this miraculous victory snatched from despair, freedom to reach for *my* dreams, *my* goals, this late in life. I think about how most people search for their river of dreams, but I'm living mine. No more boss. No more house hanging around my neck. From now on I'm free to travel when I want, where I want! I'm living life on *my* terms. Life is *so* good.

My whole body is dancing in the Rexall's modified recliner that is my seat of power, high above mere cars and pickups, the mysterious and macho cockpit of techno-gadgets mine to command, just as soon as I can figure them out.

That's when Murphy shows up. One of those mere cars pass by, the passenger hanging from his open window, frantically waving and pointing back at my rig.

What the...?

I check my offside mirror. Is that smoke? Good lord, that is definitely smoke, rising from the rear passenger side. I kill the music and pull over. I'd seen a few cars burning on the roadside over the years, read of deaths from car fires. My heart bangs away in my chest. I couldn't stop fast enough.

Turning off the engine, I grabbed the fire extinguisher as I released the door and jumped to the ground.

Smoke rose from the rear tire well in a thick column. No fire, but I wasn't taking any chances. I struggled with the plastic band on the extinguisher handle. It wouldn't come off. I jerked and twisted. Nothing.

Cripes, what good is a fire extinguisher if you can't use the damn thing when you need it? Filled with terror, I almost wet my pants. Any second now, flames would explode from all that smoke. I held the cylinder tight and gave a giant yank on the band. It broke loose and I blasted the huge dual tires, saving some of the foam in case the flames I feared burst—please God, don't let it happen—from the smoking wheel.

My hands trembled. I crouched lower and shifted the extinguisher to release another gush of foam from a different angle. My overactive imagination created images of towering flames engulfing the entire rig. I muttered a few more prayers and sprayed some more and watched the smoke slowly dissipate.

There I stood, watching my home smoke, stranded along the highway. In the middle of nowhere, in a desert with heat well over a hundred degrees. Alone. Why was it again I wanted to RV full-time?

Hours later, I still pondered that question standing in the smelly shop with the sexy mechanic. Tension ate at my stomach, dollar signs rattled around in my brain as my vacation high leaked out drip by drip in a growing puddle of oil, and all I could do was stare at my RV, propped up on a set of megajacks.

I'd owned the damned thing less than a week.

"I'm glad you have someplace to stay," John said. Then he gestured toward the bits and pieces of my home scattered on the soiled concrete floor. "We'll get this reassembled in a jiffy and parked so you can offload whatcha need. First, let's head back to the office and get the parts ordered before today's deadline. Don't want to add an extra day to your wait."

No siree, no extra days allowed. I wanted my home back. I wanted my stuff!

Walking across the lot to the sanctuary of the air-conditioned office building, I told myself to think of this experience as shaking out the bugs. Every new venture had bugs, right? Used vehicle like this, should probably expect more. That didn't help the knots in my stomach so I tried another angle. Look, it's simply a major home repair, like fixing the roof after a storm. My stomach churned.

"Where you headed next?" John interrupted my anxiety attack. "If we've got a shop nearby, we offer free follow-up on this here work, and a 20% discount on any other maintenance or repairs. Save you some bucks."

Hmmm, saving bucks sounded good. "I'll be in the San Francisco area in a couple of weeks."

He threw me a sexy grin. "Hey! Got us a shop in San Rafael. I'll get you a brochure."

"Appreciate that," I said, relaxing some more. Discounts seemed very appealing with my new version of home repairs.

A little while later I also appreciated his offer to send someone to help dig for the things I needed to take with me, although I happily turned down his offer of transportation. I had my own idea of transportation in mind.

Billy, the friendly young man John sent my way, crawled out of the Rexall's undercarriage on elbows and knees, unloading boxes from storage. We'd been chatting nonstop since he arrived.

"So you're a fulltimer," he said as he placed another box at my feet. "I want to do that someday. Travel full time, see the country. Where're you going from here, Ms. Hannon?"

I pawed through the box, smiling to myself. Curiosity seemed endemic to RVers, me included. So far, I'd held more conversations with strangers than...ever.

A gawky towhead, taller and skinnier than I, Billy had grease smeared on his face and shirt, his hands blacker than John's. His uniform shirt hung loose over bony shoulders, bagging pants suspended low on his narrow pelvis by spit and a prayer, crotch at his knees.

I pity the whole generation of females deprived of the male form by this abysmal fashion. Not that Billy had much to display at this point, but he'll get there. Dressed like this, who'll care?

This wasn't the right box, either. I spotted a box of CDs that would have been nice before the ordeal with the seized bearings began. "Hand me that box, Billy, I'll take the CDs inside. I think the box I want is that last one in the back. Now what was it you asked?"

"Where're you off to next?"

"California. I'll be staying in Napa Valley near Calistoga for a month or so, near where my daughter lives. Ever been there?"

"Naw. Don't travel much, even though my dad owns this place. I mean, we're all about RVs and traveling, right? But we don't like, travel much ourselves, you know? I will someday, though."

8

Youthful dreams always touch me. Adults seldom live them, but seldom lose them either. Listening to Billy as he rambled on about what he'd like to see and do, I wondered how much of my dramatic change in lifestyle was about recapturing my own youthful dreams.

The thought gave me pause. At my age, living youthful dreams seemed exciting, but was it wise? Then again, since wisdom had sent me down a career path that so recently crashed and burned in a forced early retirement, did I really care? Maybe mid-life was a good time to stop doing what was wise and start doing what I truly wanted.

Billy lifted out the last box. I dug down. There it was. My old backpack, the black nylon scuffed and the buckle twisted. I had lots of hiking miles on that puppy, both stateside and abroad.

We shoved all but the box of CDs back into the compartment. I locked it, and hurried around the motorhome to the rear rack where my transportation awaited. It was almost five o'clock and I wanted to beat the rush. Commute traffic was a terrible time for another maiden voyage.

"Awesome bike! Here, I'll get that down for you," Billy said, and disengaged the straps and clamps holding the sexy, bold Kawasaki Ninja 500R to the rack. Dust couldn't completely hide the sleek, tilted split-body frame of the powerful sport motorcycle.

"Thanks, Billy. I have to admit, I'm a little intimidated by the whole process," I confided. "It's fairly lightweight for a motorcycle, but the rack seems a little tricky."

"Nothing to it. The lift does all the work. Undo the locks and safety straps here and here, hit the button, and stand back. Just don't release the bike until it's down."

I watched him work, so young and competent. As the lift began to whine, I admired my pride and joy—one of my own personal youthful dreams I'd given into at the last minute. "So you like my bike?"

"You bet. I've ridden my cousin's, she's got one just like it. It's the shit. Sorry, I mean it's hot."

Assuring the blushing young man I wasn't offended, we both watched the lift touch the ground. Billy unlatched the bike, pulled the front tire aside and rolled it off the rack. Looked at me. Frowned. "Uh, it sure looks new. Ride much?"

Ignoring his question, I grabbed the backpack. "Oh, it's new all right. I'll run inside and get a few things together." I turned to walk backwards. "You want to take it for a spin?"

"For real? Cool!"

I dug the key out of my pocket and tossed it over, enjoying his huge smile. "I'll be about ten minutes."

Changing into sneakers, a purple shirt and khaki slacks, I pinned my hair securely in a flat knot on top of my head, slung the fat backpack in place, and vacated my home. Billy sat waiting for me when I came out, the motor rumbling. He'd polished off the dust. The bike screamed of speed and adventure, its angled lines lower to the front as if poised to thrust the driver forward. The red-striped titanium body gleamed; the black engine a bold contrast between the split pieces, the glittering chrome muffler tilted upward the same angle as the split body and strips.

I took a deep breath. I'd dreamed of having a motorcycle when I was a kid Billy's age. My nephew Nickolas assured me I could handle this one now at my age. Carrying my prized hat, I locked the door and went to find out.

Billy dismounted and held the motorcycle upright, staring at me. As I stopped to anchor my hat with a long hatpin, his face broke out in wild delight.

"Wow," he said, and kept grinning.

That seemed to cover it. I smiled back. "Well, I can't stuff it in the backpack, now can I?"

He just shook his head. I mounted, jammed down hard on the bright red, wide-brimmed hat. A long grosgrain ribbon circled the base and looped in an elegant double bow. An arrangement of flowers clustered along the crown and flowed over the shaped felt brim to dangle graciously near my ear.

Take that, Hell's Angels.

I revved the engine, let it quiet. The last instructions from Nickolas, my ever-confident young nephew, rang in my head. One gear down, five gears up. I repeated it as a mantra. Throttle and front brake on the right, clutch on the left. One gear down, five gears up. "Thanks for your help, Billy. Hope I see you around."

"Sure thing, Ms. Hannon. Drive safe," he added with a sassy grin.

Smartass. I laughed and nodded.

Taking another deep breath, I engaged the clutch lever with my left hand, joggled the gearshift down one notch with my right foot, and gently swiveled the right hand grip for a wobbly start.

No time to worry about the left foot, the rear brake. Coordinating three appendages was more than enough. A little more speed and the cycle stabilized. My feet skimmed the ground for about twenty yards, until I thought to put my sneakers on the foot pegs.

That felt better. Once out of Billy's sight, I'd practice using the brake lever. Maybe go up a notch on the gearshift to second gear.

For now, all my prayers centered on a six-inch solid steel shaft sticking in my best red hat.

Chapter 2

The experiment in braking proved successful. That is to say, I managed to slow the machine to a near stop, whereupon it commenced wobbling like crazy. How irritating. Why couldn't it be like a regular bike? I don't remember wobbling on a regular bike.

Then the motorcycle started to fall over. Out shot my feet. Whap! They hit the ground.

Oh. Thank goodness, I didn't have an audience. That could change once I swung around the sales office, so I concentrated on getting it together. Clutch lever with hand, toggle down one gear with foot.

This time I sped up and shifted—grip clutch hand lever, toggle foot up one—into second gear, whizzed by the sales office at a brisk trot and pulled up to the entrance onto Boulder Highway. It's more street than highway, but I didn't intend to get in a traffic lane, just cruise along the edge. Pretend I was on a real bike.

A car waited to turn left. I pulled up beside it to turn right. Traffic zoomed by. Lots of traffic. I braked okay, I got that part right. Only I forgot about downshifting, forgot about the clutch lever. The engine stalled with a death rattle. The kids in the car pointed and laughed as the damn motorcycle jerked and wobbled. I started to fall.

Whap! Feet again.

Silence. I concentrated on breathing. Sweat ran down my face, my purple button-down shirt was soaked through, my hands trembled and my legs shook. Maybe I should've taken a practice run before the salesman loaded it on the RV the day before I left Seattle. My nephew's instructions and the owner's manual seemed to have left out a few things.

I licked dry lips. The red hat gave me strength. Like Anne Abernathy, known as Grandma Luge, the oldest woman in Winter Olympic history, going for gold in her special Red Hot helmet, I thought of Red Hot Ladies everywhere, and straightened my spine. All I needed, I decided, was practice.

Waving at the kids as their car turned, I found neutral, hit the starter, went through the gear thing and eased out onto the side of the road.

Second gear was fast enough. My hat fluttered about my face, straining against the hatpin as the big trucks barreled by. Some people honked. Some pointed and waved. Laughed. I laughed right back, knowing my heart was strong and the pounding probably wouldn't hurt me at all. Why not enjoy the ride? I was going faster than I ever did on a boring regular bike, without peddling! How cool was that?

Boulder Station came and went. The largest building around, for a casino, it looked...well, blah. After staying at the MGM Grand, my dazzle expectation was perhaps a little high.

The RV Park had to be close, though, and on the same side as the casino. Thousand Trails, yes, there's the sign...only I was on the right side of street and the exit was on the left.

I know, I know. I shouldn't have panicked. Should have taken the next exit. Instead, I checked the traffic behind me. The main cluster sped by, then the stragglers. I could see the next surge waiting at the light: starters at the gate.

The window was short, the open space narrow, the timing critical. I waited, looked back. Not yet. My exit loomed closer. I looked back again. Now! I shot out across the three lanes of traffic, threading the gap, aiming straight for my exit.

I was not driving my Acura.

As if in a dream, I felt trapped in slow motion, only horror of horrors, I *was* in slow motion! All I could do was lean forward, hold onto my hat, and practice levitation. I swear to God it worked. Why those people were so upset, I don't understand. There was plenty of room to pull around me. Road rage, I suppose.

Frankly, I had enough to worry about when I saw that the exit immediately looped into a sharp u-turn, which I approached far too fast.

Leaving my red hat flapping in the wind, I used both hands to grasp the handlebar, frantic to control my wild, exhilarating Kawasaki Ninja. I'm not good at estimating distances in feet, but whatever the distance to the on-coming traffic at the end of that loop, I had to come to a full stop by the time I arrived. That wouldn't take long.

Heading into a tight curve at this speed with an uncertain surface of loose rocks dotting the pavement, I wasn't about to risk experimenting with downshifting, but I did remember the clutch lever.

I hit the curve and braked. Loss of momentum messed with the bike's balance, so I leaned into the curve to compensate. The busy street rushed toward me. I squeezed on the brake lever. Squeezed hard. Then harder still.

Heart going gangbusters, I whooshed to an abrupt stop. The back wheel popped off the pavement a few inches, throwing me forward. Jeezel bezel! I'd stopped at the perfect spot, my feet coming down at the perfect time.

When I eased across the road—this time blessedly clear—I smiled, already planning my next trip. In a proper helmet, I bet I could hit third gear, no problem. After that, all I needed was a long straight road. Then I'd go for fifth.

A few minutes later, I pulled up in front of Gwen's motor-home and sat admiring the spiffy new forty-foot Phaeton. My modest and aging Rexall was a dull rock beside this gleaming jewel.

Exhaustion washed over me, leaching my body of energy. More than the stress of the last few minutes, the last few hours, the last frantic weeks and tense months came crashing in on me. Getting to Las Vegas, getting to Gwen's, had been my focus for three miserable months. At last, I was here.

Gwen must have heard me coming. The door burst open and out she came in a rush. "You made it! Are you...my gosh, look at you!" She stopped, put her hands on her hips and laughed a big, booming laugh that rocked her back on her heels. At least it revived my spirits.

Seeing Gwen all tanned, looking bright and marvelously healthy revived them even more. She'd put on weight, thank God, and done something to her hair, made the pixie cut whiter, or maybe the tan did that. She filled out the tank and shorts more, too, like the old Gwen. She looked good.

"Pretty neat, huh?" I said, patting down the flowers. Making sure I still had flowers.

"I'll say."

I started to dismount.

"Wait, wait," Gwen held out a traffic cop hand and shouted back at her husband Shay, just stepping out of their rig. "Will you get the camera, sweetie? For the scrapbook," she tells me.

Knowing Gwen and her scrapbook, I settled back down. As Queen Mum for the Red Hot Ladies Club chapter in Seattle she'd named the Dazzling Darlings, she wouldn't dare pass up this photo op. I had to admit, it would make a good story for our DD newsletter. Bet she sent it into National Hotquarters, too.

At least the short break gave me time to observe my friends a little closer, soak them in a little deeper. Shay had also acquired a tan, the first I'd seen on him during the almost three years of our acquaintance. The tanned bald scalp above his salt-and-pepper fringe matched his tanned knobby knees. Don't think I'd ever seen him in shorts, either. Nope, I'd never seen those knees.

Tall and lean with a comfortable middle-aged pouch, Shay's shoulders sagged a bit from too many hours hunched over a desk, but his dark eyes behind those stodgy glasses gleamed bright as ever. In fact, more than ever. He looked...they both looked fresh and relaxed.

A knot of worry loosened inside.

Gwen's questions continued spilling out as Shay clicked away until a couple out walking their Pomeranian headed our way. The Pom and the woman arrived first, both excited and nearly prancing. Towed by the long leash, the man followed.

Sparkling and smiling, the woman watched me while she addressed Gwen. "Hi, Gwen. This must be your friend from Seattle. How wonderful, having another Red Hot Lady here. We'll have to hold some official events! I bet we can get some local ladies to join us. I'll give them a jingle. Hi, I'm Roxie Weisner."

Roxie pumped my hand. She never stopped talking. "Would you look at that motorcycle! You really drive that thing? Golly, Albert, can you believe she drives a hot motorcycle like that? That's my husband, Albert. This is Gwen's friend, Lotsimina. Did I get that right?"

Despite the motor mouth, I thought I might end up liking Roxie. Life filled her, overflowing in tumbled words and boundless enthusiasm. She looked in her early seventies, soft and round and comfortable with it. Gray hair short with no apparent style or care, her clothes loose, casual, and cool, her attractive face bare and walnut brown, she provided an interesting contrast to her husband.

Albert still hadn't said a word. He'd ignored the questions fired his way, nodded at the passing introduction. Somewhat older than his wife, tall, thin, well groomed and ugly as mud, he stood on the sidelines, perhaps to better observe life. He didn't strike me as much of a participant. Then again, what chance did he have?

I dismounted, set the kickstand, and answered her question about my name. "Yes, that's right, Lotsimina Hannon. I'm cursed with an old family name. I didn't pass it on, believe me."

"No, it's lovely. Lotsimina," she drew it out, all the rolling syllables, just like the punks in my neighborhood used to do, only without the taunting twang.

I laughed. "Please call me Lotsi. Glad to meet you both." When I gave Albert my hand, his smile opened up his face to show the humor and intelligence lurking inside. An interesting man, I thought, and not ugly at all.

"Look," Gwen said, "I'm sure Lotsi needs fed and a bit of rest, but if she's up to it, why don't we meet later at the hot tub?"

That idea agreed on, we disbursed, and the Evans and I headed for the motorhome.

"Here, let me help," Gwen said as I tugged at the backpack grown heavy. The hat followed. Gwen's eyes widened at the hatpin.

With a laugh, I held the long, wicked shaft upright. "Never call a woman defenseless when she's armed with one of these babies." Then I grimaced and massaged my sore scalp. "I didn't realize it'd pull like that. There's a dent right here. Ouch."

"Slaves to fashion," Gwen grandly dismissed my complaints. "It's our woman's cross."

Shay, the dear man, played the gallant. "But that hat is such a magnificent cross to bear."

I preened. I really loved that hat.

"Toady," Gwen said with perfect disdain, tilting her nose high and giving him a nice profile. Laughter came first, that special music shared with friends.

God, how I'd missed these two. Tears sprang as the laugh became a sob. I tossed my hat on the sofa and reached for Gwen. We clung to each other, the warm touch of kindness surrounding me, comforting me, nourishing me. For a few moments, loneliness receded. I wasn't adrift in isolation, in a confusing mess of jagged bits and pieces of myself. I was here. Safe.

Seizing control of my marauding emotions, I wrapped her tighter then eased back. The same height, we stood eye to eye. A thousand words rose and went unsaid. I wiped my face and half choked, half gurgled, "Where did *that* come from?"

"Come on, honey, let's get you fed and you can tell us what those bastards did to you," was her way of answering my question. Smart lady.

However, I had a more pressing question. I grabbed her hands. "How are you, Gwen? You look great. I see you've gained more weight. Can't call you hatchet-face anymore."

She squeezed my hands, smiled as I needed her to smile. "I'm great. Honest. Passing the one-year mark as cancer free made a huge difference for me. Ask Shay."

My eyes sought his, and when he nodded, that particular worry knot loosened completely. Gwen pulled me toward the freestanding dinette, passed around Coronas and lime from the largest side-by-side refrigerator I'd seen in a motorhome.

Shay watched Gwen bustle around, a soft curve to his lips. "Gwen wouldn't listen when the kids and I wanted to hold off ordering the motorhome until we'd gotten the word she was clear. Said she was, and that was that. I think she was having way too much fun, driving their Research and Development folks crazy."

Gwen plunked down a bowl of spicy thick chili she'd dished up from a crock-pot and went back for more. "Well, it was fun. After years of using motorhomes, we'd learned a thing or two about what works, what we wanted. Once I found out the Phaeton R&D boys at Tiffin Motorhomes loved to work directly with buyers, I didn't want anything else. I got the cabinet space I wanted instead of too many sinks, a desk area that's actually functional, and a real table and chairs."

Unsealing the containers of grated cheese, chopped onions, and oyster crackers already on the table, Shay pushed them my way and grinned at his wife. "Those were the easy things. Then she got down to the nitty-gritty. She must have changed the color and type of fabrics she wanted ten times, more for the cabinets."

"I did not! And they appreciated the new designs. Bet they're standard options by now."

I'd looked around while they bantered. Gwen prefers classic formal to my mixed contemporary, but her selections looked stunning: soft, elegant and functional. "It's lovely, Gwen. I hope they don't make everything standard. This is yours. When you've looked at a hundred motorhomes, you can tell when one is unique. How did you like picking it up at the plant in Alabama?"

"Shay about stroked out on the plant tour. All the flying sparks, deafening noises, and horrid smells. He went bananas. And their tools!" She shook her head. "Seriously! Must be a guy thing."

He laughed. "You liked the girlie part. Furniture and appliances."

"We both loved it. And we haven't had a lick of trouble. These last three months...." She smiled at her husband and squeezed his hand. "It's been a special time for us. We're thinking about making Shay's leave of absence permanent. He's sixty-two, and I don't want to go back to work. Early retirement can't be all bad, can it?"

She had a hopeful, uncertain look on her face. I wanted to smack her. She knew there was a huge difference between choosing to retire and being forced to retire. But hey, reasons are personal, and their reasons aren't so hot, either. I'll take mine any day.

"No," I assured her, "it's not all bad. In fact, I think retirement may be the best thing to happen to me in years."

Shay stacked the empty chili bowls and took them to the sink, snagging another round of beer as we moved to the surprisingly large living room, thanks to dual sliding room extensions. I started lusting for more slides.

"Now tell us what happened," Shay said, handing out bottles. "Gwen's been cussing Franklin for a month."

My friends settled close together on the couch and I took the rocker recliner, easing into a gentle rhythm. Despite the comforting motion, I grimaced. "So many things make sense now. I'd seen other women in management leave, heard the rumors. But I trusted my immediate bosses George and Wolfred, even though I became aware of my situation while in Italy."

Gwen frowned. "Five years ago?"

"Yeah, hard to believe. Franklin Industries requires upper management do at least one three-year foreign tour, so when I went to Florence as a new Vice President of Sales & Marketing, I didn't think anything of it. My promotions were on-track. I'd earned awards. I'd known George and Wolfred for several years. We'd worked well together, moved up the ladder together."

"You think they assigned you there as a set-up?" Gwen asked.

"No, I didn't report to them before Florence, but once assigned to their division, I think they crunched the personnel budget and targeted the largest expense. Me. They brought me in for less, gave smaller increases. They figured they'd get away with it."

"Boy, is that a familiar song!"

Shay nodded, mouth knotting in one corner. "It is. My law firm practices a gender pay differential for staff and partners both. Of course, it's not legal, but we do it." As a senior partner, he'd know.

My foot stilled, the rocker slowed to a stop. "Why is that, Shay? Women fought hard to close the gender pay gap, and we did for awhile. Now it's widening again. Why doesn't a major law firm for God's sake, practice equal pay?"

He hunched his shoulders, and held up a hand at the shocked look on Gwen's face. "I'm not proud of it, but we do it because we can. Few female employees know they're paid less because company policy controls that information. We keep expenses down, billing rates down, and profits up. The partners are happy, clients are happy, and frankly, the women are happy to have the job."

"Jesus, Shay," Gwen's anger swept a red wash across her cheeks. "How can you say that? Your own daughters worked there, and I know damned well Kim and Michelle wouldn't be *happy* making less money than the guys sitting next to them. They'd be furious! They'd...they'd...."

"Look for another job. Which they did. Now they're paid more, but probably still less than men for the same job at the new place. It sucks, honey, but that's reality."

Gwen sputtered, tongue-tied and bubbling with wrath. I'd heard his brand of logic for years, though. "He's right, Gwen." My fleeting grin felt malicious. "But as Paul Harvey used to say, now for the rest of the story."

I pushed off with my foot again, rocking. Much of the emotional pain I'd gone through agonizing over the situation I'd never share, and legally I couldn't say anything to anyone. These were my best friends, and I had to talk to someone. This was too big, too powerful, to bury completely.

"You're right about knowledge, Shay," I said. "Most women suspect, few know. They can still file a sex discrimination suit and win, but without that knowledge, they're afraid. So companies officially prohibit discussions about salaries and litigations, but they can't always stop employees from talking."

"Who told you?" Shay asked with a sneaky grin.

I chuckled. "My predecessor in Florence not only boffed his admin assistant, he bragged about his salary. I inherited her. She assumed I'd be impressed for some reason and told me. To think I owe my final triumph to sex, ego, and pride. I'd like to thank her."

"Oh my," Gwen said, and snickered. "But if you knew, why didn't you leave or complain to Human Resources?"

Shay knew. I saw it in his eyes. I shrugged. "New VPs don't leave. You need time in grade. And HR is the last place to go, despite what they tell you. They protect management, not employees."

This was painful, more than I'd anticipated. I rocked faster. "I confronted George. He gave me a song and dance about the weak economy. That I needed to wait for my turn. They'd take care of me."

"Your turn...you mean when you transferred to Seattle?"

"That's what I thought. When it didn't happen, I asked again. This time Wolfred and George both met with me. Wolfred had charts. He still blamed the economy, but in the coming reorganization, I'd have the new Sr. VP position. My name was in the box. Until then, I needed to be patient."

"That's before I went through chemo, right? You worried you might be transferred when you got the promotion."

"Yes. Only this spring the position went to a young man on his first tour as VP. Wolfred dangled another position. Then my workload decreased, assignments went elsewhere, my staff was reassigned. I saw the handwriting."

"What'd you do?" Gwen promoted as I fell silent, lost in my reflections.

Blinking back to the present, I bathed in the compassion I saw in my friends' faces. "My knowledge gave me a weapon, and when they didn't play straight with me, never intended to, I used it."

"Smart girl," Gwen smirked, and Shay nodded.

"Smart enough to go loaded with documentation. During the hearing, Wolfred first argued I had less responsibility than my predecessor did, when in fact I'd been given two regions, with less staff and budget. But no pay increase. All on record."

I almost chickened out on this part, but I needed to say it. Even I could hear the thin, painful edge to my voice. "When I kept forcing their settlement amount higher, Wolfred claimed I'd become incompetent. That they'd already hired my replacement."

Silence trickled by, then Gwen spoke with sad indignity. "Honey, that is so crazy. It's not in you to be incompetent."

She hadn't seen me on the Ninja, I thought, but I knew what she meant.

As usual, Shay was more realistic. "It's not an uncommon tactic. Overload a targeted employee, cripple resources, and blame the employee for the consequences, thus creating the grounds for dismissal."

Gwen turned to me. "Why were you targeted like that?"

Ah. How many nights had that question kept me awake? I'd finally come to a bitter but unavoidable conclusion. "It's not about me at all. My management put no value on loyalty and experience. Women work cheap, but young guys work cheaper than senior women. And women seldom retaliate."

Gwen threw a hostile look toward Shay, who shrugged. "She's right. And with the risks low, the benefits high, it'll keep right on happening, too."

"That's one reason I fought this. They'd lied to me, strung me along as if it was business as usual. But at the hearing, when they assaulted my competence, my integrity— that...that burned to the bone!"

Seared by a fresh flood of anger, my foot halted the rocker and I snapped upright. "Twelve years I bled out *my life* for them! I fought hours past when my lawyer stopped, and I got every cent I wanted, exactly what they'd screwed me out of."

Triumph rose, slammed against the anger, then ebbed into a bleak acceptance. I sighed. "But I realize now, if it'd been ten times that, it still wouldn't change the way they do business."

Pensive, Shay nodded. Gwen looked sick.

I hadn't meant to upset them. I'd taken great strides in healing my pain. Pushing off the rocker, I tried to lighten the mood. "Hey, I won this round. Others can, too. After all, feisty ladies never quit, they just join the Red Hot Ladies Club."

Shay raised his right hand, palm facing me, and intoned, "Live long and prosper." His fingers twitched. He looked at them, concentrated. The little finger moved. With his other hand he pulled apart the last two fingers, leaving a wide V between the two sets of double fingers, and sat there grinning while we laughed at his pathetic Vulcan salute.

Later that evening, we met Roxie and Albert in front of the motorhome and walked to the pool and hot tub area. Roxie bubbled about a sightseeing tour the following night given by the RV Park.

Gwen added her pitch. "I checked earlier; they're not full. We'd cruise the Strip first, then head down to Freemont Street, and end up on the hills above the city at a temple. Wanna go?"

She had me at cruising the Strip. During the convention, I hadn't seen it all and the bright lights beckoned. We were still discussing arrangements when we arrived at the narrow passage to the pool area and formed a single-file line.

The pool gate opened, and Roxie greeted the man warmly as he held the gate for us to pass. I couldn't see him as Gwen stood talking with him, but his voice intrigued me, sight unseen—a warm, rumbley sound. I knew he'd be smiling.

I stepped around the gate, following the lure of that voice. One look and my heart stuttered and kicked up a notch.

"Trent," Gwen said, "I'd like you to meet Lotsi Hannon. She's here for the next two weeks. Lotsi, Trenton Wallace."

Gorgeous. Heavily grayed, his wet hair fell in softly curling ringlets almost shoulder length—long enough to sink my hands into—tumbling around a tanned face, comfortably lived in and sexy as hell. The man stole the polite words from my lips and the air from my lungs. This wasn't the mild flicker of interest I'd felt for John the Mechanic. This instant, burning heat struck like a body blow.

Trent's easy smile faded as he turned to me. Dark Ghirardelli chocolate eyes flared and reached toward me. Sucked me in.

Oh, yes, please! I thought, and let go.

Chapter 3

I spun off into Trent's eyes, into a quiet space filled only by each other. Deeper I drifted, seeking more of him, opening to him, feeling his intensity caress me like a physical touch.

Tingles lit up through my body, sparkles of sensation awakening secret pathways. I could feel him inside me as deeply as I was inside him, pulse-to-pulse, heat-to-heat.

Gwen touched my arm. My lungs sucked in air. Words began to register from the garbled sound of her voice. "Lotsi? Are you...?" Wrenching my eyes free, I saw her begin to smile with a devilish glee I didn't trust at all.

"Ah, well. Let's see," she fumbled, as neither Trent nor I said a word.

Trent captured my attention again, his face serious, intent. A drop of water beading on the end of his hair diverted my gaze, and I watched the clear pearl fall from a sexy spiral to his bare chest. Aw, man. The urge to follow it with my tongue sneaked out to grab me. My body thought that was a great idea and tightened all over, clamoring for action.

Attention fastened to the glittering track, I envied the drop coursing over those firm muscles, through that spatter of dark age-streaked hair, over that golden skin. Somewhere the drip ran out but my eyes kept going down, over the taut abdomen, taking in the loose cut trunks—thank God, I'd have died on the spot if they'd been Speedos—and over the long, strong legs of a runner. Then back up.

Somehow, I'd seen or felt his eyes exploring my face, lingering at my breasts beneath my thin swimsuit, but they'd returned to catch mine sliding back from his nether regions. My nipples tightened harder. A flush heated my skin.

Trent's eyes began to twinkle as heat turned to humor. An intimate, knowing curve softened his lips. Good golly, Miss Molly. That wicked, sexy look snuck through what barriers I had left and inflamed sexual desires I'd thought closed away forever. I felt my breasts swell as the nipples pinched tight. My womb spasmed in an almost forgotten response.

Red alert! Red alert! My heartbreak radar screamed at me, but nobody was listening. I was too busy smiling right back at the source of all the sexual commotion.

Lust attack imminent! Commence evasion tactics! Lust attack imminent!

Forget it. Alarms were flashing but no higher cerebral function was going on at all.

Gwen cleared her throat and broke into my stupor, voice loaded with amusement. "Trent, ah, you've finished your swim but perhaps you'd like to drop by tomorrow for tea? Say, about ten o'clock?"

I knew I'd catch a load of teasing for my reactions, but still couldn't seem to do anything. Except watch his lips. That soft curve twitched, stretched wider. I felt mine widen in response, a perfect mimic.

"Sure," he said. "Be glad to."

As his lips shaped the words, I swear mine sought to move with them. Incredible.

This wasn't right. I blinked several times, met his eyes. Molten chocolate syrup poured over me, entrapped me. He nodded once as if to acknowledge my response and left. We had not exchanged a single word.

A pool of silence gathered around our small group. I tossed my head, caught the various looks aimed my way and slammed up my defenses.

"What?" I snarled, then spun around and stalked toward the hot tub, struggling to shake off the haze clinging to my thoughts. What the hell was *that*?

Smirking, Gwen got in her first lick. "Was that what I think—?"

"No!" I used my best drop-dead look, but had no real hope it would work for long. The palm trees and garden areas around the partially shaded pools held no charm. I climbed into the large hot tub, submerged my ears, closed my eyes, and played ostrich.

Shocked, stunned, and not a little horrified, I hadn't a clue how to handle what had just happened with Trent. A perfect stranger...*yes, yes, he's perfect! No, no! Get your mind away from perfect. He is not perfect. He is one of them. He's not only a man, he's a gorgeous male specimen of perf...he's...too good to believe. There. He's the kind you don't trust. And you don't trust any of them, anyway, but you especially don't trust a man who looks like*...oh, this was bad. Real bad.

For a woman who just looks, I'd blown my whole philosophy of acceptable behavior. There's no way in hell I'd ever think about "just looking" as a benign, safe occupation again.

What was I to do?

I sat up straighter and looked around. My companions talked to each other, met my glances with casual smiles. Well, Albert's hound-dog face nodded, a little. Companions became friends just that easily, and friends are the greatest gift to discover at times like these.

Gwen and Roxie sat on either side of me. Female radar kicked in and they focused on me. Waited.

"Okay," I said, letting my embarrassed confusion show, serious as spit. "I'm a big girl. I've been around. I played in the sexual Olympics when making love was going to save the world from war machines and cure loneliness. When scoring points against the Establishment meant orgasms, not bombs. Know what I mean?"

Head bobbing, Gwen choked back a startled laugh. Roxie stuffed fingers in her mouth to stifle a chorus of giggles. I ignored the men and frowned at the women. "I'm serious. This was before free love met safe sex and died."

Waving a hand, Gwen said in a quivering voice, "I got that part. So what's your problem with...with Trent?" Laughter bellowed out. "Sorry, sorry," she said, sucking it in.

When I was sure she wouldn't lose it, I went on. "So, maybe I haven't had non-personal sex in fifteen years, but I remember good. And I never experienced anything remotely close to what just happened." I let my head fall back against the tile, so close to tears my voice shook with it. "How am I supposed to play tiddly-winks with someone like that when I've got these sexual superhormones raging out of control in my body?"

I heard Gwen mutter "Tiddly-winks?" as Roxie patted my hand under the water. I sighed, a shuddering wind of despair. "It's not right," I said, letting the tension go. "At my age. Something morphed...I know...it's a gene mutation!" I sat up, excited. "They say being fifty is like being thirty, right?"

Gwen rolled her eyes. "She's off again...what are you talking about, Lotsi?"

"Come on, you're the one who told me about it! I've never watched Oprah. We live longer, healthier and that's supposed to mean we have the same potential at fifty that prior generations had at thirty. Remember?"

"What's that got to do with a gene mutation?"

My hands splashed in the water. "Work with me here. If fifty is like thirty, then...at fifty, we still have years, decades, of thirty-something sex ahead of us. But give me a break, you can't tone a hormone like you can a muscle, now can you? So when the fifty-something sex drive starts to run down, the genes mutate and create sexual superhormones! There you go."

Shay scratched the thinning hair on his head. Albert actually smiled at me. My gal pals looked puzzled.

"I don't think I've had any superhormones running around in me lately," Gwen offered. She looked at Shay. "Have you?"

"Ah, no, I don't think so. Sorry."

The three of us looked at the Weisners. Roxie shook her head. "Me neither."

Albert's face drooped even more. "Sorry."

They all looked back at me. "Well, you're all married. Maybe having steady sex delays the need for superhormones. Maybe you have to—oh, I don't know—dry up a bit sexually, before the gene starts mutating. Then, wham! It lets you have it." I zoned for a second. I might be on to something, I thought. Pretty mind-boggling. I mean, that wasn't normal lust I'd felt. No way.

"Something happened," I said, more to myself. "Maybe I'm not such a sexual waste, after all."

"Lotsi!" Gwen's body jerked, face outraged. "How can you say such a thing? You're a lovely, fascinating, sensual woman and don't you forget it!"

"Yeah, yeah, tell that to the men I know."

Albert responded instantly. "You know the wrong kind of men. Those who are breathing work best."

Shocked, I looked at the gentle smile he offered, his kind eyes. He stole my heart, right there. "God love ya, Albert, that's the nicest thing I've ever heard."

"See?" Gwen poked me in the side.

Everyone seemed to like his comment and his smooth, quick delivery. Clever man. I think we'd underappreciated Albert until that moment.

The next night, a growing crowd gathered in front of the park store, waiting for the Evening Lights Tour departure time. Shaded tables and benches held some of the people. A few perched on the edges of large planters. The rest wandered or stood idle.

Roxie titillated our group with the evening's coming attractions. "Freemont Street has billions of lights, flashing like a humongous video canopy stretching for blocks and blocks. Wait until you see the scenes they have, flashing from end to end. It's amazing, isn't it Albert?"

Albert nodded.

"I heard the bus guide is really entertaining and knows his stuff," Gwen said.

"Me too," Roxie flashed a wicked grin. "He's been here forever and my friend said he'd tell us all kinds of interesting tidbits. I can't wait."

Yeah, I knew the feeling. I'd been waiting to spot Trent, missing from our knot of friends. He'd agreed readily enough to come on the tour when Gwen mentioned it this morning at her impromptu tea. He hadn't stayed long, nor spoken much. To me, that is.

He'd had a fine discussion with Shay and Albert about their golf games while his eyes kept flicking my way. I'd been prepared then, my evasion tactics of Indifference and Brush Off finally operational. If he'd just talked to me I'd have engaged Get Lost, but for some reason he'd stayed back. Maybe he'd gotten the message already.

The tour van waited at the curb as departure time approached. I couldn't see Trent. I waited some more. More folks trickled in, looked like a van full. Still no Trent.

While most of the diverse group was older, two newcomers filling in the space next to us appeared more diverse than usual. The ebony giant caught and held my eye. I probably came to mid-chest. And boy, what a chest. And arms. And neck...okay, this guy screamed football, some kind of lineman. Not that I'm an expert, but he looked big and tough.

When I finally reached as high as his face, he smiled at me, amiable but well guarded. I banked on the amiable and said, "I love your hair. It sure is unique."

His smile bloomed, transforming his ordinary face to handsome as it came alive. He rubbed a hand over the tiny bleached swirls of buzz-cut hair, so short it looked like patterned peach fuzz all over his head and in a stripe around his chin.

"Thanks," he said in a voice surprisingly baritone for such a large man. "Saves me from shaving cuts."

"As if you ever worried about a little blood," his companion teased, a sensual smile resting on his full lips. A foot shorter, beanpole to redwood, everything about the man was sensual, his movie-star looks and his bedroom eyes, the curve of his lips. While his large partner dressed casually in khaki Dockers and sandals, he dressed impeccably in black Armani and loafers; classy, sexy, and gay.

The big guy laughed, drawing eyes to the rich sound. "True, but usually someone else caused the blood, not me. I'm not into self-inflicted wounds."

Before I could follow up on that intriguing comment, the driver interrupted with a general announcement about the tour and a ten-minute boarding call. I scanned the crowd, the approaches. No Trent. Damn, that burned. I was determined to seize the opportunity tonight to slap a big Not Interested sign in his face. I wanted no part of sexual superhormones on the prowl. His or mine.

Although considering my idea that too much sex inhibited the mutation he'd cursed me with the instant I'd met him, he certainly should still possess the regular kind. Then again, Trent was probably *born* with superhormones.

Gwen caught my eye and looked compassionate. She thought he was a no-show, too. I should be relieved, except I needed to make that statement clear to him, fast.

If only I'd had the chance this morning. But no, the men spread out in the front of Gwen's RV where the double slides opened up a generous living room and the women clustered in the kitchen area expanded only by a long common slide.

Isn't that the way it always went? My eyes fell on the gay couple. I wondered which group...I spotted Trent approaching.

His eyes had me nailed. I froze. For a few seconds, the world stopped. I was the gazelle in the tiger's path, the rabbit inches from the eagle's talons. Trent's presence spanned the twenty or thirty feet between us and enfolded me in his essence, in his power and determination.

For those few seconds, everything in me rejoiced, welcoming him inside to fill a space I hadn't admitted was empty. He hit all my female buttons with a one-two punch that took me down for the count. His looks struck me first. Those slightly overlong curls framing his face looked so good in gray—I could hate him for that alone—and his handsome face, where the delicate touch of age added lines of wisdom and strength to his character. His killer body, strong, trim. Firm. Male. All male.

Then the force of his eyes struck, those dark gateways that unleashed his intensity and spoke to me. I may not have heard words, but I got the message.

This man wanted me. Every step announced he came closer to take me. A few seconds, I was on the mat under his barrage of sensuality, ready to spread wide, a willing TKO.

The crooked referee, my superhormones, called out the count to complete surrender, and my body screamed, *Yes! Yes!* My mind embraced the sexual heat battering my senses and shouted, *Yes! Yes...ah, wait a minute, I mean, No! No!*

I heaved myself up from the mat. Emotionally bruised but with my dukes up and ready, I turned my back, frantically searching for the dammed No Trespassing sign.

"There's Trent," Gwen trilled, as if she'd never doubted him. Traitor. She smiled and looked smug.

Trent stopped beside me. "Lotsi. Good evening, everyone. Had to take a business call. Looks like I'm not too late, though."

I posted a rather wilted sign and nodded a cool greeting. My heart still raced, my body still hummed. How could his mere standing beside me affect me like this?

Dammit, I needed the sign to work in *both* directions!

Turning aside, I smiled at the ebony giant and his friend and tried to think about what we'd been talking. Oh, yes, blood. "So, if you didn't bleed from self-inflicted wounds, what did you bleed from?"

When the driver called for boarding a few minutes later, Erwin the Giant and Tremaine and I were becoming buddies. I was right. Erwin was an ex-pro offensive lineman, Tremaine an art gallery manager.

As my group began to shift, I realized I had a problem. We would naturally fall into three sets of couples as we moved toward the boarding line, certainly as we settled into the dual seats on the bus. No way was I sitting with Trent. I had to change the dynamics before we were automatically locked in as a couple.

"I'll see you at the other end," I said with a casual wave, and took off for the bus, catching a glimpse of Gwen's puzzled frown and the narrowed glint in Trent's eyes.

Good, I thought, rather pleased with my exit. I'd have to make it right with Gwen later, but for now, I'd avoided an awkward situation and finally posted my Not Interested sign with some teeth.

"Whoa there, Stretch," Trent said as he caught up with me in three paces, snagged my arm and pulled me to a halt.

Startled, I looked up as he hooked his elbow under my arm in as smooth a move as I've ever seen. I didn't trust that grim smile he faked, not for one minute.

"Not going to a fire, are we?" A lifted eyebrow dared me to protest as we finished the last few yards at a leisurely pace, clamped side by side.

"Sorry," I muttered, although I wasn't. "I tend to walk like I'm clocking the mile. Which I usually do...." We reached the end of the line and I tugged against his arm.

He firmed his grip. "On the job or for exercise?"

"For exercise. It's a problem, sometimes." God, I couldn't believe I was babbling, half-mumbling with embarrassment. Where was my poise, my sophistication? Apparently, Trent affected more than my libido.

"Not for me," he said, handing me into the van.

I started to sit at the first available seat beside a single lady, but Trent gave my shoulder a gentle push and we kept going until he urged me into an open double at the back. I wasn't happy with myself. I couldn't pretend to post unwelcome signs and then sit with the man in a puddle of sexual confusion. My mind jumped back into the sparring ring.

He leaned close, close enough I could smell him, a subtle whiff of male cologne and...male. "Lotsi, are we working at cross-purposes here?"

My eyes flew to his, met his steady look as if he searched deep into mine for answers. Maybe he did.

"I...ah...." I wanted to say bug off, but I couldn't. *I* wanted to bug off, but I couldn't even do that. Damn. It wasn't his hand that guided me where he wanted me to go. No hand would have, could have stopped me sitting elsewhere if my traitorous heart hadn't wanted to go exactly where he put me. I looked away.

Double damn superhormones. Sneaky bastards, every one.

His breath heated my forehead as he spoke soft and low, his back blocking out the people across the aisle. The high seat backs shielded us from people sitting behind and in front, creating a private space of intimacy. "I thought you were as interested in me as I am in you. Now you're sending these mixed signals. Why is that, Lotsi?"

I couldn't answer.

Trent laid his hand against the side of my face and lifted it until we looked at each other. "Tell me."

Responding to the touch, the openness he offered and demanded, my heart surged and flooded my system with blazing arousal. My breasts ached, my sex moistened, seeking the promise I felt flow from him. I craved his touch, craved to touch him. To appease this...this aching need. Egad. How could the body jump ahead full-throttle before the mind decided to shift into gear?

Parts of me pulsed while other bits and pieces swelled and throbbed, opening my body, opening my soul to the long years of loneliness and pain tucked away in some musty corridors inside. A mere brush against those memories and sanity returned.

I clamped down hard on my wayward body. "Trenton, I...You're going too fast! I'm not even sure I *want* to be interested!"

His thumb brushed across my lips as his softened and curved upward. "Let's find out."

Chapter 4

Trent's hand on my face urged me closer and his mouth lowered toward mine.

Good god, he's going to kiss me right here on the bus! My eyes widened. Heat rushed to the surface of my skin. I had no breath as I scowled and managed a weak protest. "Trenton!"

The black centers of his eyes swelled as he drank in my response. His intense gaze stroked across my face, my lips, lingering ever so slightly at the shallow rush in and out of my chest. Then his eyes lifted, watched the rising panic heating my face. His lips twitched. Easing back, he dropped his hand. "All right. Slow it is. But Lotsimina, you are interested."

"Lotsi," I corrected, trying to reassert a semblance of control.

"Oh, no. You called me Trenton, with that certain little sound to it. That's yours now. I take that same liberty with your name. Your full name, Lotsimina. That's mine now."

Closing my eyes, I tried to block the waves of intimacy flowing over me. I couldn't take any more of this erotic torment. I was wrecked, totally wrecked. Yet he was right. I had said his name that way, the way he'd just said mine.

He'd turned down the intensity when he spoke again. "Is Lotsimina a family name, or did your parents get creative?"

I blinked and verbally lunged for the conversational bridge between sexual implosion and social safety. "A family name. My maternal grandmother had the name, and on back as first or second names for generations. Mother escaped, but she resurrected the practice for me. I didn't pass it on, and neither did my daughter, so maybe it'll die out gracefully now."

"That would be a shame. It's a beautiful name, full of dignity and fire. Lotsimina," Trent rolled the name off his tongue, precise and robust. He settled back into his seat taking my hand with him and holding it on his thigh, as if it were a normal thing to do.

"Lotsi, now," he grinned at me, "that's spunky and fun. All of those traits are in you. I find the combination intriguing."

My mind scrambled, stirred by his heady words and the thrill of my hand caught between his leg underneath and his hand on top. "And, ah, is Trenton a family name, too?"

"No. My mother read it somewhere." His thumb slipped beneath my palm and slowly moved back and forth. "It has not been a great first name."

The nerve endings in my hand tingled, echoing into other places and my response died in a gasp. Licking my lips, I started again. "Trenton is a wonderful first name! It reeks of family tradition and, ah, history."

"You think so?" He looked startled when he turned, then he mused, "Well, my daughter named her son Michael Trenton Fielding, but it sounds so...hyphenated, I didn't think...." Relaxing against his seatback again his smile flirted and teased. "So, you like Trenton as a first name, huh?"

An image swelled and came alive as a little girl wrote 'Trenton' on a hundred Valentine hearts for a little boy who wrote 'Lotsimina' on a hundred back. Maybe then neither would have thought their names a burden and unworthy of passing on.

I cleared my throat. "Yeah, I do. You didn't name a son Trenton?"

"No. Two daughters, and I wouldn't trade them for anything. My brother Leon has carried on the Wallace name."

"Leon Wallace. Another fine name." I caught the slight furrow between his brows and couldn't resist the opportunity he handed me. "Leon," I drew the name out and gushed, "Did your mother pick out Leon's name, too?"

Frowning, Trent studied my eager face and then he pretended to pout. "You're not supposed to like my brother's name; you're supposed to only like *my* name!"

At my burst of laughter, a pleased glow radiated from his handsome face, and again his thumb stroked my palm, an unhurried movement that conveyed a need to touch, and a need to show the sexual pot still simmered.

Lured by the warmth flowing from his sensual caress, I pushed the sway of the van and the driver's preliminary patter further into the background. We were thirty minutes from the Strip and Trent seemed as willing as I to create our own little world along the way, answering my question about his family.

"Yes, Mom insisted on naming both of us. My father's family used Tom, Steve, and George a lot, and she wanted different names for *her* boys."

That probably explained where much of the teasing came from. "She probably thought Tom, Steve, and George were perfectly good names, but knowing moms, she wanted special names for her special boys."

"Oh, we were special all right. That's why she gave us a week's detention when we ruined her flower beds with the soapbox racers we made when we were nine and eleven." God, his little boy grin about killed me. "I was the engineer at nine, you see, and I tried to tell her we just needed to adjust the steering before we came down the hill the next time."

As his tale unfolded, I studied him as one would a moving sculpture, absorbing the contours of his features and the motions of his form. Prominent cheekbones created a soft hollow beneath them, light and shadow changing as he turned. A strong chin, squared in front, bristled now with dark shadow, shifted with speech and the bunching of facial expressions. Animation suited Trent, his vitality and presence a key component of his appeal. He was handsome enough he turned heads. He'd certainly turned mine, and I enjoyed every moment I could spend looking at him.

His body, too. I took my time, leisurely watching the muscles of his fine chest and arms ripple and move under the polo shirt as he used both hands to speak with gestures and elaborations. Each time he'd slip it back around mine until it began to feel at home there in his, sheltered and somehow...cherished.

The concept didn't feel as foreign or fanciful as it might have earlier, but I couldn't trust it, not really. It was enough that I laughed and egged him on to more stories just to hear his voice, feel it whisper over my skin and dip into my valleys.

He wanted to know about my daughter, so we shared kid stories. He'd been a single parent a long time, and that raised the topic of the conflict between parenting and working at demanding jobs. We found a lot of common ground, a footing beyond the explosive chemistry that kept me slightly off balance.

I don't know how long I sat there softly smiling and staring at him. Long enough the silence registered. A sexy look crossed his face and he raised my hand to his lips. I watched it float there, seemingly disconnected from my body until his lips pressed against the first knuckles and his tongue speared into the valley of my fingers, moist and warm.

An electrical charge zinged down my arm and slammed into my chest, igniting those blasted hormones. The sensual buzz I'd become used to burst into an erotic fire. Desire rushed through my body, warming my skin, melting my core and pooling between my legs. If I could just get used to the whiplash, this wild explosion really would feel incredibly good.

Looking over my hand, Trent absorbed every response, his dark eyes intense, flaring with heat. He spoke against my hand. "You're more comfortable with me now."

I smiled. "Perhaps."

He turned my hand over and pulled it higher, his mouth sucking and licking slowly on the pulse point of my inner wrist. When my blood hammered against his lips, he raised his head. "You're more comfortable with me now, aren't you?"

Turning my hand again, he rubbed the top gently, ever so gently, over the rough stubble on his cheek as he waited for my answer. That might take awhile, as shallow, quick breaths made conversation impossible. The erotic intimacy of his action puckered my nipples, clenched at my womb.

"I—" Moistening my lips, I saw the hungry intensity of his gaze sharpened. "Yes, I suppose so."

At my admission, Trent's eyes lowered to half-mast and his lips pulling back in a quick grimace as a shudder ripped through him. Fixing that compelling attention upon me once more, he shifted as he had before to shield us from view and moved closer.

"I want you, Lotsimina Hannon," Trent whispered, lips brushing the heart of my ear as his fingertips feathered through my hair, tucking the strands behind the sensitive curve. "I hope you get comfortable enough to take me real soon, because I sure as hell can't get to you fast enough!"

I nearly climaxed at his words, a spasm clenching my channel tight. This man was too dangerous for my own good and I felt the panic rise again. I hadn't realized my eyes had closed until they flew open, and there he was, waiting. "Trenton...."

Watching his pupils dilate with arousal at my one word was unbelievably exciting. Here was pure, unfeigned physiological proof of this gorgeous man's response to me, little ol' Lotsi Hannon. Powerful Lotsi Hannon. Evidently sexy as hell Lotsi Hannon. I-I couldn't resist him anymore. I didn't want to. Maybe I needed to reexamine things here.

My ex-husband's friend asked him one time what he'd looked for in the women he'd dated. "A cervix," my ex responded in a memorable comment. In the years of my celibacy, I'd had men take a run at me, motivated by what I'd privately begun calling the cervix factor.

Maybe it was time to truly believe I *wasn't* done with life, and that my sexuality wasn't dead yet, either. Maybe it was time to consider the attraction of the...the penis factor. A wave of embarrassment rose, but I refused to give in to it. Serious attraction seldom came my way. Well, it'd never come my way, not like this. If age brings wisdom, then I'd better wise up and accept the gift sitting in front of me, but I needed to get control of myself and accept him on my terms.

My lips softened, melting into an upward curve as I tilted my head and breathed the words, "I'll work on it, Trenton," near his lips and moved back.

His smile became entirely too predatory to suit me and as he darted forward my hand thumped against his chest. "You don't want to get cocky."

A startled laugh erupted from him. "God, no. I want to get lucky. Those are mutually exclusive conditions. What you're seeing is pre-appreciation of getting lucky."

This close to him, I could see flecks of gold in his dark brown eyes, feel the heat simmering in their depths, soaking into my hand pressed flat against that muscled chest I'd so admired earlier.

"Like I said. Cocky."

He glowed with cheer, his eyes danced, lips curved in a sexy grin. Having all that male ammunition aimed at me was wasting cannon shot on a butterfly, but I wasn't about to let him know that.

"No, baby," Trent purred in a sensual rumble. "This is the joy of a man who anticipates being thankful for everything he hopes to get. Very soon."

My hand rubbed back and forth, moving of its own volition. My eyes dropped, watching the subtle movements. Jeez. My mind had just decided to ease into first and my hand was burrowing under the man's shirt. In a tour van. In broad daylight. Reluctantly, I removed my hand and settled back into my seat. "I said I'd work on it, but don't expect to get lucky *very soon.*"

He groaned. "So I'll be even more thankful! Diabolical, woman. Now you're torturing me with more joy!" The shameless tease didn't look tortured as he leaned back as well. He looked awfully cocky. I think he'd listened to my body, not my words.

For the first time, our attention joined the tour as we entered the Strip. As Roxie and Gwen had predicted, the driver knew Las Vegas, the stories behind the scenes, the history, and the scuttlebutt. The Strip took on a glamour exceeding its bright lights, as human dreams and passions entered the mix. However, there's a dark side to Vegas, and he also gave us a glimpse of that in his commentary.

Near the middle of the main run down Las Vegas Boulevard, Trent took my hand in his and rested them entwined on my lap. I smiled to myself and left them there.

Passing the Stratosphere, we left the trolley route, the glitter, and the high-rise buildings behind. This was the land of Elvis wedding chapels, pawnshops, cheap rooms, and bars on storefront windows. A sobering no-man's land stuck between the two blazing Vega spotlights, the Strip and Downtown.

In one way, I felt relieved that reality had intruded on a surfeit of contrived fantasy and oversweet stardom. An urban sherbet to cleanse my dazzled palate.

Yet if my dazzle quota had dimmed, it brightened again when the driver dropped us off at the Golden Gate end of the Freemont Street Experience. The four blocks, or six, counting the two ends, surrounding the light show extravaganza already had me jacked up. A bazillion flashing lights in gigantic starbursts and enormous banners. Shops stuffed with strange merchandise and often-stranger shoppers. Towering Indian and cowboy statues. I was ready to dive in.

As the light show didn't start for almost ninety minutes, we regrouped outside the van. After some sharp looks from Gwen, which I ignored, and minimal discussion, we decided to amble over to the Golden Gate for dinner before touring the streets.

When we turned, Trent's hand curved around my waist in a subtle gesture, a guiding touch that brought me to his side. Instinctively I stiffened and shot him a startled look. He gave me his bland face, dark eyes glittering and sinful lips aware. A man touching his woman. Gawd. My heart pounded. Trembling fingers grasped the long straps of my bag anchored on my shoulder. Demolished in one casual, intimate touch. So much for my control.

Further down the block, lovely feathered and beaded masks inside a shop caught my eye, and I paused a moment, gaping at the astounding displays. They were nothing like the little imitation Mardi Gras masks I'd seen for years. Of course, I'd never been to New Orleans, either.

"Look at the feathers on that one," Trent said, his hand a soft pressure at the curve of my shoulder and neck, urging me to turn right. The wonderfully gaudy mask on the far wall certainly had the longest feathers I'd ever seen but it was Trent's fingers sliding over my skin that caught and held my attention.

I flicked my eyes up to his. He studied me, not the mask, his eyes growing more intense watching my small gasp and parted lips.

"It's, um, lovely," I mumbled, turning back to the mask.

"Yes, it is," he whispered so close to my ear his breath heated my skin, and this time there was no mistaking the caress of his fingers on the inside of my elbow and the shiver that coursed through me.

We rejoined the trek to the casino, but his touches continued. Never obvious, never lingering long, just a simple message to look here, to move there. God, he was killing me. My body thrummed in constant arousal, waiting for the next small touch, eagerly accepting a claim never spoken yet clearly made.

The Golden Gate's line at the deli stretched around the inside perimeter but moved at a steady pace. Roxie spotted some Red Hot paraphernalia hanging on a display rack along the way. "Hey, that reminds me. I talked to a local Red Hot Lady this morning at Sam's Town."

She frowned at me and then asked, "You been there yet? No? Well, Sam's Town is a fun casino down from Thousand Trails—got this huge forest in the middle of it—and like Boulder Station, they specialize in these humongous meals. Cheap, too. Albert and I eat at one or the other place a lot. Always see someone there from the park, especially at breakfast, don't we Albert?"

Albert nodded.

Roxie barely paused. "Anyway, the Red Hot Lady was a kick. She had her hat on, so naturally I went over to talk to her. Says she meets Hot Ladies from around the country that way."

I traded amused looks with Gwen. We often used the same technique in Seattle. Wearing a hat, especially when in full regalia, is an invitation for other members to network and an icebreaker for the curious.

"I'll bet," Gwen said. "Vegas attracts lots of Red Hot Ladies, and sometimes the local chapters act as hostesses or ambassadors."

"Yeah, that's what she said," Roxie nodded and Trent's hand pressed low against the small of my back, moving us closer to the deli cases. "Her group is hosting a dance Monday night, a Sock Hop. And you know our ladies, they're going all out on the theme, let me tell you. My goodness, the music! The Platters, Dion and The Belmonts...who else? Albert, you remember. Who else did we listen to?" She poked Albert, her face a study of concentration.

"Everly Brothers," Albert responded.

"That's right! They were great. I still have some of the old records, you know, we play them every once in awhile, don't we Albert? Someone's going to do Wolfman Jack, and Casey Casem or maybe Dick Clark as the DJs, and they're gonna duke it out...you know, like Duke, Duke, Duke, Duke of Earl," she chanted and played an air drum.

She had us in stitches. One of the ladies behind us chipped in. "Remember poodle skirts and saddle shoes?"

"Yeah," her companion added, "And men in tight pants with their collars flipped up." She wiggled her white eyebrows, her inner devil peeking out in her smile.

Gwen laughed and threw Shay a flirty look. "I bet the guys will call themselves Rat Johnson and Captain Marvel and have rum and cokes and snow cones."

Shay flashed back a teasing grin and predicted root beer floats and penny loafers.

I noticed Trent looked increasingly puzzled. Oh, oh, I thought, trouble in River City. I'd avoided thinking of the age thing, but he *was* the youngest one here.

"Tell me about this...huh, ladies club," he said, eyeing the large matching bags Gwen and I carried. Simple totes in white canvas, an appliqué of our own Red Hot Lady in a sweeping red hat dominated one side, with our chapter name, Dazzling Darlings embroidered in a purple appliqué underneath. On the other side, our names were hand-stitched in small purple lettering near the top.

"You don't know about the Hot Ladies?" Gwen chuckled. "How could you have missed all the ladies in strange purple outfits and red hats? There are so many of us these days!"

He shrugged. "I've seen them, but that's about all."

"Well, the women over fifty wear red, under fifty wear pink. We always have some Pink Ladies at our events. There are over two million of us worldwide, celebrating being older by having fun. I make all the ladies in my chapter one of these bags. We have huge banners with Miss DD—that's what we call our symbol—on them, for our chapter to carry at conventions and such. Lotsi was one of my first members."

Trent looked at me. "You're not old enough to wear red," he said, apparently serious.

Naturally, that should have stroked my ego, but my stomach iced over and I looked away. I'd known, just known, he was too young for me. Despite the dread, this had to happen sometime. "Yes, I am. I'm fifty-eight."

A grapefruit lodged in my throat. I felt the weight of his gaze but couldn't make myself look as I stood stiff and silent, waiting for his reaction. I wondered if the mesmerizing little touches would stop, now that he knew.

Trent shifted closer, circling my waist with a firm arm until I looked up. His eyes awaited mine, soft, peaceful. His hand rubbed up and down in a tiny caress. Without a word, he made his acceptance and his continued interest plain.

Now I felt foolish, and so disturbingly relieved I ducked my head, blinked a few times and moved up the line.

"So, are we going?" Gwen asked me, and I ran the conversation back in my mind. Oh, yes. The dance.

Shay added his encouragement. "We might as well. Monday Night Football doesn't start until the following week, so what else is there to do?"

I laughed. "What a guy! Sure, sounds like fun. And if Trent can go, he'll, ah, get to see some Red Hot Ladies in action."

"I'll be there." Trent's rumbley voice never sounded more assured or more welcome.

One worry knot eased and another snarled as the next question arose. Just how much younger was Trent, anyway?

Chapter 5

The next morning, the three golfers, Shay, Albert and Trent, had a seven o'clock T-time. Sunday morning! At that hour, we women were not yet civil, which encouraged the men to leave quietly. An hour or so later I took a tour around the park roads, greeting fellow campers out walking dogs or putzing around their rigs.

Since one of my primary objectives on this excursion was to determine if a full-time life on the road agreed with me, I'd watched the other travelers along the way, talking to them about the joy and grief of fulltiming. Without exception, they loved the life. Of course, I cautioned myself, those who didn't were long gone. However, the reasons why they remained on the road struck me as interesting.

They did it for the freedom, freedom from a fixed home, a fixed lifestyle, a fixed weight upon their soul. They did it for pleasure, the pleasure of seeing new places, meeting new people, making new friends. For the spontaneity, the satisfaction of being able to pick up and go wherever, whenever. Even when they didn't.

I don't know where I fit in that profile. I recognized its lure, though, and its pull grew stronger. Once I did what I needed to do with Kaitlynn and Bianca, I'd planned on heading out thataway, whichever way I'm pointing at the time, and see what I shall see.

Now...now there's a Trenton Wallace-shaped question mark looming inside, anchored somewhere deep. How could that be? Despite the addictive casual intimacy we'd fallen into, I'd known the man for only a couple of days, and yet, I'd known him forever. Despite the temptation, part of me insisted I didn't need nor want his kind of distraction and upheaval in my life.

Why now, for Pete's sake? Why not ten, fifteen years ago when I'd considered looking for someone? Tried to look for someone. But no, no one suited, no one stoked my furnace, no one got the...the penis factor going.

What was I to do with him now?

The jaunt around the park yielded no answers to the Trent question mark. It was too huge, and even more disturbing, too important. I couldn't wrap my mind around it. Perhaps I never would.

When I returned to the motorhome, Gwen was bright-eyed and bushy-tailed, planning a trip to the Swap-Mart. "It's insane," she said, "Booths of all sizes and all kinds of stock cramped into one gigantic building. You'll love it."

A Swap-Mart? "And we're going there because...."

"Lotsi, don't tell me you've never been to a Swap-Mart before. I knew you were deprived, but sheesh! Well, consider it part of your new lifestyle. Every retired person, fulltimer, and Hot Lady goes to Swap-Marts of one kind or another."

"Hey, I'm all three, so bring it on!"

"Attagirl. We'll get you up to speed in no time. There's no telling what we'll find, but I'm looking for something with a fifties feel for the dance. Hmmm, maybe a new hat. What did they wear in the fifties for a hat?"

"Pillboxes, maybe? We'll have to ask Roxie."

By the time we'd talked to Roxie—she'd worn kerchiefs in the fifties, not hats, but did remember pillboxes with little half veils—we ended up with five ladies in Gwen's Lexis SUV.

Riding in the SUV reminded me about the towing issue. I'd sold my Acura RL because the gears or something made it unfeasible to tow behind the RV. Shay's Lexis had the right stuff. The concept of towing a vehicle intimidated me. Heck, I couldn't even park my rig in one of those tiny spaces yet, how could I corner or back up with a vehicle attached back there?

After the assurances I'd received about how easy it would be to ride my Kawasaki Ninja, I figured I'd better snag Shay for a serious discussion on the subject. For now, the spiffy motorcycle suited me fine as a get-around vehicle. I had to fit in a few more practice sessions, that's all.

Five hours and several overstuffed shopping bags later, we returned to the park exhausted. We'd found fifties stuff all right. We had enough to hold our own sock hop, which naturally Gwen planned to do when she returned to Seattle.

We had long felt skirts and miles of net petticoats, bobby socks, pillboxes for the ladies and Panamas for the men. No penny loafers or saddle shoes, though, we'd wear our own flats. I had a lightweight sweater twin set in my rig I'd wear. If Gwen didn't find a suitable top by tonight, we'd be back shopping tomorrow.

I crossed my fingers and wished her luck. Serious shopping with Gwen took endurance and cast iron feet.

Shay woke from his nap and passed along a message from Trent asking me to drop by if I was up for a walk. My exhaustion fled. I stashed my stuff, changed into walking gear, slipped a small bottle of water in a belt holder, and left in less than ten minutes. Not that I rushed or anything.

Clear cerulean skies had heated the day to the mid-nineties. Definitely not as comfortable walking as this morning, but I didn't think we'd be aiming for our aerobic target zones.

Following Shay's directions, I spotted Trent's RV near the end of the last row, a forty-two foot Mandalay with four slides. I hadn't seen one before and I was anxious to check it out. The grand investment this baby required was more than I was willing to place on an experiment. Although if a certain turtle finds she likes toting her shell around....

Still standing at the door, I discovered my curiosity competed with a reluctance to enter Trent's home. I'd never considered the intimacy of entering someone's personal space. Not having crossed a man's threshold for fifteen years, considering it now placed a certain nervous anticipation on the act of knocking.

I knocked.

My heart kicked into gear when the door opened almost beneath my hand and Trent welcomed me with a huge smile. He hadn't been napping. Relaxing perhaps, and so mouth-watering in bare feet, bare legs, and...and bare chest. God, what that man could do for a plain pair of khaki shorts.

"I'd begun to wonder if you'd chicken out," he said. "I should have known better."

Almost doesn't count, does it? "Yes, you should have."

He stepped back. "Come up."

The entrance arrangement of the bus-style motorhome never seemed so awkward. The steep steps rising in front of the passenger seat, the small area at the top that forms a narrow isle between the seats seemed crowded as he waited there, watching me come up. If I'd kept going, I could have squeezed past him and gone on down the aisle. Maybe. He had arms. Sneaky ones, too.

I stopped. I needed to see him, just for a moment, to melt into those hot Ghirardelli eyes and watch the flecks of gold dance in their depths. This close, almost body touching close, I could smell him, a faint aroma of fresh civilized products and warm primitive man. The need to touch his bronzed skin, to run my fingers through his masculine pelt hit like a shockwave. I fought it off, keeping my hands to myself, but my eyes roamed freely.

There, at the base of his throat, his heartbeat throbbed faster and faster. The pace his bare chest rose and fell quickened and stuttered. Fascinating. Then a muscular twitch response rippled over his body, his hands clenched, and his equipment surged and grew down where no lady should look.

Focusing upward again in self-defense, I saw his gaze linger at my similar places. The flushed hunger on his face sent a shaft of arousal piercing deep inside. Heart racing toward fibrillation, breath fast and shaky, my sex swelled and gushed. "I...oh, god...what you do to me. I can't take much more of this."

Tearing his eyes from my peaked breasts, the sensuous glaze in his eyes turned predatory as he leaned closer. "We can cure this real easy. Real quick." A slashing grin. "And then real slow."

It took a moment for my heart to restart and with it, my self-defense alarms finally kicked in. I needed to back us both down before I imploded. "Oh, I'm sure we could,"—I held my hand up to stop his forward movement—"but it's too soon. I didn't mean to...I only wanted—damn." I dropped my hand and slumped there, so frustration and inarticulate I wanted to shoot myself.

Humor softened his face, and this time I didn't stop him when he stepped close and drew me into his arms in a gentle hug. "Yeah, me too." Then he pulled back. "Let's go for that walk, shall we? I'll only be a minute. Have a seat and...." He broke off when I took my first true look at the inside of Trent's RV and my lips pursed in a silent Wow. Here was another droolable RV, spacious, elegant, and sensible.

"Or take a look around," Trent teased, following me into the center of the open living area. "You haven't seen a Mandalay before?"

"No, and I love it! Look at that desk." Hooked already, I moved closer to check it out. "A real desktop area! Have you seen the so-called desks in most rigs? They're a joke! You have file-sized drawers! I'm dying here. And your printer actually sits where you can use it...wow."

Trent's light-hearted laugh drew my attention. He stood with his hands on his hips and devilment on his face, so sexy he made my heart sing.

"Now I know where your priorities are," he said. "You haven't even looked at the kitchen!"

"Oh, I'm the same way in the kitchen, believe me. If something is used, it should be efficiently usable. That's why I love this desk. It's my favorite feature in Gwen's Phaeton, too. All of the others I've seen stink! Do you use it much?"

"Yes, I do. When I'm working, anyway."

Funny, we'd never talked about work. That's usually the first thing that comes up, back in my former world. "Oh? What do you do?"

Trent kept pace with my meanderings through his motorhome. "Nothing spectacular. I do some consulting for the company I sold a few years ago. I've been fulltiming since then. Seems to work well for me."

We did the complete tour, and I have to admit, the Mandalay was spectacular. The bathroom arrangement was the best I'd seen, and the kitchen pantry was ingenious. Darn. Now I'd have to choose which one was my favorite, Gwen's Phaeton, or Trent's Mandalay. Well, not *Trent's* Mandalay...a new one. For myself. Someday. Maybe.

While I extricated myself from my mental quagmire, Trent slipped on a polo shirt and a pair of cross-trainers, and we went for an easy stroll down to Sam's Town. We talked more about our families and raising children.

He had two girls, younger than Kaitlynn, starting their families in Santa Barbara. I discovered his wife had died ten years ago, and that had to suck worse than divorce. That led to our social lives, as in relationships, which I managed to gloss over with a generalized "nothing serious for some time." He nodded, saying that no relationships had stuck long with him, either, and then he looked into my eyes, and said with that serious intensity of his, "No one's knocked my socks off before now, either."

I ignored the sparky burst of exciting tingling shooting through every nook and cranny. It's just a line, I scoffed, you've heard similar from lounge lizards looking for company that night. Trent just packs more punch, that's all. Yet I wanted to believe. I-I just wanted.

He started to say something into the silence, then let it pass. We kept it causal after that, fun stories of vacation camping. Arriving back at his motorhome, I stopped outside. He turned, waited, then quirked an eyebrow and asked if I'd like to come in. From his half smile, half smirk, I figured he expected me to say no. I did.

For the first time, he reached out to me, cupped his hand behind my neck and slowly rubbed the bones at the base, up and down. "I find it impossible not to try and change your mind. Do you want me to?"

"Are you asking if I'll agree to be seduced?"

"Lotsimina, you have an interesting way of seeing things."

I'd wanted him for hours, days, but just the way he said "Lotsimina" in that deep, sexy way of his made me breathless and achy. "I could say the same thing about you. After all, you asked the first question."

The pressure of his hand urged me closer. "Maybe I shouldn't ask. Just take."

"Oh, I love your lines. You're so damn good at this."

His X-rated lips curved a little more, his hand urged a little harder. "Does that mean its working?"

"No," I lied.

"Liar," he said softly, watching my mouth, the rise of my chest as his hand caressed my neck. Pure lust radiated from him, licking over my body. Meeting my eyes, he smiled a male-to-female smile so hot it went through me in a blaze of fire, branding me, claiming me. An image exploded in my mind. I could see him taking me as if viewing from a few steps away, but at the same time I felt the heat of his naked body sliding over mine, felt my desperate need to open myself to his penetration, his possession.

A shudder ripped a keening moan from the depths of that need. My knees began to buckle. I thought the world went black for a second, but it was only my eyes fluttering closed.

I heard him mutter, "Christ," and his hand tightened at my nape as the other gripped my arm. Nothing tender there. He grasped hard to hold me up and shook me. "Lotsi! If I touch you another two seconds I'm dragging you inside, I swear to God."

My eyes slitted open. A harsh, savage tension etched his face, his eyes nearly black. I wanted to slurp him up.

His hands shifted to my shoulders, fingers digging into my flesh. "Move your butt now, or I'm taking it as a yes, do you hear me?"

I moved. A slow, careful step back. His hands stayed on me. "I hear you," I whispered. Then with more conviction, "I'm, uh, I'm fine now."

He studied my eyes before he let me go, running a hand over his head as he muttered and paced, throwing glowering looks my way. I was thoroughly disgusted with myself for losing control over my own body, but I began to resent his attitude. He'd started it. What the hell did he have to complain about?

Irritation filled his voice. "Do you have any idea what seeing your woman respond like that does to a man?"

What? I started to blow about his being awfully presumptive with the "your woman" part but just couldn't get the words out. I growled right back at him. "And you think saying something like that helps *me* out? Get a grip, Trent. I'm the one fighting these damn superhormones here!"

"What are you taking about?" Trent frowned and stopped in mid-pace, dropping the hand he'd used to scrub over his jaw.

"Never mind. It's nothing," I lied again.

"Lotsi? Is that you?"

The uncertain questions came from behind and I turned to look. Smiling her cherub's smile, her hair neatly styled, wearing make-up and matching blouse and slacks, a seventy-something lady stood on the other side of the road and down a couple spaces. My goodness, what was she doing here?

"Charlotte! I don't believe it!" I ran to hug her, almost faint with relief—I didn't want to explain about overactive hormones thank you very much and dreaded that Trent would insist.

"I thought it was you!" Charlotte called out. "My, isn't it wonderful, running into you all the way up here?"

How had I missed her camper? I saw it over her shoulder mid-way down the row, the only Class C in the park. Probably the only one in 90% of the larger parks nationwide. The short, truck-style camper with a bed over the driver suited her to a tee. That's why she'd had it for twenty-some years. Small, unpretentious, frightfully organized, Charlotte was one of the most content people I know and a secret guru for my new lifestyle.

Charlotte kept throwing glances at Trent, who'd followed me to her space. She'd probably gotten an eyeful of our little interaction. Keeping an arm wrapped around her, I turned. "Charlotte, this is my friend, Trent."

Oh yeah, she'd seen us, all right. She had that knowing glint in her eye that said she knew exactly how good a friend Trent was. "Trent, meet Charlotte, The Pumpkin Lady. She winters at the Slabs, what they call boondocking—I'm too much of a backwoods camper to call open desert RV camps the boondocks—you've been fulltiming for...how long?" I asked Charlotte.

"I'm a newcomer, barely twenty. For my friend Carl, over twenty-five years." Charlotte laughed, but then frowned as she glanced over at a giant forty-two foot bus jockeying into place across from her toy.

The driver shouted out of the window to the woman standing nearby.

"They've been at it for twenty minutes," she lowered her voice, although the people couldn't have heard over the distance and the racket the driver was making. "I saw them come in. That's a tight space for that size bus. Makes me happy with my little home. I feel sorry for them. Well, for the wife anyway. He's made six or eight attempts to back in. Had her out directing the last few times. Apparently he doesn't take direction well."

"Goddammit, Martha, you can't see anything from that side! Get your ass over there!" Leaning out the window, the red-faced man pointed. She moved to the other side. With a couple of feints forward and back, he appeared ready for another thrust.

"It's not easy," I said, growing nervous watching and thinking about it. "I've driven my motorhome all of four days now, but haven't had to back into a space yet. And the other parks had larger spaces than here."

The long motorhome started backing slowly. Gesturing with her hands, the woman watched the driver inch the bus toward the hook-ups. The clearance between the coaches on either side looked incredibly tight to me, growing smaller as the big rig moved back. How could anyone fit something that large into such a tiny space?

I was terrified, thinking it could be me at the wheel. This was my greatest fear about fulltiming on my own, breakdowns included.

"Those spaces in the other parks were huge, in fact," I amended. "Really huge. Personally, I like the pull-throughs." I could hardly watch, but I couldn't not watch. I'd get my own rig back in a few days. It wasn't that much smaller.

"I told you to get a Class C," Charlotte's smug voice purred.

"Yes, you did." I sighed. "Wish I'd listened."

"It's not that bad," Trent said. I could tell he was laughing at me. "Just takes practice. You need to focus on placing your rear tire next to the stubouts. Forget the rest."

"Easy for you to say. But the spaces here...Gwen said Shay could park my rig for me," I admitted. "Just this once."

"Richard!" Martha's hand signals changed, grew frantic. "Richard, you're going to—"

A dull crunch echoed. The bus stopped. Perfect silence reined, then the door snickered open and out came a furious tubby, snarly bear. "What the hell's the matter with you, Martha? Can't you see the damn post?"

Since even a fool could see the damn post was on the side he'd made her leave, he shut up and went to inspect his crumpled rear fender.

"I'll park your rig," Trent announced, eyes intent on mine, unsmiling. The little emphasis on "I'll" spoke volumes. Any other time, I would have refused point-blank and parked it myself, whatever it took. The crunch replayed in my mind. To ask Shay now would be churlish. I nodded.

Charlotte invited Trent in to see her hobbit home. When I insisted, she dug out some pictures of the pumpkins she'd painted for thirty years, and newspaper clippings detailing awards, interviews, and the famous people who'd come for her pumpkins year after year.

Unfortunately, I needed to get back to Gwen's. When we were outside, I gave Charlotte another hug and invited her over in the morning to meet my friends. A blistering curse from Richard the Jerk across the street cut through the park. He'd managed to park while we were inside and was working at the sewer and water hook-ups. Another curse rang out. Then the shocking scent of raw sewage hit us.

Trent laughed quietly, his face lit with the devil's own delight. "Look at his roof. He's mixed up his water and sewer connections, back flushed his holding tank right up the vent."

Spreading across the roof and dripping down the side flowed a growing tide of toilet paper and waste.

Trent smirked. "I'd say the man is definitely not a happy camper."

Chapter 6

The next morning I searched for my Rexall in the acres of concrete jungle between the repair shop and office. Assorted campers and RVs sprouted haphazardly, and I found mine lurking behind a brightly painted behemoth. As I walked closer, I noticed the steps were extended. How odd. Surly I'd retracted them before I left. Although I'd been excited about the motorcycle, so maybe I hadn't, but the mechanic would have noticed. Wouldn't he?

Oh, well. I'll get used to the external steps eventually. Diesel pushers with the engine in back and the passenger door entry have interior steps, but my old gas rig has a front engine hump between the seats. Passengers use a mid-section entrance and external steps. More than one person has cautioned me beginners like me damage them if we leave them down and hit a driveway or some other obstacle.

I'm sure switching back and forth between the two types of rigs wouldn't help form good habits, but even more dangerous, hanging around Phaetons and Mandalays tempted my sybaritic tastes. Maybe I should trade up. I sighed. No, my old gal might not have all the bells and whistles, but she's my first rig, and she suits me fine.

She did look a little forlorn parked out here, but I intended to break her out as soon as I could. For now, I needed my twin set for the dance tonight and pictures for Gwen.

I dug a digital camera out of my Miss DD bag and took some shots of the long length down from a front corner, walked around the front to the other side. Focusing on the little display screen I played with the zoom button and took a few shots. I didn't register the man pawing through my undercarriage storage bin until I heard a sharp voice lash out, "What the hell are you doing?" and saw a tiny man on the screen stand up and face me.

Of course, when I lowered the camera, he wasn't tiny at all. Especially when he took a few steps toward me, his face surly and mean, his arms bulging and fists clenched. He looked freaking *huge*.

"I was just—" I stepped back then caught myself, snapped my spine straight and demanded, "What the hell are *you* doing in my storage bin?"

A young man ambled around a back corner. "Hey, Ms. Hannon! How's it going?" The cheery kid with the droopy drawers, Billy. I gave him a tentative smile, relieved at the interruption. The older man didn't seem threatening now, and indeed, with twenty or thirty feet between us, he probably never had been. Single women develop excellent imaginations, but still....

"Have you met my Uncle Charlie?" Billy said. "Ms. Hannon, this is my uncle, Charles Benson. He helps out here sometimes. Ms. Hannon burned up her wheel bearings last week," he explained to his uncle. "We're waitin' for parts."

Billy paused, looking at the open bay and back at Uncle Charlie. "What're you doing?"

So, even his nephew questioned his actions. I waited for Charlie's response. After a sparse nod to me, he gave his nephew a begrudging answer. "John wanted the jack. Thought it was in this bin, but it ain't here."

The boy frowned, swiped a sleeve over the side of his face, absorbing some sweat and smearing some grease. "Naw. Tools are in the other side." He turned back to me with a teasing grin. "So how're you doing with the Kawasaki, Ms. Hannon? Did your hat survive your wild ride?"

I laughed, tucked the camera in my bag and fished around until I found my keys. "Kind of you not to ask if my Ninja survived. And you know very well I didn't have a wild ride. I barely got out of first gear!"

"Well, there's wild and then there's wild," he said and joggled his brows. "I thought that hat was totally wild, you know?"

His wonderful smile charmed me so I played it up. "I'm starting a new fad in helmets for older ladies, you see. Since everyone knows old ladies never go fast, who needs those ugly things when they can wear our stylish hats instead?" As Billy described my hat in glowing detail to his puzzled Uncle Charlie, I thought of my penchant for fast speed—my last ticket was for over a hundred—and vowed again to shake loose some practice time with my current hot road machine.

For now, I needed to rush. I had a dance to prepare for. I had a date to prepare for.

I wasn't sure I liked that idea at all.

"Your room looks wonderful. Straight out of the Fifties!" I assured Sherry, the beaming Queen Mum.

The local Red Hot Ladies had indeed gone all out with the school dance theme. Banners lauding the Class of 1957 decorated several walls. Crepe paper streamers abounded, pom-poms decorated the walls and various hands of happy senior cheerleaders who worked the room. Red and purple dominated, of course. Even ladies in poodle skirts and the like managed to have red and purple somewhere.

Sherry's queenly figure showcased a class sweater, long full skirt and saddle shoes. A jaunty red tam with purple feathers set atop her bouffant hairdo, pink scalp showing through the henna rinsed, hair-sprayed helmet. She'd used a heavy hand with her makeup and glittering bling. The gaudy red pins and jewelry clashed just a tad with her decades-old-style outfit.

As the Queen Mum leaned closer, she screwed her colorful face up as if confiding a state...er, a royal secret. "I got most of the stuff off one of the Internet sites, you know. Even the food. I couldn't believe all the junk they had. Cost a leg, let me tell you, but Bertie insisted."

She nodded toward the makeshift soda fountain table across the room. "That's my husband Bertie over there. Looks like Fonzie, don't you think?"

I struggled to find the resemblance. Maybe if I subtracted forty or fifty years...no, I still couldn't make the leap. He was having a good time, though, serving root beer floats and snow cones from behind the laden table, a long line of cheerful elders waiting their turn.

"Bertie graduated high school in 1957," Sherry said, as if that explained it all, and perhaps it did. "He's having so much fun with this event I think we'll do it every year. Where'd you say you folks were from?"

Although we'd needed several vehicles to transport us all, we'd come in together, so perhaps she thought we represented one chapter. Sometimes a group from one or more chapters will caravan or bus across several states to attend interesting events.

"We're from the RV Park," I said, "over on Boulder Highway. We've several Hot Ladies with us. My Queen Mum and I are from Seattle. Our other guests, well, they're from all over."

Roxie came over, and after greeting her hostess, told me that Trent was looking for me. Since Roxie had dragged him onto the dance floor as soon as we'd arrived and kept him there, he needn't sound as if I'd gone missing.

"He's some dancer," Roxie added with a wink. "That boy's got the moves. Takes a crane to get Albert on the dance floor, you know, and I gotta tell ya, he don't move like Trent."

With another wink, she shooed me away. I took her comments as an apology or explanation for absconding with my date. Not that Trent was my date. I'd gotten my head straight about that. We'd joined a group of friends at the dance. That's all.

I arrived at the double table our group had staked out as our base. Erwin, hot and laughing, passed me towed away by a tall, Amazon-sized woman twenty years his senior.

Gwen laughed behind her hand and watched him run his partner out in a sexy swing move. "After the first dance, the ladies haven't let Erwin sit out a single dance. He flirts outrageously with all of them. And you should see Tremaine."

I followed her eyes, watched, and bit my lips. "He'd better have insurance."

She looked puzzled. "Broken hips?"

"No, heart attacks. Some of the ladies haven't had that much excitement in thirty years!"

Tremaine wore his hair slicked back in a perfect ducktail. He looked more Latin than Black tonight, trim and elegant, emanating smoky sex in his signature black Armani. He played the ladies, careful with the shaky ones, adventurous with the hardy ones, bold with the younger ones, beguiling them all. They were lining up, the pinks, the reds, and the unaffiliated.

Albert was the only man at the table. I started to ask about Shay but saw him leading Charlotte the Pumpkin Lady back our way after dancing to a crooning Pat Boone.

"Hi," Trent's sexy voice sounded inches away. My heart tumbled to the pit of my stomach. There was a general shuffling of chairs and Trent ended up beside me. Close

65

beside me. I ordered my body and thoughts to toughen up and put some space between us.

No date, I reminded myself, trying to ignore the thought that I'd probably be in his arms tonight, sharing a small chunk of floor space with the most inflammatory man I'd ever known. He not only got me hot, he made me burst into flames...and I'd decided playing with fire was a dangerous thing to do, and playing was what he wanted. Flattering maybe, but dangerous.

I pictured a meteor, flaming through the atmosphere, consumed by the fire until only a pitiful scrap survived when it hit the earth and buried itself deep and alone for eons to come.

God, how depressing. But a good image, I thought. Better use it to remind yourself you're no one's shooting star.

Roxie came back with Sherry and a few other locals, and Gwen and I were drawn into the usual Hot Lady chitchat. Trent stayed through it—valiant man—and Erwin was sitting out a breather, when Roxie asked Sherry how she'd become a member. After Sherry replied, she asked Gwen the same question. It's a common question, but I wondered if my friend would fluff it off, or tell the whole story.

Gwen caught my eye first, and her lips twitched, half smile, half grimace. "I don't often tell my story, because it's not an easy one, but here goes. Two years ago, I fell down the stairs and broke my leg in nine places. While I was being prepared for surgery, they took a chest x-ray, and found I was riddled with cancer. The really shocking thing was that I'd had two chest x-rays taken during the previous year, but my doctor didn't read the radiology reports. Twice. So I had the surgery, recovered from the fractures, and then went into cancer treatments."

Shay wasn't usually around when Gwen told her story. Pausing now, she took his hand, shared one of those husband-wife looks of empathy and support. "Chemo was hard on me, especially the last of the three rounds. Real hard. Shay took me home to New York to visit my family afterwards. I was gone five weeks.

"When I came home, my daughter...." Gwen's eyes glittered and blinked. "She'd left a hat stand on my dresser, with a beautiful red hat on it. There was a copy of the poem, Warning, and a note from my daughter, telling me, 'Here you go, Mom. Now go have fun.' I made my first year as cancer-free three months ago. That's why Shay and I are on this trip, to celebrate the life we have together."

I'd seen people respond emotionally to Gwen's story, not only her trials but also her daughter's affirmation of love. Tonight, seeing the way she and Shay shared her triumph, was even more poignant. Sherry's comment especially caught my attention. "You've been given a special gift. I wish we'd all learn to celebrate the life we have together."

Like a compass seeking north, I turned to Trent, found him watching me. For a long moment, his probing look held me captive, and then without a word he lifted my hand, kissed the back soft and slow, and laid it on his thigh.

Now how could I resist that? I was becoming addicted to the eloquence of his silence.

Fortunately for my peace of mind, we started dancing, and with a few pointers from the older set, we worked on moves I'd never seen. The Slop, the Hand Jive, the Bop. I remembered doing the Bop, but not like the Dance Police showed us. In 1957, they did a more formal version, more like swing, not as vigorous as we worked on in the next decades, yet more demanding. All the dances that night were more in step with your partner, but a step away from your partner. It was a blast, and put the kibosh on Trent's tendency to slide in and pull tight.

Ricky Nelson, Jerry Lee Lewis, Chuck Berry, and of course, the early songs of Elvis populated the night. The Dueling DJs, with their pseudo-rivalry kept the music pumping, Buddy Holly, Perry Como, The Everly Brothers...and the music packed the floor. Roxie hounded

Albert, until in a pique, she flounced off and danced and flirted with every man who wasn't nailed to a chair.

One of the last songs for the evening was Mr. Blue, by the Fleetwoods, and Trent didn't hesitate. He spun me out to start and when we came back together, he wrapped his whole body around mine and we danced heart to heart, breath to breath, scent to scent. No fancy tricks, no feely moves, no pushy behavior. Just close.

I felt his every heartbeat, his every breath, and knew he felt mine, escalating each other's response. When my breath hitched, his arms pressed me even closer, so close I felt the pulse of his sex pressing against me. Without thought my body shuddered and my hips surged closer. For one insane moment, I wanted to shift my legs, create a nest and let that thick, hard shaft slide inside....

His head drew back and he whispered, "Lotsimina?"

I looked up. What he wanted to ask echoed in that word, in his eyes. I heard the answer my body wanted to give loud and clear, but my head screamed even louder that I'd avoided relationships for a reason and I'd best be careful. "Not yet," I whispered. "Please."

He didn't hide the disappointment, but repeated, "Not yet," and kissed my forehead.

When I went to bed that night, I relived that dance many times, and when I dreamed, I soared through the night as a shooting star, and reveled in the blazing flight.

The dream's memory stayed with me as I walked to Sam's Town the next morning. Cooler temperatures and restless feelings encouraged a brisk pace. I went for a second circuit. The way I felt, I needed to burn up a treadmill. I needed to slam some weights around. I needed a damn gym.

Yet it wasn't iron I wanted to pump. It was Trent.

I'd left for my walk early, within minutes after Shay joined the men for their golf game. They had a foursome this morning. Erwin's boisterous laugh, muted by the early hour, melded into a male harmonic of greeting as the men congregated at Shay's SUV.

I found myself listening for Trent's voice in the mix, hanging on to each sound as it vibrated through me, exacerbating the persistent need I could barely suppress to see him, touch him. This attraction for Trent wasn't going away, it was getting worse. What was I going to do about it?

Physical activity usually clarified my thoughts but so far, the only thing coming out of my walk this morning was a bad case of frustration and a good sweat.

"Look, you're making this more difficult than it needs to be," I spoke aloud, using the empty sidewalks to my advantage. I'd learned the fine art of talking to myself from years of living alone. I have the best conservations that way, and can argue from both sides without hurting anyone's feelings.

"This is your new life. You like him; he likes you. Go for it!" Yeah, well that was the easy side.

"But I just met him! And even worse, I'm only going to be here for less than two weeks! What am I supposed to do, jump into bed and then say hey, it's been nice, bye?" Now that side truly sucked.

Okay, so now we have the opening statements. Time to dig deep.

"This is about sex. The best sex you've had coming your way in the history of ever. What's wrong with enjoying yourself? There's no harm here, no foul. You have needs, you know you do. You can't pretend you don't anymore. You can't ignore them."

"Oh, yes I can! I'm damn good at doing just that! And I'll tell you what's wrong. I let this happen, then what? Do it again at the next campsite, with the next guy I get the hots for? I'm not cut out for brief encounters. I didn't start this new lifestyle to become a court and spark junkie, hooked on the latest piece of hot chemistry that comes along. I'd rather have nothing than something that superficial!"

"Yeah, well, it's not like your long-term relationships spared you from superficial. On their part, anyway."

"Great, rub it in. So I've been around that block a few times and it didn't work. Didn't matter whose ass hit the door first. They didn't work. That's not going to change my need for relationship sex into suddenly embracing recreational sex just because I haven't been getting any. And what else can this be? Tell me that."

No rebuttal. I took a deep breath, felt the ache press deep and hard, fought down the useless tears. Nothing has changed for me. Buying into this attraction would lead to the kind of personal pain I've spent fifteen years avoiding. What's different is the temptation. Trent.

I'll put my portfolio at risk—for the right temptation. But my heart?

I'm not buying into your company plan, Trent. I'm not playing your shooting star. I'm not changing my lifestyle that much.

End of discussion.

The first person I ran into when I returned was Roxie, charging down the street toward Gwen's spitting fire. Albert had gone golfing.

"I thought they'd scheduled games for all week," I said, confused.

"Yes, but that was before last night!"

Goodness gracious. When Roxie did chirpy, her face, her voice, her whole body expressed exuberance. Now she did mad the same way. Thunder rolled across her face, icicles formed on each word, and belligerence radiated from every cell.

A mental review of last night's activities left me clueless. "So what happened last night?"

"What happened? I'll tell you what happened! I left Albert last night, that's what happened! The nerve of that man. You saw him! He refused to dance with me all night long. Then after we got home, he had the *audacity* to say I'd made a fool of myself with other men. I should act my age, he says. Well! I've had enough of that old fart. If he wants to act like he's dead because he's seventy-two, that's fine. I'm not, and I won't act like it!" With a toss of her head, she dared the world to disagree.

"No, of course not," I hastened to reassure her. See, I told myself, they've been together for fifty years and they still can't get it right! My decision to stay clear of intimate relationships, especially recreational ones, made me down right cheerful. "You said you've left him?"

"I did. Spent the night with Charlotte. I went home to see if he's ready to talk about it, but noooo! He's out playing golf with the boys! Probably didn't even notice I was gone. It'll be a cold day in hell before I go back now!"

We went inside, explained the situation all over again to Gwen, and then Roxie decided that since Albert had gone gallivanting around, she would too. Nothing would cheer her up more than a nice excursion with her friends. She whipped out her cell and made short work of setting her plan in motion. The three of us and a couple ladies she'd met the night before would deck ourselves out in full regalia and descend on the MGM Grand for a cruise through the casino and a decadent lunch.

I'm sure shopping was included in there somewhere.

Now, five bodacious babes in various purple outfits, magnificently decorated red hats, red-feathered boas and enough assorted jewelry to sink the Titanic create a collective field of dramatic energy. With Roxie's mood the driving force, dramatic edged toward reckless. We were going all out. Outrageously expensive and slathered with sophistication, Emeril's at the MGM was the obvious choice.

71

Because Emeril's has a limited lunch hour, we headed there first. The New Orleans theme and Cajun food brought up the Red Hot Ladies Club national convention in New Orleans cancelled because of the flood. Since most of us had been to its St. Louis replacement or right here at the MGM in Las Vegas the year before, we reminisced about some of the wild RHLC events and our favorite crazy costumes. Then the wine arrived.

Roxie poured out the first bottle of the pricey golden nectar and ordered the second before we finished looking at menus. "Too bad Charlotte couldn't join us," she addressed me, hanging onto her wine glass like a lifeline. "I know she's not a Red Hot Lady, but before I went to see what's-his-name this morning, she told me about your visit. In February, wasn't it?"

Poor Albert. He had some serious sucking up to do.

"Yes, Valentine's Day." I turned to the lady who hadn't attended the conventions and explained the reference. "Grandma Luge—she's the luge Olympian from the Virgin Islands, Anne Abernathy—was a speaker at both conventions, sort of a before and after. Man, what a gutsy woman. I can't imagine getting that many broken bones and going back for more. This was her sixth Olympics, the oldest woman ever. And she's one of the funniest women I've ever heard. She's a great Red Hot spokeswoman."

"Yeah, she is. I saw her on some talk shows," the local woman said. "Too bad she was injured during the trials. Our chapter was all set to watch her event together, but when she was eliminated, we did a Grandma Luge Recovery Valentine's Party instead."

"Well, when I heard her event was on Valentine's Day, I remembered Charlotte's party. She winters in the desert at one of the no-frills RV sites, and puts on a huge Valentine's Party every year. We'd set up a Red Hot event for Grandma Luge, but like you, we changed it a little, and had a wonderful bash. We were worried about Anne, though, so it made seeing her in St. Louis even more inspiring. Just her being in the Olympics was a special statement about older women, not just Hot Ladies."

"Darn right!" Roxie crowed, her glass jolting as her elbow slipped off the table. "Juss because we're older, don' mean we're ol' sticks. Some of us can still kick up our heels, by god. Right, girls?" Roxie led the toast, polished off the last gulp of wine, and promptly ordered another bottle.

By the time we finished lunch we were just a teensy bit tipsy. Perhaps that's why I was a little too bold when I recognized the most unlikely person wandering the casino floor.

Chapter 7

"Why, it's Uncle Charlie! Charles...Benson, I believe. Billy's uncle."

Our group had dispersed a few minutes before. Gwen, with a firm grip on Roxie's arm, and another lady went off to shop; the others beelined toward the slots. I headed into the bowels of the casino in search of Starbucks. The trilling rattle and clash from the cavernous slot rooms dimmed behind me as I passed the baccarat and high-stakes poker dens, the shops where people—God watch over Albert's charge cards—can drop their winnings and then some.

I spotted Billy's uncle near the security desk. His face blanked as he stared at me. Did he forget, or did the red hat and purple gown freeze his brain?

"I'm Lotsi Hannon, with the motorhome?" I prodded Benson. The man looked sharp in an elegant dark suit and silk tie. Sharp, but befuddled. Why was that? Sure, I looked different, but so did he, with his hair gunked back with gel, nametag and a black ear bud—what was he, a pit bull? No, a whatchamacallum, pit boss or something—but I certainly knew it was the same man.

My voice sharpened. "From yesterday, at the shop?"

"Ah, of course. Ms. Hannon. Sorry, didn't recognize you with the hat," he said, glancing from the offending article to my bag, which he probably remembered better than he remembered my face. Men forget an older woman so quickly.

I laughed. "Fair enough, I almost didn't recognize you in the suit. Pit crew?" I nodded toward the nametag.

"Security," he snapped, and then looked displeased.

Ha! Security probably preferred to remain invisible to customers. A man's ego trips him up every time.

"Sir?" A younger version of Benson—suit, nametag, ear bud—stopped by his side.

"Excuse me," Benson muttered. Turning away, they engaged in a quiet conversation.

Intrigued, I watched their dynamics. Benson clearly held the superior position. Hey, maybe there's a possibility here. Older women as security...being invisible could be an advantage. I bet it's primarily surveillance work, and given a good pair of glasses, nobody has better peripheral and rear-view vision than an experienced mother or grandmother.

The young man sped off, and Benson turned back to me.

"Are you head of security?" I asked, ready to start grilling him in earnest about potential opportunities. One never knows what could come in handy, after all.

His cell beeped. Scowling, he reached for his belt holder. Before he could flip it open, he muttered, "Shit," and reached for the other hip. "Gotta run," he said, and took off, yanking a walkie-talkie from under his jacket as he placed the cell to one ear and the walkie-talkie to the other.

Hmmm. I bet the ear bud was yakking at him, too. Who needs that? Forget casino security work.

I saw Trent leave Gwen's RV the next morning and head down the road, presumably for his own rig. Boy, was I in for it now. He didn't see me. I'd parked my newly liberated home by the store and walked over, cutting through the back. No use hanging at Gwen's until Shay came home now. She would have told Trent I picked up my rig this morning. How did everything get so damn complicated?

My plan was working. I'd avoided Trent all day yesterday. Most of the day was involved with the excursion at the MGM. After dinner, I took my Kawasaki Ninja for a spin, worked on my shifting and balance for awhile and then caught a movie. I figured once I was in my rig, I'd stay busy cleaning and rearranging my stuff, organize the storage bins, spend time away from the park with Gwen and Shay. He wouldn't stay interested long.

However, the unfortunate understanding that Trent would park my rig still hung over my head. I'd hoped to avoid this too. Now he knew I would arrive soon, and that Shay was gone. What excuse did I have for not allowing him to park my rig?

What I needed to do was park my own damn rig!

I headed back to the store. Carla, the clerk, was an RV Wonder Woman. One of the four and a half million female RVers, she'd been a fulltimer for eight years. She would help me figure out something. I needed a field, a parking lot to practice in. Look how much a little practice helped with handling my motorcycle. I'd even gotten it into third gear! Having some proper instruction beforehand might have helped, though. Maybe Carla knew an experienced RV driver who could go with me, teach me a few tricks. That would work. I could do this.

Erwin and Tremaine browsed through the gift racks. I stopped to talk. Maybe I could ask one of them...no, bad idea. Golfing buddies were a bit like girlfriends, right? You don't ask one to go behind another's back.

While we chatted, Richard the Jerk and his wife, Martha came in. A calm and pleasant woman, I'd enjoyed talking to Martha when our paths crossed while she walked her cocker spaniel, so I introduced her to Erwin and Tremaine. The Jerk took one look at Erwin's blond cap of swirls and thin fuzz line on his coal black chin, cocked an eye at Tremaine's spectacular good looks, sniffed and turned away. We all ignored him.

Erwin's bright smile flashed over my shoulder just before a hand clamped onto my upper arm and Trent's voice growled in my ear. "Excuse us, please. We need to talk." Then he hauled me out of the store.

Pissed, I tried to pull loose. He tightened his grip and tugged harder. "Jerk," I mumbled, but went along until we were outside. "Dammit, Trent, let me go!"

I'd have protested more but I glimpsed a line of grinning spectators at the windows. Okay, this was not the place to square off. Trent pulled me around the corner to the pool passageway, near the gate where I'd first laid eyes on him. Oh, that burned.

He faced me and his hands gripped both shoulders. "You have two choices," he announced, voice deep and growly. "We can hash this out right here, right now. Or we can go park your rig."

How fierce he looked. Face stretched tight in sharp angles and thunderous brows, narrowed chocolate eyes darkened almost black and glittering with angry determination. Why did this dangerous side of him attract me as much as his sexy charm?

Dangerous was the key. I considered my options, which were more than he'd provided, and made a quick decision. "My rig is the Rexall out front."

"Smart choice."

When he dropped his hands, I spun around. I'd gone three steps when he snatched my wrist.

"Slow down, Stretch," he said, sliding his fingers down to tangle with mine. He didn't let go until we were inside my camper and he'd shut the door behind us.

"Space number?" He held his hand out for the keys, and when I gave him a number a few down from his, he twitched one eyebrow and didn't say a word.

I watched carefully while Trent parked my RV, studying technique. After all, I had to learn this stuff, but I don't know how he did it. As if small spaces and narrow roads

77

weren't enough challenge, many spaces had extra vehicles jutting onto the roadway at odd angles. With an enviable calm assurance, Trent jockeyed around several times, aligning the long bus with some mysterious instinct, then took it back into the perfect position in one steady motion.

Amazing.

The rest was a snap. We worked together and had it leveled, hooked up, slides extended and the air cooling in less than twenty minutes. Watching him soon became less about learning and more about need. I sensed every move he made, even when I wasn't looking, building an awareness of him until I felt synchronized to his breath, his body, his thoughts. That's silly, I lectured myself, unnerved by the seductive intimacy of the feeling, but I couldn't shake the connection.

Trying to establish some distance, I set out some kitchen gear and then started opening and closing doors around the room, digging out a few items as I found them. Trent looked puzzled.

"I can't remember where I put everything," I said, and laughed. "I call them my homey touches. A couple of plants, some rugs, a few family photos and knickknacks." I put the small treasures into the places I'd planned for them, made a few adjustments.

"Nice photos," he said, examining them closely.

"I'd noticed all the fulltimers had personal homey touches, so I had mine ready. This is my first real stop, so I haven't set them out before." I looked around, pleased. "I think I like it."

As strange as it seemed, the few personal items made the small space feel a part of me. Maybe I could find a special place again. A home. The feeling was so alien, so powerful, my eyes welled, and I turned away, hiding the pain, the hope. The dream.

Trent's arms wrapped around me, turned me to press fully against him. The contact burned through my nervousness, laid bare my vulnerable underside. When he didn't press for more, I relaxed and opened to him, took him in.

Burrowing into the haven of his neck, I smelled the musk of his skin, melted into the heat of his hard body. Long hours thinking of him, avoiding him, had banked a tiny fire deep inside. The last hour together had fanned the coals to glowing embers, but with the touch of his body, the smell of his flesh, the embers burst into flames, heating my sex, fogging my mind, and I welcomed the sensual haze.

Closer. I needed to be closer. As if in answer, his arms wrapped tighter, strong bands of flesh around me. My tongue slid inside the notch of his collar, slowly swept up the column of his neck. Hmmm, delicious.

"Lotsimina." Trent's breath brushed against my ear. Lips nibbling, I couldn't resist a gentle bite, right there where he tasted so good. He shuddered. Oh, god yes. I wanted more of him. "Lotsimina!"

"Hmmm?"

He started to move me back but I held on. "No way, love. We need to talk."

What for? Everything was going great right now. Then the sensual fog lifted enough as we eased apart to know he wanted an explanation for why I'd avoided him. Damn. I shouldn't have given in to his allure. I should have kept my distance.

I tried a little humor to regain lost ground. "I thought that was the woman's line."

"Smartass." Trent sounded pleasant, but tension simmered beneath the surface. "Looks like we took another one of those giant steps backward since the dance the other night. Want to tell me why?"

"Not really."

"Tell me."

I licked my lips, searching his face for an answer that wasn't in him but in me. I didn't find it there, either. My shoulders fell in defeat. I couldn't lie. He wouldn't let me avoid him. It was time to face reality. That usually drives off suitors faster than the L word, anyway.

"When I'm with you, when we touch, everything seems golden. Later my mind comes back online, and all the warnings and cautions take over again. Self-preservation, I guess."

"So this is about fear? Your fear of what, relationships? Commitment? I didn't take you for a coward."

What he'd probably meant as a sexual goad was something far more sinister to me. Out of nowhere, a dark pit opened and I fell, tumbling into my past. Demons arose, skyscrapers of pain, betrayal, anger. My deepest adversaries. Perhaps I'd never bested my demons, but after a lifetime of battle, I'd brought them under control—mostly—and no one, *no one*, was going to belittle or undermine my hard-won victory.

I jerked out of his arms and stepped back several paces. "Goddammit, don't you dare call me a coward when you don't have a clue about what I've gone through! You think a coward runs when she faces the fire. Well, fuck you. You stand in the goddamn fire long enough, often enough, you're not a coward to run, you're a damn fool to stay! And *I'm no fool!*"

Rigid and shaking, my fingers clamped into fists, I stood there facing him. In him were all the men I'd compromised for, prayed for, sacrificed for, fought for, begged for, and by damn, suffered for. Never again.

Because when only the ashes remained, not a single one had so much as noticed I'd given him anything worthwhile. I for damned sure valued myself more than that.

Trent faced me without moving, without yielding. Weighing, watching, his strength testing mine. I waited for one of the typical male reactions that played in my mind, none flattering.

"No, you're no fool." Calm, reasonable, his reaction disarmed me. "You're a woman warrior with strong and powerful guards on the outside, and a loving wounded core on the inside. Tell me something." He walked toward me. "Are your fierce guards still protecting you from harm, or are they now preventing you from reaching out for what you want?"

He stopped an inch away. Waited.

I couldn't respond. He'd exposed too much, left me stripped all the way through. I stood rigid, breath coming in shallow gasps, heart racing as if its very pace could outrun what I saw in his eyes. Naked truth rested there, not in a challenge, not in a taunting dare, but in acceptance. Tenderness.

Oh god, oh god, oh god, my mind whispered, praying, panicking, pleading. Everything in me longed to accept what he offered. What did I want? I knew only one thing. I wanted him.

I struggled to tell him. To reach for him. I couldn't move. I opened my mouth, but no words came out. I begged him with my eyes.

Trent's gaze sharpened, diving deep as if he searched for hidden treasure. His hand cupped the side of my face. "What do you want, Lotsimina Hannon?"

His soft demand struck my defenses, my inner guardian, full force. I felt something yield and weaken. A glass barrier enclosed me inside, thick safety plate glass, with jagged lines radiating outward from the impact of his words, rippling into a crazed spider web pattern. I swayed, breathless. Trapped behind the glass. His eyes were all that held me upright. A terrible want filled me. I needed him more than I needed that safety.

A tiny sound ripped out of me and broke off. What I wanted most now was on the other side of the wall. Trent's words had struck a blow, but I must bring it down. My heart reached out, pushed with the force of the immensity of my desire. The inner wall collapsed into a million marbled pieces, cutting the strings in my joints and I sagged against the only solid reality I knew.

"You, Trenton. I want you." I whispered, entreating and offering at the same time.

Trent swung me up into his arms, and I whirled, floating, until I felt cool leather press against my back and legs. Then the heat of his body covered me, his hands gripped my head and his mouth fed on mine.

In one powerful beat of my heart need overwhelmed me. My lips, my tongue hungered to taste, searching his mouth for the Holy Grail, his flavor bursting through me, wild and bold. I felt his muscles tighten and move under my hands, against my body. Ravenous, I arched under him, seeking more.

Then the rough pads of Trent's fingers began feathering over my face, stroking down my neck, across my shoulders. Fire followed in their wake.

I needed those fingers lower, easing the ache in my breasts. "Touch me, Trent. Please, please. Touch me."

"Here, sweet baby? Touch you here?" His hands slipped inside my blouse and cupped the tender mounds.

"Yessssss." A shaft of desire struck to my core. My legs flinched together and my hips undulated, begging, pleading. Through my bra, his palms circled and rubbed.

His fingers captured my nipples. Squeezed. Released. Squeezed again, pulling, milking the tips. A dam broke loose inside, flooding me with sensations too intense to hold back. A short, savage cry rang out. My whole body convulsed and shook as orgasm pulsed through me.

"My God, woman, you're going to explode all over me when I get inside you, aren't you?"

Ripples of little explosions still rocked my body. The shocking power of the experience had stopped my breath. I think it stopped my heart. I know it stopped my mind, or I would never have blurted what came tumbling out. "No, I don't think so. I've never been very good at this."

Trent stilled in my arms. My body registered his quiet. One beat, two beats. I went on alert. Oh, god, what had I done?

He moved back enough to read my eyes. "Not good at...."

"At...at this, the sex thing. I never got it right. For me, that is." I rushed to assure him. How do I get in these horrible conversations with him? "I know a woman is responsible for her own or-orgasms, so I know it's my problem. I just concentrated on satisfying my partner...oh my god. Shut up, shut up, shut up."

Scalded by mortification and frozen by shame, I tried to climb over Trent, frantic to get away. Momentum carried me over the top, but his arms grabbed hold of me and we tumbled to the floor together.

Struggling to control the sobs breaking free, I waged a savage battle, feet, hands, elbows, twisting and shoving to get away. Terror drove me. This was all his fault anyway—destroying my barriers. What the hell, did he think walls protected in only *one direction*? I couldn't allow him—couldn't allow anyone—to see what threatened to erupt from that hated abyss.

Trent's voice began to filter in. "Shhhh. I've got you. You're okay. Let go, love. I've got you now. Lotsimina, listen to me. Let it come out, baby. I've got you."

I let go. Wrenching crying jags aren't easy to endure. Once released, they had control, not me. I suppose that's why I've never allowed them to start around anyone. Vulnerability is complete, the body defenseless, emotions wide open.

When the jag tapered off and reason returned, his hands were doing incredibly soothing things on my back, under my shirt. Tiny soft strokes, whispers of contact. His lips pressed slow kisses where he could touch, simple kisses to comfort.

I knew I was a mess. I used my shirttail as best I could. It was hard to meet his eyes when I drew back, but I saw only concern and warmth.

"Poor baby," he said, drying off my cheek with his hand. "You look exhausted."

Shrugging, I acknowledged the lethargic haze that weighted me down. I couldn't begin to process what had happened.

His lips curved, then widened, and then a throaty chuckle gushed out. I saw a gleam in his eyes and braced myself.

"So. We've got some retraining to do."

I frowned. "I don't think—"

"That's right. Don't think. Explore. Experiment. Most of all, experience what I will do to you, what we will do together. I don't want you...no, I *forbid* you to do anything to me. Unless I tell you to. You'll follow my lead on this, Lotsi. And I warn you, we have a lot of ground to cover."

"What arrogance! It may have been awhile for me but I—"

"How long has it been?"

Shit. Trust him to zero in on what I didn't want to discuss. "Awhile."

"How long, a year?"

I didn't answer.

"Two years? Three?"

I looked away, began buttoning my shirt.

"Lotsimina. How long."

I mumbled at my buttons. "Fifteen years."

Now *he* was quiet. I tucked in my shirt, swiped at my face some more. Fluffed through my hair. Looked up.

His eyes were furious. "Fifteen years. You're as sexually explosive as dynamite but you've denied yourself sex for fifteen years? You must've beaten them off in droves. It's not healthy, woman! What were you thinking?"

Leaning into his face, I poked him in the chest. "You're the one who has all these superhormones going, pal! I'll

84

have you know I haven't denied myself anything at all worthwhile, so don't bellow at me! Personal sex works just fine for *normal* hormones!"

Rubbing under my finger, he smirked. "Superhormones, huh? These the same ones that attacked you at my place? They just happen with me?"

I sniffed and moved back, tucked my feet into a half-Lotus and leaned against the couch. "Don't get smug. They have nothing to do with you. It's the fifteen years. I think there's been a gene mutation, triggered by the...the drought. Not a complete drought, but...you know."

"Gene mutation." Trent sat beside me, draped an arm across my shoulders and pulled me closer.

"I knew it was a mistake to get into this. It made perfect sense at the time. Okay, it's the fifty is thirty deal. That's an Oprah thing. We live longer, yada yada, so now our fifty is like their thirty. But I figured my sex hormones couldn't adjust when you...so they mutated these superhormones...just shut up!"

Trent was laughing so hard he should have choked. I decided to help him. I put my hands around his neck, but choking morphed into the sweetest kiss, leaving me rosy and soft, a lump of hope and ragged feelings.

I couldn't take any more. I needed time to sort things out. Breaking the kiss, I offered a small smile, my hands still threading through his wonderfully silky hair. "I told Gwen I'd be over...probably ages ago."

"All right." His lips touched mine again, nibbled gently. "See you tonight?"

"Yes," I said, and the answer seemed very right.

Already I felt the excitement of the evening to come, a giddy sense of hope and anticipation more fitting a teenager than a mature woman.

It felt so good.

Chapter 8

"You'll never believe what's happened, Gwen," I hollered at my friend as soon as I opened the motorhome door. Not hearing a reply, I thought she must be in the bathroom.

Anyone who had seen me on the walk over would have assumed I'd been drinking. Dorky smile on my face, muttering to myself, bursting out in spontaneous laughter. Another soft burst escaped as I latched the door and hopped up the steps, eager to tell Gwen how...how special Trent was. Maybe there was more than just chemistry happening between us. And that—

"Gwen? My God, what happened? Gwen!"

Sprawled on the kitchen floor, dress hiked up, arms flung out, all I could think of as I ran closer was the cancer had done something, the cancer...cancer....

Cancer doesn't do blood. I stumbled and halted a couple of yards away. Blood matted Gwen's head, pooled around her.

Gwen's blood.

"No, no, no, no," I chanted as I stared at Gwen's face, her graceless sprawl on the cold floor, and I knew. I hadn't gone this long through life without seeing death, but I'd seen death in a hospital bed, in a funeral home. Not on a kitchen floor.

A numbing stupor crept over my mind and body. Wobbly-legged and awkward, I took several steps closer and fell to my knees. I wanted to wipe the streaks of blood from Gwen's face. Put her battered head back together. Make it all go away. A kiss to make it better.

My hand reached to straighten her dress, to do something to give her dignity and respect, but all the years of TV cop shows and murder mysteries intervened and my arm dropped, listless.

In a crushing wave of despair and apathy, my shoulders hunched and my head dipped forward. Dry sobs rattled my bones, shaking some sense into me, and I managed to snap out of it.

No time for this shit. Gwen's dead, but some bastard did this. And by God, he's going to pay!

Now that I'd fixed on a goal, I knew what to do next.

"911. 911. 911," I muttered. "My phone, where's my phone."

In jerky, disjointed movements, I reached my feet.

"Purse."

A sluggish mind remembered dropping my Miss DD bag and I turned around. There were two bags. One on the floor by the couch near the bright splash of Gwen's hat from our impromptu Red Hot event yesterday, the other by the front seats near the door. That one's mine, I reasoned, and went to place that terrible call.

Afterward, I couldn't leave Gwen, couldn't turn my back so I waited on the couch, phone clutched in my hand.

Shay, I thought. How can I tell him? All the joy of their trip, their celebration...Oh, Shay. Their girls...I pushed it aside. Can't deal with everything. Just this.

What would Gwen want, what would she do?

Crystal sharp and bright, I remembered Gwen saying, "That's why Shay and I are on this trip; to celebrate the life we have together."

At least they had that. They had that. Cancer didn't end their time together, but at least they had that. It helped. A tear slid down into the crease of my nose.

I took a deep breath, let it out, and called Shay.

Chapter 9

To date, my personal experience with police had involved receiving speeding tickets. Some officers were even human enough to warrant a genuine smile as I took my licks. Nothing prepared me for the caliber of the cops that descended on the park.

All those shows and stories lulled me into expecting at least professional compassion, a certain steely competence and efficiency. The cool indifference displayed from the first cops on the scene shocked me. With the mere glance at Gwen, one cop began a walk-through of the motorhome while the other took me outside, had me wait by the door. He then ignored me, talked on his shoulder mike, the car radio, chatted with the other cops as they arrived.

Soon four cop cars, two fire trucks, and an ambulance clogged the drive. Personnel scurried through the open door with bags and equipment, oblivious to the surreal cacophony of crackling radios and flashing lights.

"Who caught this one, Franks or McInnaw?" one of new cops asked my guard.

"McInnaw," he said in a bored voice, a hand resting on a cocked hip as he watched cops rope off a perimeter with yellow tape.

"Better than Franks. He's got a burr up his ass lately," the man smirked. "I hear the Lieutenant's been riding him."

Laughter erupted from inside. I'd heard them arguing over the opening NFL game next week, calling out point spreads and bets. I wanted to scream something vitriolic. Didn't they realize that Gwen—my special, wonderful friend Gwen—was lying dead at their feet?

Yet despite the hateful disrespect, their chatter forced me to stay balanced between numbing pain and an urge to flee in howling bitter rage.

People from the park milled around. Erwin and Tremaine were there, and Charlotte. "Is Gwen okay, Lotsi?" she asked across the yellow barrier.

I shook my head no and started to speak, but could only shake it again and press a hand against my mouth.

The cop roused and frowned. "Hey, no talking."

Shay arrived, frantic and demanding to see Gwen. The cops pushed him back. Furious, I took a step toward the police line. "That's her husband, for God's sake!" I hollered.

With a disgusted glance at me, my guard waved at the cops holding Shay, who rushed toward the RV door.

My guard barred his way. "You'll have to wait out here, sir. You can't go inside."

"Lotsi?" Shay turned to me, confused as a lost child.

I wrapped him in my arms, an inadequate refuge for his shock and grief, tears of sympathy flowing as I held him. Through a blur, I saw Trent arrive, anxious eyes fixed on us as he tried to talk his way closer but to no avail.

Seeing Trent sharpened my worry and dried my tears in a hurry. Would he have problems with the cops? I'd seen him leave Gwen's rig. I didn't question his innocence—did I? No, no question there, really—but I worried the cops would hassle him unless someone had seen Gwen alive after he left her RV.

And Shay. Didn't they always suspect the husband? Shay had dropped me off at the RV shop and went off by himself to check out houseboats at the Bass Pro Shop. The park's front entrance is often unmanned. Registered campers had an access code for the gate. Would the cops think he doubled back? My confidence in real cops was sinking by the minute. Where was Columbo when you needed him?

An unmarked car with a dash light nosed in, disgorging a tall, cadaverous man with a mustache and thinning dark hair, his tie pulled askew, an impatient air about him. Hmmm, maybe we'd get somewhere now.

He eyed Shay and me huddled together and nodded at my guard, who responded, "Detective McInnaw."

McInnaw tilted his head. "Who are they?"

"The woman called it in. He's the husband."

Hearing the comments, Shay dashed a hand over reddened eyes and pulled himself together.

"I want to see my wife," he croaked in a watery, hoarse voice.

"I'm sorry, sir, that's not possible at this time." The detective glanced around the busy area and the knot of anxious friends, sighed, threw the cop a look. "Couldn't you find a better place to hold them?"

"No, sir. It's a camper. Just the main room and bedroom."

"Ever hear of a squad car, Officer?"

Tired of standing in the heat and alarmed by McInnaw's solution, I offered my own. "Excuse me, Detective McInnaw. My motorhome is one row over. If it's all right with you, the officer can wait there with Shay and me."

McInnaw's flat eyes examined me for a moment, face devoid of expression. "Appreciate that. Officer?"

We were still at the dinette nursing fresh coffee when McInnaw arrived almost an hour later. The detective declined refreshments and joined us at the table, while the cop leaned against the kitchen cabinets across the aisle.

The questions were direct at first, our statements simple, but my mind was in turmoil. What should I say about seeing Trent? Just because he hadn't seen me didn't mean someone else hadn't noticed me noticing him. However, if I was the only one that saw him at Gwen's, then I'd make his life miserable for nothing. Or was it nothing? What if...no, don't get paranoid. Surely even a seasoned killer couldn't have murdered someone and less than half an hour later been so lov...so tender with me. Could he?

Arrrgh, this was crazy making! Damned if you do, damned if you don't. I riled at my choices, but in the end, I told McInnaw, feeling guilty and anxious as hell.

McInnaw nodded, scribbled a note and then threw me for a loop when he asked, "Did you touch Mrs. Evans, move her, check for a pulse, anything at all?"

"No. I knelt by her. I started to—" Lord, I almost said, "make her decent," but Shay would go bonkers with worry. Thinking back, I thought her clothes had been disarrayed from falling, not from...well, I didn't want to go bonkers, either. "—to check a pulse, but I could see she was gone."

"You mentioned seeing two purses and being confused. Your purses look exactly alike. Why is that?"

I explained about our bags, our Dazzling Darlings chapter in Seattle. I began to feel like some interesting bug, the way the detective's dull eyes sharpened, narrowed with focus as he listened, his facial expression never changing, never expressing any thoughts or reactions. Was his attitude professional detachment or his lack of human caring? Perhaps for him the two meant the same thing.

McInnaw made more notes and the lifted his head. "Did you move her purse, look through the contents, or remove anything?"

"No, of course not! I told you exactly what happened. I saw both bags, but I knew which one was mine. Besides, all we have to do is check the names. That's why they're there."

"You didn't unzip the bag, remove the wallet?"

"No, I did not."

"Can you describe Mrs. Evan's wallet?"

Her wallet? What's with that? Are they thinking burglary? "Yes, it's a black, smooth leather clutch, overstuffed usually. I don't know the brand. Why, is it missing?"

Ignoring my question, he turned to Shay. "Mr. Evans, can you describe your wife's wallet? Did she usually carry cash, credit cards, a checkbook? Mr. Evans?"

Shay gripped a cold mug of coffee, body hunched forward, occasionally swaying as if his mind went away, his eyes open but empty. Probably a good place for him to be right now, I thought. Away.

Clicking back with us, Shay roused and said, "Black. It's black. She likes cash. She usually starts with, I don't know, maybe two, three hundred dollars and spends it down. We use one credit card, better mileage points that way, but she has a checkbook. Is something wrong?"

"Did she keep it in that bag, or someplace else? Maybe she switched purses sometimes, put it in a drawer for safekeeping, anything like that?"

"No, she's been using the one bag this entire trip." Shay's demeanor sharpened as his legal mind cleared. "What's going on, Detective? I insist you tell me. Now."

Irritation surfaced on McInnaw's blank-slate face, then submerged. "The bag appears to have been disturbed. The wallet is missing. I'd like you to go through the camper carefully, see if any other items are missing."

The detective asked Shay some pointed questions about where he'd been, what he'd done during his absence. "Basically I daydreamed. Looked at boats, thought about...about Gwen and me—" He looked away, blinking. After a moment, he cleared his throat. "I bought a pair of sandals, had lunch."

"Do you have receipts?"

"Receipts? Yes." Shay put his lawyer's game face on. "I can save you some time and provide a current photo if you'd like."

A faint twitch to McInnaw's lips acknowledged Shay's sardonic tone. "Appreciate that. If you'd have the receipts and photo available in the morning, I'll pick them up. Where will you be staying?"

"I'd like you to stay here with me, Shay," I said. He nodded.

Taking that as his answer, McInnaw stood. "Until then," he said, turned to leave and paused. "Oh, yes. Ms. Hannon, when you saw..." he glanced at his notebook, "Mr. Wallace leave the Evans' RV, was he carrying anything?"

Shay and I talked to his daughters, Kim and Michelle, making tentative plans for them to fly down in the next few days. Then Erwin and Tremaine arrived, followed shortly by Charlotte and Roxie. The police had questioned them all, their reward for hanging at the scene, I suppose. Trent hadn't been released yet.

Shay didn't talk much, but the activity around him kept him occupied. I'd asked him quietly if he'd like me to send them away, but he shook his head. "No. No, they're fine."

Plans for an impromptu dinner jelled, with Tremaine and Charlotte dashing out to collect various items. While I dealt with chores, Roxie became Shay's emissary, seeing to his needs, talking softly around and to him.

Albert showed. His hound-dog face and steadfast calm seemed a comfort as he and Roxie set aside their differences and double-teamed Shay, helping him start the difficult process of dealing with death, talking about Gwen and their life together. I knew from losing parents and friends that mourning mingles tears with smiles, often at the same time, and we mingled both liberally.

Tremaine fixed hors d'oeuvres, Erwin and Charlotte had the rest under control, so I tried to concentrate on washing salad greens instead of the personal panic attack brewing below the surface.

What horrid things could be happening to Trent? I didn't trust that McInnaw person an inch. Something about his eyes bothered me, the way they never revealed any life beneath their opaque surface. I'd bet dollars to donuts he wouldn't hesitate to pin Gwen's murder on Trent if he could. Maybe I should worry about rubber hoses and thumbscrews.

The background music and kitchen clatter must have masked his entrance, for I heard Trent's voice not far behind me.

"Naw," he said, apparently answering someone's question. "But I may need a lawyer."

I whirled around, every drop of blood draining from my face. The colander crashed to the floor. My heart raced so impossibly fast the room swayed, and I threw out a hand to clutch the counter.

Trent grabbed my arms. "Jesus, Lotsi," he said with a worried frown. "I was joking." He looked around, smiled at Erwin and Tremaine. "I have to drag her off again, so excuse us for a few minutes."

Which he did by hiking me up against him until my feet left the floor and walking through the passageway into my bedroom. He set me down long enough to latch the pocket door, then grabbed me tight and buried his face in my hair.

"I'm sorry, sweetheart," his soft rumble purring against my ear. "I didn't mean to scare you. You weren't really worried, were you?"

"You've met McInnaw. Of course I was worried!" My hands rubbed up and down his back. I couldn't get close enough to quiet my heart, close enough to ease my hunger. My lips sought his, soothed the panic and fear, and fed my need for this one man, this beautiful, enthralling man who drove me insane every time he touched me.

Trent twisted us around and I landed on top as we tumbled to the bed. A dark and wild passion raged in me, voracious, mindless. I was desperate to escape the hole in my world, desperate to reaffirm the vital new feelings Trent had awakened in my life. My hands pulled and tugged, reaching his skin, racing lower, releasing barriers until I held his pulsing, hardening penis in my hand. Oh, God.

Instantly we both froze, little shivers rippling through our bodies, lungs fighting for air. Trent's fingers, buried deep in my hair, tightened their grip. His tongue, thrust deep in my mouth, withdrew.

I couldn't release him. My want was fifteen years—no, a lifetime deep. His erection twitched and grew harder beneath my fingers. My hand tightened, burning from his flesh.

"Lotsi." Trent whispered against my lips. "Don't move, love. Don't move."

I whispered back, "I need you," and felt a deep shudder rip through him and echo in me, tearing loose a moan I buried in the softness of his mouth. My hand stroked down, measuring, testing. Sweet heaven, hot silk over steel. My body released a wet flow between my legs. I went for more.

Trent's muscles convulsed into motion. I blinked and found myself lying under him, my hands pinned by his on either side of my head. Erotic pain hardened his face. Dark eyes bore into mine. "Lotsimina, in two seconds I'll either come or be buried inside you. You don't want that."

Reading the emphatic "yes, I do" in my eyes, he shook his head, lips curving. "No, you don't. Your body needs this, but your mind won't understand when we're done. Trust me, sweetheart. This isn't the time."

I knew he was right. Between one heartbeat and the next, I burst into tears, words tumbling out amidst a spasm of broken sobs. "Oh, God, Trent, she was lying there, her head bashed in. The blood, the blood...why, Trent? Why Gwen? For God's sake, why Gwen?"

My fists hammered out the last words against Trent's chest, pounding out my rage, my pain, my utter helplessness. He rolled again, bringing me on top where his hands could soothe, his legs entwined with mine. His lips pressed again and again across my face as his whispers washed over me. I remembered a lifetime ago—this morning?—I'd heard similar words, in similar comfort.

"Go on, let it out," he said, "I'm here now, love. Damn cops. Couldn't come earlier. But I'm here now. Let go, sweetheart. I'm right here."

I hadn't realized how much I needed this. Needed him. His touch on my back, his hard body beneath me, his smell surrounding me. I needed his warmth, his words. He filled me. Anchored me. Strengthened me.

With a last shaky inhale, I relaxed against him. "I hope this doesn't become a habit, my crying all over you."

His chuckle bounced me around on his chest. "I'm not worried. I think you're a champion holder-in, not a weeper."

Tucking my elbows against the warm platform he provided, I propped my chin in my hands and looked down at him. "Normally that's true but lately—" I'd done a lot of raging and weeping the last few months, but this...this brought pain to a whole new level. My eyes leaked. I laid my head back down and breathed deep. Trent ran his fingers through my hair, a gentle scalp massage of infinite sweetness.

"Did McInnaw give you a hard time?" I asked after a moment.

"Just some persistent questions. I'm not worried. This morning, when I saw Gwen—I didn't tell McInnaw this—she teased me about you, told me if I was stubborn enough, I could have you, and if I wasn't, I didn't deserve you."

I lifted my head, startled. Curious.

He smiled into my eyes, and then his voice firmed. "I told her when it came to you, I was the most stubborn son-of-a-bitch you'll ever know. You'll have to tell me to get lost and convince me you mean it before I'll let you go."

I'd seen enough now to almost believe him. My face heated. I ducked to hide a watery grin and didn't say a word.

Moist air from Trent's soft laugh bathed my skin. He slapped my rump. "Come on, Lotsimina. Time to get a move on."

Later that night, my RV emptied of all but Roxie, who insisted she'd help me keep Shay company. I put Shay in my bed, and she and I made up beds in the living room. We talked for a long time, but even after Roxie dozed off, I lay there, staring into the night, too numb to think, too wired to sleep.

At first, the noises didn't register. Then I knew. Without a thought, I went to him. He'd taken off his shoes and lay on top of the coverlet fully clothed. Men have it so much worse than women, I thought, seeing and hearing Shay battle against his need to mourn his wife.

I didn't say anything. What was there to say? I lay beside him, held him while we wrung ourselves out, lost souls protected by darkness, bound by the woman we grieved.

The next day went by in a kaleidoscope of jagged vignettes. Murder victims, it seemed, lost all rights to dignity and a normal family burial.

"I'm sorry," the funeral representative said in saccharine tones. "The police haven't released the body."

I jumped McInnaw at the door when he came for the documents. "Of course we haven't released the body," he explained with an edgy grittiness. "The investigation is still on-going."

"When will Gwen be released?" I asked, refusing to let Gwen be relegated to "the body". "The family needs—"

"I'll notify Mr. Evans at the appropriate time. Tell him we'll hurry things along. I'll pick him up this afternoon at three o'clock for a formal identification of the body."

I could learn to hate that man.

Then the vultures circled. A few reporters slipped by the front gate—scary thing, that—and knocked on my door. Their only reward was a "No comment" as I shut it in their face. I didn't answer my cell unless I knew the number calling.

Trent hadn't left my RV all day, chatting with whoever dropped by while Shay mentally drifted in and out. Thankfully, I kept busy as hostess and as impromptu mediator when Albert came to see Roxie, but when McInnaw took Shay to the morgue, I started to come unglued. Damn all those TV shows. I couldn't help but see Gwen on a slab.

I'd walked Shay to the door, and stood there, sort of lost, wringing my hands and hurting, until Trent came to me, gave me a one-armed shoulder hug, brushed a kiss over my forehead, and whispered, "Come sit down, sweetheart."

He sat down beside me on the couch, using my hand to rub his leg, giving non-stop tactile comfort as Roxie picked up the conversation McInnaw had interrupted.

"I'm not still mad at you, Albert," she said, uncomfortably caught between wanting her husband's understanding and wanting to fulfill her own needs. I suppose that's why she'd asked us to stay. "I told you that last night. But Gwen's passing changed something for me, and I-I want to work this out. I'm needed here, and I'm not ready to come home yet. Can you accept that?"

Mournful sharp grooves etched Albert's long face, the bags under his eyes dark and pronounced. "I need you too, Roxie, don't forget that while you're thinking things over. Don't throw out the comfortable shoe for a new style that catches your eye."

"Oh, Albert, you make me sound frivolous. I'm not looking for a new beau, I'm...I'm—you just don't understand!" Roxie jumped up and hurried into the bedroom, closing the pocket door behind her, leaving a distressed and bewildered Albert staring after her.

"She was flirting with that Henry Lakehurst," he said. "Told me he had enough energy to shake his bootie at a dance, she just might see how he liked to shake his bootie in private."

Naughty Roxie, I thought, secretly pleased the seventies hadn't stopped her from rubbing sparks off her man. Evidently, she'd fanned the flames with some innuendos, and now with Gwen's death, she'd lost the opportunity or perhaps the inclination to collect on the heat she'd created.

"I don't think you have to worry about Henry," I said, not wanting to spill too much but unwilling to prolong Albert's pain. "Roxie's been very upset about Gwen. Even though Gwen was younger, she'd gone through her cancer scare, and she'd come to terms with life in a way I think Roxie needs to think about. She just needs a little time."

I tried to convey reassurance in my smile, and maybe it worked, as he nodded and sighed. When Roxie didn't reappear, he threw a last longing look toward the closed door and stood. I invited him back for the evening gathering.

Phone calls winged back and forth to Seattle. I'd spoken to both her daughters, and to Evangeline Campton, Gwen's Royal Assistant for her RHLC chapter, Dazzling Darlings. Evangeline, otherwise known as Lady Tacky, Duchess of Ever Camp, was desperate for further information. She'd received calls from other chapters wanting to help honor and celebrate Gwen's life. I needed to hash out some firm plans tonight.

With that in mind, I ran outside to jump on McInnaw again when he brought Shay back, catching the detective before he could pull away.

"Just a minute please, Detective," I said, pausing to give Shay a hug. "My bedroom's all yours if you want to rest, or join Trent and Erwin. They've already popped a beer and are talking football."

I knew Shay and Gwen were avid sports fans, and normally Erwin would be a football fan's wet dream—an ex-pro lineman sitting in the living room talking shop. Tonight I wasn't sure what Shay needed, solitude or football, or simply background noise and warm bodies moving around.

Shay nodded and I went over to McInnaw's sedan, put my hand on the door and after a few rounds of push and shove about the needs of the crime scene vs. the family, I got the motorhome released to us by noon. We'd have two hours to get it cleaned and ready before Kim and Michelle arrived, but we'd get the job done. I took my hand off the car. McInnaw gnashed his teeth in lieu of a smile and departed.

Football won. Parked in my recliner with a Sam Adams, Shay listened to Erwin's colorful and exuberant stories about training camps and pre-season games, egged on by a lively Trent. Oh, goodie, I thought. Four more days of pre-game hoopla.

Joining the kitchen brigade, I found Tremaine searching though my spices and the contents of the tiny pantry, checking his menu and calling out items for Charlotte to put on the grocery list. The length of the list made me nervous.

"Tremaine, honey, can I see that?" I asked, taking his menu in hand, "Wow! I'd love to have you do Superbowl Sunday. But for tonight, let's see if we can compromise a little, okay?"

He struck a pose and pouted. With his dark angel looks and elegant style, he could pout in my kitchen any day. "No chips and dip," he insisted. "Or cut up veggies." His lip curled in a sneer.

When I agreed, he uncurled his lip. Charlotte offered her special deviled eggs, and he brightened. By the time we'd worked out a menu with everyone contributing a favorite dish he beamed, kissed his fingers and saluted, exclaiming, "Bene appetite!"

My, what a trial, but so adorable. He had all of us women shaking our heads and smiling, willing to do about anything to make him happy.

Then Tremaine and I went shopping. I'd just found a wonderful assortment of cheese and sundried tomato ravioli when the thief struck. In all my fifty-eight years, I've never had my purse stolen from a shopping cart. Never known anyone who had. Tonight my luck ran out.

A loud crash yanked my attention from the freezer case. My cart banged against a glass door as the thief wrestled with my Dazzling Darlings bag, caught in the seat wires. The pimply-faced fat kid threw me a frantic look as I yelled. He tugged again and the bag came free.

The thief took off in a mad dash.

"Stop, you sonofabitch!" I screeched at the top of my lungs. "That's my Red Hot purse!"

Chapter 10

I ran after the purse thief, screaming insults and commands all the while. The kid's short fat legs couldn't keep up. I shut up and ran harder, gaining ground. With one last, panic-stricken look at me closing in, he burst from the store, leaped into a waiting car and peeled out.

"Lotsi!" I heard Tremaine pounding up behind me. In rigid fury I stood staring after the car, chest heaving while I sucked wind. I didn't think about the license plate number until too late. "My God, Lotsi, what happened?"

"Oh, Tremaine. It's awful, just awful," I crumpled against his chest when he reached for me. "He stole my Miss DD purse, the one from Gwen. There wasn't even a damn wallet in the bag! It's just not fair. It was from Gwen!" I fought back sobs, trying to catch my breath. "Now it's gone too!"

"There now, sweetie," he cooed and patted my back. "There now." Then his voice changed. "It's all right, folks, we just had a thief. She'll be fine."

I rubbed my face, took a deep breath, and took care of business, all the while boiling with hurt and anger. Tremaine stayed close, patting my shoulder or my hand as I told the manager what happened.

"But he didn't get your wallet?" Tremaine asked as though looking for a ray of sunshine.

"No, I'd stuck my driver's license and bankcard into a pocket when I went out on the Kawasaki the other day and left the wallet on the shelf." I pulled the edges of the cards from my pocket. "I grabbed the cards tonight but took the bag with me from habit." That burned. If only I'd left it at home.

Maybe the manager felt relieved about the wallet, but he sounded so damned condescending. "Well, at least he didn't get anything important."

Not important? I almost punched him. "I'd give that kid a hundred bucks to get my bag back. Two hundred. He could hold it for ransom and name his price. The bastard."

The guy didn't understand, but Tremaine did, and patted my shoulder again. "The bastard," he echoed. "I'd like to smack him for you." His eyes hardened into narrow slits. "I'd like *Erwin* to smack him for you!"

God bless him. I laughed and thanked him for the lovely thought, but asked him not to mention the incident. No way would I let this nastiness hurt Shay any further.

Friday morning began with a tight agenda. During our planning session the night before, Roxie had suggested calling a couple of her local Red Hot Ladies to help clean and stock Shay's motorhome. Not that there was much square footage to clean, but that awful black fingerprint residue coated everything, and we wanted the larder well provisioned with decent meals, not packaged frozen entrées. We were coordinating that effort when Charlotte knocked once and threw open my door. •

She stopped as soon as she'd clambered up the steps. "Oh, Lotsi," she said, near tears, hands clinching and wringing between her breasts. "I'm so sorry, but they've arrested Trent!"

"What?" I bumped against the dinette as I lunged to my feet. "You mean for Gwen's...for Gwen's...how could they be so *stupid*?"

Charlotte rushed forward. "I'm sure they'll realize their mistake soon."

"McInnaw?" Roxie snorted. "Get real. That jerk wouldn't admit to an error if it bit him on his—"

"Surely he's not *that* bad," Charlotte rushed to reassure her. "He *is* with the Las Vegas police, after all. They're some of the best, aren't they?"

I blinked, traded glances with Roxie.

"Uh, that's on CSI, Charlotte," Roxie said. "McInnaw wouldn't make it on TV."

Hmmm, scary thought. I wrenched us back on track.

"When did they arrest Trent? Did he talk to anyone? Did you see him being arrested?" My mind raced over options, who I could call, what worm had lodged in McInnaw's twisted brain.

I'd told McInnaw about seeing Trent leave the motorhome, but we'd met not long after that at the store. Erwin and Tremaine were there, I'm sure they mentioned the same event. Trent hadn't changed clothes, hadn't been upset—wait, he had been upset. At me. For avoiding him. Had McInnaw read something else into his actions?

Charlotte spoke fast, her voice growing stressed again. "I just saw them. I was walking through the park, and saw Detective McInnaw speak to the police driver and then Trent left in the police car."

"Was Trent handcuffed?"

"Well, I-I don't know. Yes, I do. He sort of waved to me as they passed. No handcuffs." She looked relieved, her face curving into her normal pleasant lines for the first time. "That means no arrest, right?"

"I think that's what it means. But then, I watch CSI." I still wasn't happy, but my heart stopped knocking in my chest. "What is McInnaw thinking?"

Someone pounded on my door. Hard. I peeked out the window. "Well, well, speak of the devil," I said, and let him in. "Yes, Detective?"

He came up the steps, glanced at my friends, and with his give-away-nothing face, said, "I'd like you to come with me downtown, Ms. Hannon. I have some questions to ask you."

No way. I'm sure my eyes bugged out. I know my stomach iced over in fear. My heart skittered and raced. What was going on?

"And you can't ask your questions here, in my own home?"

"No, ma'am."

I stared into his flat eyes. There was nowhere to dig, nothing to grasp, no hint to pursue. If I wanted information, I had to go along with him. I wondered what he'd do if I refused. I was perverse enough to find out, except for Trent.

"Do you stand by your word to release Shay's motorhome by noon?" I asked.

Heat flashed in those black depths. "Yes."

Nodding, I turned to the goggle-eyed ladies standing at the table. "Go ahead with the plans for cleaning. Between the two of you, I'm sure you can suggest some dishes to prepare. Please remind the ladies to use disposable containers, nothing large; the side-by-side freezer isn't very wide. And everyone has to be out by 2:30."

"Okay."

"We'll take care of it."

Grabbing my wallet, I almost asked McInnaw how long I'd be gone but he'd probably enjoy stonewalling me. I turned back to Roxie. "If I'm not back in time, please ask Erwin or Tremaine to take Shay to the airport."

She nodded.

The trip downtown seemed longer than it was. I kept my thoughts to myself and my fears at bay. McInnaw used silence as a weapon, or perhaps he was too bored to care about civil niceties. I debated the question until he settled me into a coffin interview room, bleak and confined.

He made a production of recording the preliminaries, and then leaned toward me, elbows laying on the table, hands loose, drilling me with his cold gaze. "Tell me about your relationship with Trenton Wallace."

Frowning, I considered my answer. "I don't think we have a relationship. I have an interest in Trent, and I believe he has an interest in me."

"How long have you known Mr. Wallace?"

"Since the night I arrived in Las Vegas, a week ago today."

"Did you meet him before then? Perhaps while he was on business in Seattle?"

"No."

"Did Gwen Evans approve of your interest in Mr. Wallace?"

"I...what...yes, she approved." I didn't like the shape of that worm I began to see festering in McInnaw's brain.

"Was Mrs. Evans jealous of a man coming into your life? Did she quarrel with Mr. Wallace—warn him to stay away from you?"

I jumped to my feet, body thrumming with fury. "How dare you insinuate something so despicable about...about all of us!"

McInnaw straightened, gloves completely off. For the first time, I could see the mean, implacable core of the man, the cop. "Sit down, Ms. Hannon. Now! I'm not done with my questions."

Slowly falling into the hard chair, I balled my fists on my lap, piercing flesh with my nails. "You aren't asking questions, you're making vile suppositions about a dead woman because you don't have a clue what's really going on!"

His head inclined. "That's my job, finding the clues. Were you and Gwen Evans lovers?"

"No! We were friends!"

"When did you first meet Mr. Wallace?"

"Last Friday night."

"And yet you were seen kissing him two days later?"

The questions went for hours. McInnaw would leave the room for long periods, and when he returned, pick up where he left off. I envisioned Trent in another coffin room, taking his turn at being hammered with the same sort of garbage.

Would Shay be next?

At last my inquisition ended. No one would answer my questions regarding Trent. Emotionally battered and exhausted, I returned to the park in time to thank the generous Hot Ladies who'd pitched in to help. Shay and I left for the airport. It'd seemed prudent for Shay not to drive, but now I mistrusted my own state of mind.

I agonized over how much to tell him. What was best, spare him the ugly details or prevent him from being blindsided?

He took the question out of my hands when he said, "I imagine you and Trent had a rough time in interview today. Are they seeing a conspiracy or just one of you acting out of passion?"

That lawyer's mind, lawyer's experience—I think I admired Shay more at that moment than at any other, hearing the compassionate acceptance in his voice, feeling the non-judgment straight from his core. It pinched at my heart.

"I think they're leaning toward the theory that Gwen and I were lovers, she was jealous of Trent and he...killed her in an argument over me." I brushed at the tears that eased down my cheek. "Pretty heady stuff, considering how boring my sex life was until recently."

Shay patted my leg. "Don't let it get to you, honey. I suspect my turn is coming soon. For me, the motives will probably be insurance, adultery by either one or both of us, or euthanasia. I'm sure they've ordered the results of the last medical tests, talked with Dr. Burkowitz. They're waiting for the insurance report, talking to our friends and associates. They're doing their job, Lotsi, unpleasant as it is for us."

I didn't want to get chummy with McInnaw just doing his job. I'd looked into his eyes, seen what was inside. "Are they all like McInnaw?"

He thought a moment. "No. Not all. There are decent cops. I knew an ex-cop once. He told me when he first joined the force he wanted to help. Then he looked at the suspects, and he realized some of them were just plain assholes. Then gradually they were all assholes. Then he realized some of the assholes were cops. And one day, he looked in the mirror, and he saw an asshole staring back at him. That's when he got out."

We were silent. Then I said, "Maybe McInnaw hasn't looked in the mirror yet."

Standing apart near the passenger gate, I watched the Evans family draw together in their adversity, strong for each other, supporting each other, and marveled at their unity. I'd seen their closeness during Gwen's long ordeal, the unwavering support of Kim and Michelle from and for both their parents, and now I saw it draw tighter still into the three remaining family pillars.

What made some families draw together and some fall apart, I wondered, an aching pain compressing my chest. I loved my daughter Kaitlynn, and I'd always believed she loved me. So why did the collapse of my marriage with her father drive a deepening wedge between us, as if we stood on opposite banks of a divide and despite numerous attempts to bridge the gap, we continued to drift apart?

Did divorce drive bonds apart that death cemented together? No, I'd seen it work the opposite in some cases, for both situations. No, it came down to Kaitlynn and me. We'd each made personal choices, our actions becoming habits. Maybe in the next few weeks, the next few months, we could begin regaining the closeness we once shared.

God, I hoped so.

Seeing Shay and his girls, I never felt the loss more, nor yearned more to hold my Kaitlynn and Bianca with even a part of their intensity. First Kim and then Michelle turned to me and opened their arms. I joined in their circle and thought my heart would break.

My intentions to let Shay and the girls have some quiet time before congregating with our new RV friends for dinner went awry when the friends dropped by to meet the girls and check on Trent and me. Only Trent still hadn't returned, and everyone stayed as an impromptu vigil.

When he arrived at nearly five o'clock, I introduced him to the girls and immediately shooed everyone out until dinner at seven, including myself.

Trent latched onto my hand before I'd taken half a dozen steps. "There you go again, Stretch," he said, hauling me back into a slower pace. "We need to talk. Your place or mine?" His dark eyes twinkled.

"It's not funny, Trenton Wallace." I fought for possession of my hand. He won. Dammit, he knew people were looking. For chrissake, Martha and Richard the Jerk had just passed Erwin and Tremaine who were ahead of us, and judging from the sympathetic concern on her face as she approached, she was going to stop and talk. I tried to retrieve my hand once more. Stupid man, I thought, but melted inside when he squeezed hard in warning.

I returned Martha's greeting and answered her questions, and waited until we'd walked a ways before snarling in a quiet undertone. "You're playing right into McInnaw's insane suspicions!"

He walked so close our shoulders bumped. "I knew you'd worry about that. I won't have it, Lotsi. He's stirring up muck, hoping to strike a nerve and make someone panic. We have nothing to panic about, and I won't let him dictate our private life." He laced our fingers together. "We need to talk."

Trent's refusal to back off, his insistence to keep our relationship moving forward did a number on my body, and it scared me. God. How could he have this power over me?

I tried to think, but I was past thinking. Past talking. I wanted to jump him and dive right in. I wanted to run the other way to protect him from McInnaw. Most of all I wanted to ease this throbbing tension in my body, to get out of myself for awhile and find some peace.

Halting, I turned toward him. "I can't, Trent. Not now. I'm about to jump out of my skin. I need...I need a workout. I need to take my Ninja out for a spin. I need—"

Trent cut me off. "We both know what you need. I can give it to you." No smirk, no suggestive innuendo, just a simple statement of the truth burning in his beautiful eyes.

Oh, yeah, feed my lust! Fire licked through me, a painful burn to my breasts, my womb. I pushed it aside. "With eyes out there watching to see how long you stay? No way. Don't even go there."

Now his mouth curved. "Lotsimina."

"No. I'm taking my bike out."

His face softened even more as his gaze danced up and down my body, resting at prominent points, stoking those fires. "On one condition. We get your keys together, and I take one kiss. Only one kiss. I'm about to jump out of my skin here too, you know."

I cocked my head. "That's an inducement?"

He pulled me a half step closer and his voice lowered to a growl. "That's a warning. Inside or out."

Laughter burst from me. Despite...everything...going on, there must be something working right in my life to have this outrageous man right here, right now.

"Inside then, by all means."

He waited by the door while I searched for my keys, never taking his eyes off me. I found them in the catch-all drawer, tucked them in my shirt pocket, and returned to stand in front of him, my face heating as I drowned in his dark chocolate gaze.

Toe to toe, he waited, lips gently curved, eyes caressing my face, my eyes, my lips. Then he turned serious, brushing the back of his fingers across my cheek. My lower lip. "Don't run from me, Lotsimina. Please don't run from me. Give this a chance. Give us a chance."

He started soft and took me deep, into a kiss of molten blood and raging heat. His mouth demanded everything I could offer. Hungry and hot, his tongue searched for mine, caressed the inner cavern, skimmed every surface, sucked every drop he could wring from my lips. Then he licked them back and forth, and began all over again.

His arms slid around me, then wrapped tight, hands clenching my buttocks, lifting me against him to cradle his growing erection, his long fingers delving deeper into the heated space growing soaked with my juices.

My hands went on their own mission, spearing through the silk of his hair, running over his broad shoulders and down the rippling muscles of his spine. I wanted those hands on the pulsing shaft buried between our bodies, driving us both crazy, but I focused on the kiss. One kiss.

I could have sworn I'd never been kissed before, never known a man's passion, his needs, his demands. When Trent touched me, I came alive with a wild freedom, a flight into uncharted desire and complete sensation, until my world centered on the merging of our two bodies, until my breath failed and my pelvis rocked against him and incoherent sounds begged for more, pleaded for mercy.

"Trenton," I heard myself say in a weak, hoarse voice, over and over. Just "Trenton."

He held me in a fierce grip, completely surrounding me with his scent, his warmth, his heartbeat racing as fast as my own, two drums beating one rhythm.

I had to wet my mouth to speak, and the words still came out soft and raspy. "I keep forgetting about these damn superhormones."

Trent's voice rumbled through me. "I rather like them, myself."

Curled into his chest, my face pressed against his throat, lips touching the wildly beating pulse point. My tongue tasted him there, right there, and he shuddered. Hmmm, this could become a favorite spot.

"Oh, yeah. I like them just fine," he said, even more gravelly than before.

I smiled, and did it again, slow and deliberate.

With more of a growl than a curse, he shifted me again, pressing my back against the wall, lifting my legs to lock around his waist. He laved my entire face with his lips and tongue until I held his head in place and frantically sought his mouth with mine and I went under once more.

Trent's hips powered my against the wall, setting a cadence against my mound, his body seeking an entrance our clothes barred, his hands assailing my breasts, my hips, my breasts again. Feverish. Frantic. I threw my head back, *thwack*, and released a long wail of pure, frustrated, female need.

With one last convulsive thrust, Trent quieted, slowing his hands and then easing my legs down. His kiss gentled until he nibbled and licked in soothing strokes, his hands buried in my hair, splayed around my head and moving in tiny intimate, erotic motions.

"That's two kisses," I whispered against the softness of his lips.

"Nuh-uh. You kept interrupting my one kiss with words. Besides, my kiss isn't over until our bodies separate. And I've got to tell you, sweetheart, separating our bodies sounds awfully painful right now."

"Ahhhh." My lower body reacted to his words by rocking against him, needing that thick shaft inside me. The sensitive hard tips of my breasts rubbed his chest as I arched into him, unable to prevent the gasp and moan that followed.

"Trenton, I can't...I can't stand any more. I ache so much it hurts. It hurts." My forehead dropped to his shoulder, and I fought the waves of arousal pouring over me.

"Shhhh, baby, its okay. I'm sorry, sweetheart. I didn't mean to make you hurt, not when I can't fix it. Are you sure you won't let me—"

"Don't ask!"

"Okay, okay." He drew in and released a giant breath. All the while, his hands rubbed soothing caresses up and down my back as the tension drained from our bodies. Then he took my lips in a kiss so gentle I felt my heart splat at my feet and tears welled in my eyes.

When he stepped back and dropped his arms, he saw the tears, and blocked my hand from wiping them off. He captured the moisture with his fingers, sucked them off and touched his salty lips to mine.

"Now then, Lotsimina, pay attention. You've got your reasons for denying us both what we want and need from each other, and that's okay, for now. But you're going to come to me. Soon. And when you do, I'm going to make you pay for every minute you've kept us waiting, and hurting. You got that?"

"Well. Is that a threat or a promise?" I asked, aroused and offended at the same time.

"You'll have to figure that one out. Or wait and see." Trent's evil twin was back, the teasing sexual smirk in full bloom as he opened the door. He waited with me until I'd straddled and started the Kawasaki, and strapped on my red and purple helmet.

He looked concerned, and his voice reflected it. "You sure you'll be safe on this machine? It's a lot of bike, and, ah, you've not ridden long."

I tried not to grin at his diplomatic effort. "Don't worry. I've only gotten up to third gear so far."

Then I engaged the clutch, toed it into gear and moved smoothly down the road. All that sexual energy pumped through my veins and I felt wicked. I figured I might take the freeway back and hit fifth gear this time. Maybe it was time for me to fly.

There is something about a vibrating, rumbling machine that calls to my blood. The throaty growl of a speedboat, the grumbly purr of a sports car...ahhhh, it sings to me. I'd found my dream machine in my Kawasaki Ninja 500R.

I eased through the park, all that growly rumble centered between my legs, merging sound and sensation with motion. Hmmm, much more of this and maybe I wouldn't need what Trent had after all! That was just first gear! Once on the street, I punched it through the gears, acceleration kicking me back, noise exploding in my head and vibrating from the bones out. I resonated with the machine like a tuning fork.

Fortunately—or unfortunately, I hadn't decided which—the smoother vibrations eased the sexual tension to a nice, alive-feeling body hum.

Cruising down Boulder Highway, I practiced my take-offs and stops. Maximum accel, smooth ending. Did a little bob-and-weave in traffic. Balance and momentum. The body attunes to the machine, the machine becomes an extension of the body. Exhilarating. Seductive. Powerful. I don't know why I hadn't discovered a motorcycle thirty-five years ago.

Spotting a supermarket, I thought of the coming dinner. There was just enough time to make a neat snack that would please even Tremaine's gourmand tastes. My special handmade breadsticks. I bet I could find the aged Asiago cheese I like, maybe a decent hard parmesan, some sharp cheddar. I think I remembered exactly where I'd stored my pasta machine.

Pleased with the selection of cheeses and fresh herbs I'd found in the store, I sauntered back to the bike. All my troubles and doubts and pain I kept pushed aside, enjoying my cooking plans, enjoying my wonderful bike. It looked so hot sitting there, the angled wedges of the titanium body poised like a torpedo. The jagged red stripe matched my helmet rather nicely, but maybe I could detail a purple edge along the bottom. Wouldn't that be cool?

I'd stored the package, put on the helmet, kicked up the stand and straddled the bench when I heard the shouting. "There she is! Cut off the fucking exit!"

A small black truck headed toward me, a burly passenger leaning out the window, pointing at me. For across the lot, another loud voice rang. "Just take her out, goddammit! Don't lose her this time!"

Chapter 11

I hit the starter, popped the Ninja in gear and didn't look back. Without thinking about whether these thugs were after me, or why anyone would be after me at all, my body reacted to *Danger!* I gunned the bike down a side aisle and headed away from both voices.

A few quick glances showed the truck and an older car speeding down separate lanes toward a converging point ahead of me. I swept around the end of a row of parked cars, pivoted the bike by nearly laying it on its side and sped back the way I'd come, heading for the opposite exit. The move had been instinctive, quick, and worked slick as spit but my heart rabbited so fast I felt faint.

Breathe deep, breathe deep. No time to wuss out now, you've got to haul ass and lose these maniacs!

I rotated the speed grip, picking up speed through the parking lot and watching for brakes lights backing out in front of me. Thank God, I swerved to avoid the two I saw.

My mind made a miraculous transition and shuffled streets and exits into escape routes. I focused on evasion tactics. I focused on the next turn, the next block, the next mile. Streets had to go. Stoplights could kill me. Kill me. Oops, don't go there, don't go there. Get off the streets, onto the freeway.

You've seen plenty of motorcycles weave through traffic, pull ahead of the pack and disappear. You can do this. You can do this.

Lake Mead Drive was not too far ahead. I could get to Interstate 95 from there and be in the wind. I just had to keep ahead of these yahoos for a couple of lights. They were determined to be difficult.

They had no respect for traffic laws, personal safety, or common sense. I'm sure we endangered hundreds of lives that day. I'd lost my early advantage at the first intersection when they barreled through a red light behind me, cars squealing and honking in their wake.

I hit fourth gear and prayed, going faster than I'd ever gone before, hitting traffic gaps I wasn't sure were there. I kept pouring on the coal and they kept coming.

Twice one or the other would pull parallel or ahead of me in an outside lane. Only the traffic in the middle kept them away, but I could see their angry, vicious faces staring at me. I evaded, I shuffled, I gave it everything I had and it wasn't enough.

When I hit Lake Meade, I knew I'd never make it unless I totally cut loose. Hey, its Vegas, I told myself. Go for broke. You wanted to fly. Now's your chance.

I stayed in the breakdown lane to avoid heavy traffic heading for the freeway. The truck stayed on my ass. This time I went through third, fourth, rammed into fifth and rounched on the gas. I hit the crowded ramp at sixty-five miles an hour and kept going.

Luck was with me. I blew past the waiting cars and onto the freeway, merging at about seventy-five and climbing. The crazy asshole behind me stuck like glue, getting some of the shouts and honks perhaps aimed at me. I got over to the far left as quickly as I could, using traffic as obstacles between us, and then I worked the lane for maximum excel. I never took my eyes off the road to check my speed. Fast. That's all I cared about.

I was flying.

A few more miles went by. No sign of pursuit. I knew I had to get off, go to ground, go home. Christ, what if they knew where I lived? Wouldn't they just wait for me at the park entrance?

No time to think about that now. I went past the Boulder exit, eased back and threaded my way right, exited and headed for the nearest stop, a fast-food joint. I had to pee so bad my bladder hurt. I parked in back, climbed off on shaking legs, and watched the exit for several minutes.

Safe. But for how long?

By the time I'd peed, I was nauseous. Vomiting helped. Still quaking inside, I sipped a soda and sat by the front window, watching the streets. Thinking.

Beyond the danger, beyond the risks, beyond what might still happen, one thought sickened me. What if Gwen hadn't been the target? What if I'd somehow, for some reason, been the real target even then?

The thought was too bizarre to believe, too insane to ignore. After all, what was more insane than being pursued by two whackos? My Miss DD purse—did that fit in here somewhere?

I couldn't process what was happening. I didn't *know* what was happening, and I was terrified of finding out. I needed to go home.

From my neighborhood walks, I knew a back way to get near the park entrance. Using the side street, I figured I could spot any watchers. The trouble was getting back to the general area of the park. I was lost.

By the time I sorted out directions and arrived at my side street near Arizona Charlie's, it was after seven. I took my time, studied parking lots and driveways, pedestrians and shoppers. Feeling safe, I darted to the entrance and buzzed inside.

I tried to quiet the terror humming inside by going about routine chores. Promising breadsticks for another time, I used the cheeses on a tray, ignored the tremor in my hands and avoided Trent's eyes. He wasn't fooled.

"What happened," he growled in my ear after cornering me in the kitchen.

"Nothing."

"Give it up, babe. What happened?"

"Not now! I'll tell you later."

Later happened sooner than I planned when Trent sent Erwin in with a fake play.

"Can I see you for a minute?" the gentle Erwin asked with a deceptive smile, indicating the passageway beyond the kitchen, the bathroom area leading to the bedroom.

"Sure," I said, stepping past him, not seeing the sneak attack until Trent propelled me on into the bedroom and sat me on the bed while Erwin shut the doors behind us. Then he crowded in with Trent, leaving me sitting there with two determined males planted in front of me with their arms crossed, identical frowns glowering down at me. The fact that Trent was about eight inches shorter and half as wide as Erwin didn't lesson his impact one iota. I felt like an elf, facing the Jolly Green Giant and his little brother.

I beat back the incipient hysteria and cleared my throat. "Well, guys, what's this all about?"

"I swear to God, Lotsi, I'm going to wring your neck if I have to," Trent snapped. "You come back from a jaunt on your bike late, sheet white, shaking like a leaf, eyes shocky, and you want to pretend nothing's wrong? Try again. What happened?"

I couldn't hold it together any longer. The story spilled out, sounding more incredible than it'd seemed at the time. Within thirty seconds, both of the men sat on either side of me, doing their own version of white-faced and shaky.

"So I slowed down, got off the freeway, waited to see if I'd been followed and pulled myself together. That's about it," I finished the tale.

The muscles in the arm Trent had locked around my shoulders bunched and quivered, his other hand kneaded mine in a crushing grip as our hands lay in my lap. Erwin's hand stroked my knee, patting or squeezing throughout the end of my story.

Silence.

"Let me get this straight," Trent said, voice suspiciously quiet, even calm. "You've ridden a bike what, two, three times?"

"Three."

"Three times. That's nice. A high-performance street bike no less. You'd even gotten it up to third gear you said, right?"

I nodded. This was not going well. Any minute he'd—

He exploded. "So how the hell does a rank beginner go from putting along in third to insane road racing at more than *eighty miles an hour?*"

"The right incentive?" I asked, my bland tone and cocked eyebrow adding fuel to the fire. Mistake, mistake, I warned myself, but too late.

Trent morphed onto one knee in front of me, hands at my shoulders for a sharp shake and then his fingers bit deep. "Don't fucking joke about this, woman." Rage twisted his face. His chest heaved; his whole body radiated blazing tension. "Just...don't."

Trenton Wallace in a towering rage was a formidable man. If it'd been truly aimed at me, I'd be a puddle. As it was, I wanted to...well, I was pretty much a puddle, but for reasons other than fear of Trenton Wallace.

"Hey, man," Erwin said, a welcome note of reason. "I think she did some amazing driving, myself. For which I'm thankful. If she hadn't...."

I could see the change in Trent's eyes. He inhaled, snatched me off the bed to press against him as he knelt on the floor, and crushed the air out of my lungs. I didn't mind. I did my best to return the favor.

"Yeah," he said. "I'm damn thankful, too."

Then he thrust me back and was on his feet, pacing in the tiny space between the door and the vanity, arms waving as he muttered curses and improbable threats. I struggled to get out of his way until Erwin picked me up like a rag doll, set me back on the bed beside him.

Not ready to forgive Erwin for the sneak play, I frowned up at him.

Erwin smiled the sweetest smile, draped a tree trunk across my shoulders, and asked what I thought of the Ninja 500. Okay, maybe I'd forgive him. We hadn't gotten far into my extolling the bike's virtues when Trent interrupted.

"We need to notify the police."

That got my attention. "No, we don't. I won't have them making assumptions and...messing with people."

"Look, I know you don't like it, but the truth is they just might make the right assumptions."

I jumped to my feet, faced him with hands at my hips. "No! I won't have Shay and the girls hammered with this. Not now." My rigid stance melted. I was begging him, and he knew it.

He grimaced, but gave in. "We need to tell the others, at least. You need protection, Lotsi."

"Please, no. I promise I won't leave the park alone. For now. Won't that be enough?"

Erwin stood beside me. "We can watch her. Protect her."

We both looked at Trent. He ran his fingers through his hair, gripping it first in his fists and then letting it slide out, one curly lock at a time as he considered the angles.

"All right," he said in a lighter tone. "We're going to be your bodyguards. You understand what that means? One of us stays with you at all times, and you do exactly what we say. Got that?" A slow smile began to play at his lips.

My head came up. Oh yeah? "Not quite, Wallace. Roxie can stay with me nights, and I'll let you know if I agree with anything you have to say to me. Got that?"

Erwin laughed a big booming laugh and fanned his hand in front of his face. "Shit. The two of you are so hot I've got to go find Tremaine."

Roxie, the Turncoat, organized another ambush the next morning. I'd told her about the wild ride the night before, and we talked through it in a much more reasonable fashion than with the men. When I told her I had an idea I wanted to check out, she asked if I was going to involve Trent.

"No way! He's too radical. He'd try to take over." Before she could speak, I added, "And not Erwin, either. Those two have some sneaky moves."

Well, she had sneaky down pat herself. Albert, Tremaine, and Charlotte showed up en masse to discuss my adventure and what to do about it. I looked daggers at her, which she blandly ignored as she served coffee and tea.

I'd been sitting at the dinette, lingering over tea. Now I understood why Roxie had bustled around after returning from her morning walk, fixing tea and a pot of fresh coffee, putting out a huge plate of cookies. The women slid into the booth with me. Albert swung the recliner around and moved it closer. Tremaine leaned against the kitchen counter across from the dinette. Then they looked at me, and waited.

So I told the whole story again, downplaying the scary characters and maybe glossing over the hairy parts of the chase. They weren't fooled. It took a full hour to talk each one of them into agreeing with me on not going to the police. I'd had an easier battle over a $200 million budget for Franklin Industries' European operations.

McInnaw ended up my closer. "After hauling Trent and me in for questioning," I told them, "McInnaw's not going to believe this. He'll think it's a stunt, and that'll make him even more convinced he's on to us. He'll never go after the real killer."

Albert's soft voice cut through my argument. "You must have considered that your assailants might be or might lead to the real killer. You'd be sending McInnaw after them."

"Only if he believed me. And he won't, Albert. Where are my witnesses? The commuters are long gone. He's not going to look for them or broadcast a request, something like that. He's going to assume I'm lying."

"And you think he'll focus even more on you, or think you're covering for Trent."

"Exactly."

Tremaine crossed his arms over the front of his pressed linen shirt, ivory today, to go with knife-pleated oatmeal walking shorts. I'd begun to think he only wore black. "Either way sucks," he said. "And it'd be so like the man. But Lotsi, we can't just ignore this attack. We've got to find out what's going on." He frowned with fierce determination.

How did this become a group project, I wondered. Did setting up camp together bond people that deeply, that quickly, that they felt we were all in this together? Or had this particular group simply clicked with one another, formed a special fellowship, cemented with this tragedy? Whatever the beginnings, they warmed my heart, even as I wished I could knock a few heads together.

I nodded and tried to placate their fears with a confident smile. "That's why I want to talk to Billy, the kid from the repair shop. I need more information."

Tremaine brought the coffee carafe over to the table for refills, looking cross and stubborn. "I think you should let Trent or Erwin talk to Billy."

My fond tolerance began to evaporate, but before I could pop off, Roxie interceded. "You think the kid's involved with this?"

"No, of course not. Not directly. But he may know something." I threw up my hands. "I'm working blind, here. What's the motive behind any of this? If it involves me, which...which is unthinkable," I had to slide over that, but the tears came anyway. I couldn't begin to face the enormous pain and guilt if Gwen had been killed for something aimed at me.

I ploughed on. "But if so, what's happened since I arrived? The answer is nothing to justify...what's happened, but I can't help thinking there was something odd about Billy's Uncle Charlie."

"What, like he was scary or psycho, or something?" Roxie asked, alarmed.

"No, nothing like that. Just something about the way he acted at the shop, and at the casino. I know it's reaching, but it's the only thing I can come up with."

Tremaine went back to the counter for the teapot. "If something is screwy about his Uncle Charlie, why do you think Billy is innocent or that he could be trusted even if he is?"

He had me there. I couldn't put my finger on anything specific, and hated to use "he's a good kid" as a rational reason for trust, but that was part of it.

"He seemed to question Charlie's actions at the shop," I finally said. "If he'd been in on it, he wouldn't have done that. It's not like I intend to confide in him. I just want to get a better feel for his uncle."

Plunking the squat metal Japanese teapot down on the table, Tremaine splayed one hand on a cocked hip. "Well, girl, I don't mind your not talking to the police, but not telling Trent about Billy is bogus. It's just plain bogus. At least let me talk it over with Erwin."

I looked at the ring of concerned faces and felt like a heel, but I couldn't let all that misplaced caring override my determination to keep my two self-appointed guardians from interfering with my plans. "No, absolutely not. There's nothing to worry about, guys. I'm just going to ask the kid a few questions."

With a brooding dark pout, Tremaine crossed his arms and frowned at me. "You're making a mistake, sweetie."

Gosh, I don't think I've ever been subjected to such intense, sexy petulance. I bit the inside of my lips to keep from laughing. "Look, I'll tell you what. If he gives me any bad vibes, tells me anything freaky, bothers me in any way, I'll talk to all of you, including Trent and Erwin. Deal?"

"Deal!" Tremaine braced himself on the table, leaned over, and gave me a smacking kiss on the lips. I caught the faint smug glow on his handsome face and knew a master had manipulated me. Pleased with the relieved looks all my friends wore, I couldn't begrudge him the victory.

However, making a deal was one thing. Getting results quite another. I was more used to gathering information by researching databases or files, requesting it from department heads, or making polite calls to outside vendors under contract than interrogating potentially dangerous men or hostile boys. Where to start?

I decided to nose around MGM Grand.

Since my hair had been pinned up both times Uncle Charlie had seen me, I left it loose and curling around my shoulders. The dark frames and small lens of my spare set of glasses altered my facial appearance. Tourist casual shorts and tank top completed my disguise. I couldn't get much further from the Hot Lady flamboyance he'd seen at our last meeting.

I prowled the lower level of the magnificent casino, winding through the endless jungle of clanging, whirling, chirping, jingling machines, bright lights flashing the astronomical sums I could win at various stations for a few quarters, pinball panels rolling and dancing with fruits and cards and video images of mind-numbing variety. No Uncle Charlie.

I cruised the felt lined tables of blackjack, craps, and roulette, past the high-stakes rooms where I'd seen him before. Still no Uncle Charlie. At the lion habitat, three young lions romping around their glass-floored playground above a milling crowd distracted me. I stopped by the Rain

Forest Café and stealthily added a package from the gift shop for my disguise and kept looking.

Finally, I stopped one of the floor men in suits. "Is Charlie Benson in today? I can't find him." I let some of my aggravation leak through.

"Don't know for sure, ma'am," he smiled at me, "but I'll be glad to check for you." He spoke to a distant source through a lapel mike, listened to his ear bud and then said, "Sorry, ma'am, looks like Charlie took this weekend off. Is there anything I can help you with?"

I wondered if I could dredge up information about Charlie or his job, but decided I'd better not to push the guise of disappointed friend too much. "No, no. I just thought we'd have lunch. Oh, well. Maybe next time."

Now I began to worry. Running into Uncle Charlie at the shop was not a repeat performance I wanted to experience, but I had to find Billy. After pondering my options, I called the shop.

"Is Charlie there? He's not at home and not at work, so I thought he might be at the shop." I spoke in a rude rush, demanding an answer.

"Charlie who?" the chirpy young voice sounded confused.

"Charlie Benson," I snapped. "Is he in the office or out back in the shop?"

"I'll check." She made me pay for being rude. Ten minutes later, she came back on. "No, he's not here."

"Thanks."

When I showed up in person, I personified graciousness, and a sweet-faced youngster with the chirpy voice directed me to Billy without hesitation.

Picking my way to stall seventeen, located on the backside near the end, I skirted broken pavement and puddles of oil and unknown fluids reeking with the promise of toxic damage. About half of the stalls contained vehicles, but only two showed apparent activity, judging from the banging going on underneath one long coach and a man in another stall concealed in black metal headgear with a brilliantly lit torch raining an umbrella of sparks. Both stalls were well away from Billy's.

Pleased with the privacy, I interrupted Billy before he could slide underneath the Gulf Stream. "Hey, Billy, can I bother you for a minute?"

The wheeled backboard paused with Billy's gangly form stretched out on his back, one hand above his head holding the undercarriage edge, shirttails in danger of falling out of his low-riders. The boy eyed me askew, and then the sun broke out in his smile.

"Sure, Ms. Hannon. What's up? Don't tell me you've got problems with those new bearings." He pushed back from the RV, stopped and stood in one smooth, graceful movement.

"No, no. Nothing like that." Staring into Billy's windowpane eyes, I saw only pleasure, curiosity, and a youthful lack of reserve. Nevertheless, I focused on his facial muscles, his body language, reading him as carefully as reading an opponent in the boardroom. "Billy, you remember the other day when I met your Uncle Charlie here by my rig?"

He nodded, brows knitting in puzzlement. "Sure," he said, pulling a red cloth from his back pocket and scrubbing at the oil staining his hands. No hint of tension or evasion there at all.

"Well, I saw him the next day at the MGM, and he seemed upset at me when I greeted him. I wondered if my running into him was a problem. You know, with his being security and all." I knew it sounded lame, but I was fishing for reactions, not social approval.

"A problem? I don't know what you mean." Billy stuffed the cloth away, looking a bit incredulous, but still without tension. "What's being in security got to do with him helping us out here?"

"With me recognizing him at work maybe? Would he be in trouble if MGM knew the head of security was moonlighting?" I kept my voice light, as if trying to offer excuses. "He seemed upset when I saw him going through my storage bin, even more so when I saw him at MGM." I shrugged.

His eyes flickered. Was he wondering why his uncle had been going through my bins, too? His voice lost all warmth, his body at last showing tension. "He's not moonlighting, just helping out family."

I was more convinced than ever this young man was not involved in nor did he know about any shady dealings concerning his uncle. Could I take the chance he wouldn't stir up trouble for me if indeed his uncle were involved?

Willing to take that chance, I plunged ahead. "I have to ask you this in confidence, Billy. Will you keep this to yourself, even from your family?"

Chapter 12

A rebellious-little-boy look flitted across Billy's face. Secrets are hard enough to keep, but when they involved family...oh, I shouldn't have stretched his loyalties so cruelly, yet I had no choice, now. "At least keep this confidential for the next week."

To his credit, Billy didn't say anything right off. I hoped that meant he'd take his promise seriously if he agreed. He tucked in the wayward shirttail and considered the question. Leaning back against the workbench with his arms crossed, he nodded. "All right. For a week."

Sweat beaded my face and ran down the back of my neck. Desert heat and nerves, I supposed, wishing for a cool breeze inside the cramped stall. Fishing a clip from a belt pouch, I rolled my thick, sweaty hair into a twist and clamped it at the back of my head and began to pace in the confines between the workbench and motorhome.

"Some...odd things have happened to me, Billy. And before you react, I'm not blaming anyone, just trying to figure out what's happening. The place I was staying at was searched. Then later my purse was stolen. And last night I was chased by two vehicles while I was out on my Kawasaki."

Turning to face him, I lifted a hand, letting my frustration show. "I can't get a handle on why these things are happening. The only thing I can think of is your Uncle Charlie. Could he be in trouble? Could he be involved with anyone or anything, ah, dangerous?"

Billy straightened, almost vibrating with tension. "I heard someone was killed at Thousand Trails earlier this week."

"Yes. My best friend. She was killed when someone searched her motorhome where I was staying."

"So you think my uncle had something to do with murdering your friend, stealing your purse, and attacking you last night?"

Didn't take an expert to see and hear his insulted fury. I tried to reach him, to calm him. Implore him, maybe. "Please, Billy. I'm trying to eliminate possibilities here. Could your uncle be involved in something over his head, someone using him somehow?"

"I think you'd better leave."

"Billy—"

He turned his back, threw himself onto the backboard and swished out of sight beneath the rig.

Heart aching with the pain and anger I'd caused, I left, certain of only two things. I'd gained no assurance of Uncle Charlie's connection one way or another, and I'd trampled on a young man's innocence.

When I returned Shay's SUV to the park, I learned he'd been notified he could take Gwen's body home on Tuesday. We torn up the phone lines to Seattle, putting into place plans Gwen had discussed with us all at one point or another.

My calls to the Dazzling Darling Royal Assistants brought home what we were doing, at least on one level. While Gwen and the family wanted a private funeral, the

DD's and other Red Hot Ladies wanted an opportunity to express their feelings as well.

Mourning is a private thing, and it never ends. Yet this was a time to honor and celebrate her life, not just mourn her loss, so with the family's approval, we'd cooked up a few special arrangements.

Now threaded through the horror of burying this wonderful woman was a joy in her transition to a greater glory, and we all felt it, thrived on it. I clung to that narrow thread as my strength.

Later Albert came over for dinner with Roxie and helped lift my spirits. For the first time, I saw Albert flirt with his wife. He started with flowers and a small smile. "So you won't forget, Roxie May," he said.

Roxie took the black-eyed daisies and blushed. Blushed! "Oh, Albert. Just like the first time. You remembered after all these years."

"I never forgot."

Then he fed her tidbits from his plate, poured her wine from the bottle he'd brought. Before long, a glowing look transformed Roxie's face into a look of feminine promise. I decided I'd go visit someone...Charlotte. Yes, I'd visit Charlotte.

Before I could make a smooth exit, company arrived, first Charlotte, and then the men trooped in, Erwin, Tremaine, and Trent. My heart began tripping.

"Hi guys, come on in and pick a spot somewhere," I said. My spacious camper became much smaller so full of large bodies, but all I could see was Trent. "Had dinner yet?"

The hours since I'd seen him last night seemed endless as a hunger for him gnawed at a secret place inside. You're worse than an adolescent with her first crush, I lectured myself, but I feasted on him nonetheless.

Roxie offered the other men a piece of the German Chocolate Cake she'd made, but Trent created a private space at the door as he stepped close, blocking me from view and stared into my eyes. His face softened. Fingers brushed my lips. "You okay?" he asked for my ears only.

"No, but I'm getting there." I smiled and tucked a silver-streaked coil behind his ear. "Come on. You don't want to miss Roxie's German Chocolate Cake."

Within a few minutes, Kim and Michelle showed up.

"Is everything all right?" I asked, fearing another horrendous event.

"Well enough, I suppose. We were out walking and thought we'd stop by," Kim checked out the crowd and laughed. "Boy, they can fill an RV real fast, can't they?"

Eyeing Erwin, I said, "Some just naturally take up space. Still got room around the edges, though, so come join us. Roxie made the most sinful chocolate cake, and we can't let the guys eat the whole thing, now can we?"

They both carried small backpacks, which I placed on the floor in my bedroom away from numerous large trampling feet. If only I'd known. The extent of that small error wasn't apparent for awhile, until Tremaine came out of the bathroom looking concerned. "Does anyone know what's ticking?"

"Ticking?" Trent said, on his feet in an instant. Erwin followed right behind. Rushing into the bathroom, the two men looked around, started pulling open doors and drawers.

"What are you doing?" I asked, rather amused at their antics. Several of us piled up at the kitchen entrance, watching the show.

"Just checking things out," Trent said. Running out of drawers, he opened the pocket door to the bedroom. His voice sharpened. "It's louder in here." Stepping through, he paused, listened.

Erwin came up behind him. "Do you think it's a bomb?"

Oh, my gosh. I couldn't believe the left turn their minds had taken. A bomb, of all things!

"Now wait just a second!" I started, but Trent bellowed right over me.

"Everyone get out!" He turned to Erwin. "Get them out. Now!" He started opening the wardrobe, the bedside drawers.

Erwin tried to push me out, telling everyone to clear out of the motorhome. Roxie's voice rose shrilly in the background. "Albert, what's going on? Is there really a bomb?"

"For goodness sake," I hollered back, slipping past my guard. "There's nothing going on!"

"Out, everyone get out!" Erwin kept repeating, waving the others back. They started streaming outside.

I darted into the bedroom. "Get a grip, Wallace. This is ridiculous! I'm sure it's nothing to worry about—"

The words froze in my throat as Trent whirled, a furious snarl on his face. He looked behind me, grabbed me by the waist and yelled, "Erwin, take her and get out!"

Next thing I knew, I was *flying across the room through the goddamned air.* Erwin plucked me from mid-flight, stuffed me under his arm like a football, and thundered through the motorhome—the walls shaking and items dancing across the countertops—and he didn't stop until we were outside.

Oh, I was mortified. I was furious. I was so angry I could have chewed woolly worms. Before I could storm back inside and do bodily damage Kim spoke up. "Oh. I bet it's the travel alarm in my backpack. I just remembered. It sounds extra loud if it lies on its side."

I stuck my head through the door and hollered good and loud. "You hear that, Wallace? It's Kim's alarm clock!"

Silence. I cocked an eyebrow at Erwin and led the troops back inside. Kim retrieved the ticking bomb-clock from her pack. "Sorry about that," she said, looking sheepish and guilty.

Arms folded across my chest and feet spread, I stared at the real guilty parties. "It's not your fault, Kim. *You* didn't overreact. *You* didn't panic. *You* didn't *throw people around.* *You* didn't cart someone around like a *freaking football!"*

Erwin muttered, "Aw, Lotsi," and bowed his head. Tremaine took a stance just in front of him. Half Erwin's width, barely up to his shoulder, Tremaine crossed his arms, lifted his nose and looked me dead in the eye.

Now how could I stay mad after that? I struggled against a grin and then threw up my hands. "Okay, so he just took the pass, but *you!*"

I whirled and stabbed at Trent with my laser-beam finger. "*You* instigated the whole thing! You wouldn't listen. You panicked and manhandled me—"

Trent swelled with an offended air. "Damn straight. And I'd do it again, too. I'm your bodyguard—"

"Bullshit! I don't need—"

"Are you forgetting your promise after the *incident* last night?" His angry eyes flickered over to Kim and Michelle, standing watching silent and round-eyed with the others.

Trust Kim to jump right on it. "What incident?"

Darn. The motorcycle incident I didn't want them knowing about. I guess I'd forced that nightmare out of my mind. For a moment, I wondered if I'd dreamed it. I took a deep breath. No, it had happened.

"Nothing to worry about. Really," I assured Kim, and looked at Trent. Okay, I had promised to let these two "guard" me to make up for not telling the police, not telling the girls, and Shay. Still...

"You didn't have to throw me around."

"I apologize. I overreacted when you wouldn't leave with the others and I took what actions seemed appropriate at the time."

His apology didn't sound very convincing, so I growled at him again. "It wasn't appropriate."

He merely tilted his head, as if refusing to argue but not conceding my point. I didn't trust those glittering eyes and the possessive heat burning in them. My heartbeat picked up and my body tingled with a sexual response I found as appalling as it was exciting.

Those dark eyes flared and then dropped to my breasts. Somehow he knew exactly the effect he had on me. Well, if he thought he had my number, he had another think coming. I'd had all the emotional drama I could stand.

I turned away. "I'm sure a drink is in order, but unfortunately, I'm about done-in with all the excitement this evening. Roxie, if you don't mind, would you please see to our guests? I'll say good night and see you all tomorrow."

Long after dark, I lay awake, empty and alone as never before. Why was I keeping Trent out of my bed, out of my heart—at least as much I could?

Oh, I know my argument about propriety was correct. I needed to protect both of us from the imaginative Detective McInnaw, but we could have managed somehow. What I really needed to protect was my heart, and I didn't know how to manage that.

I know I'd told Trent I'd never been good at sex. The truth is I couldn't pick good guys from bad guys, and I'd never been good at protecting my heart from falling in love with the wrong guy. So I'd decided all guys were wrong guys. Safer that way.

So where did that leave Trent? Where did that leave my heart?

Time was running out. I'd told Kaitlynn I wouldn't be late for Bianca's birthday, but I'd planned to be there a few days early. Now Gwen's funeral was set for Thursday. I'd be back from Seattle Friday, head out to San Francisco on Saturday, three days later than planned, but at least I'd make the birthday party. Barely.

Part of me wanted to beg for more time to spend with Trent, but I'd spent most of Kaitlynn's life putting off too many plans, delaying too many trips, taking back too many promises because I had to put the job first. I couldn't put

Trent first now. I couldn't put myself first. Kaitlynn and Bianca were too important to me.

Even if I could give myself time, what would we have? A few days, a few weeks? I don't do endings well. Maybe I should keep him away permanently. Avoid a world of hurt.

My heart ruptured then, tears flowing into my pillow. God, if not having him hurt this much now, just think what it would be like to have him and then lose him.

The idiot who said, "It's better to have loved and lost than to have never loved at all," hadn't a clue about the pain of a broken heart, one that dies again with each new day alone.

Man, was I screwed.

Sunday morning I went to church with Shay and his girls. Roxie was spending the day with Albert, planned on coming back to my place after dinner, but I hoped they both got lucky and she wouldn't show up.

In the meantime, I wanted to stay busy, so when Kim tentatively asked about shopping for some things for her kids, I jumped at the chance to take her and Michelle around Las Vegas. We weren't looking for festive. We were looking for a diversion and new shoes for Grandma's funeral. We weren't likely to get carried away by a few bright lights.

Yet we had fun together, the three of us. We drove the Strip, parked, and watched the water display at Bellagio. Then we walked past the Roman splendor of Caesars to the pirate ships at Treasure Island. On the way back, we detoured into the Forum Shops and got lost.

When sufficiently exhausted, we had acquired complete outfits for all the kids and something for the moms and dads. We even found Shay a new tie and shirt. I bought a two-foot red vase with a huge display of mixed red and purple flowers for her requiem mass, a perfectly gaudy Red Hot splash she would have loved.

Somewhere along the way, we'd started talking about their parents' travel bug. We all hoped Shay would continue traveling, if he could. It wouldn't be easy for him.

"You know your mom talked about starting another Red Hot chapter," I told them.

"No, I didn't know," Kim said. "Did you?" She asked her sister.

Michelle hadn't known either. "What for? I thought the Dazzling Darlings were doing well."

"Oh, they are. And Princess Dazz, Helen Brumweiler, will take over as Queen Mum. But this would be a special chapter, one primarily for RV fulltimers but hosting special camping events open to all Hot Ladies, where chapter members could bring Red Hot crafts and displays, put on skits and dances. She talked about all the talent we have among us. She didn't want a big hotel convention for show. She wanted a nice outdoor camp for fun."

Kim wore a huge smile, obviously pleased with her mother's idea. "That would have been lovely. I can just see her putting it together. She had a way of making things work out, you know?"

Michelle nodded, having one of those half-crying, half-smiling at the same time moments.

"Yeah, I do," I said, blinking back my own tears.

Planning to overnight the vase to Seattle, I left the girls with the packages heaped inside their RV, and walked back to my home. My foolish eyes drifted to Trent's Mandalay. It seemed quiet. Maybe he was still out with the guys or whatever he'd ended up doing for the day.

A white envelope protruded from the crack in my doorframe. Expecting a note from Charlotte, or Trent, I took it inside and threw it on the table. I needed to prop my feet up and rest my eyes for a moment. The couch beckoned and for ten or fifteen minutes I indulged myself, then my curiosity overrode my poor feet and I retrieved the message.

No name appeared on the outside, no signature on the single plain sheet inside. Just a message that stopped my heart.

If you want to see your loverboy again, take your motor-home to the Mormon temple up on Bonanza at Sunrise Mt. I'll be watching. Come alone or he ain't gonna live long, neither. 8 p.m. tonight. P.S. Check your email

Chapter 13

My hand crumpled the ransom note. Someone had taken Trent hostage, for my...my camper? My knees wobbled and caved. I landed with my butt half off one of the chairs and scrambled to sit straight.

This was a joke, right? Had to be a joke.

I started to hyperventilate. *Stop that! This can't be real!*

Well, I'd get this settled in a hurry. I rushed over to Trent's place, banged on the door. No response. Tried the handle. Locked. I banged some more. Did one of our group have a key? Why didn't I have a key?

Okay, slow down. Think about this for one damn minute. I rested my head against the warm metal. If someone has him, he's not inside. They probably aren't idiots, so there won't be clues to his whereabouts inside. You don't need to get inside.

Email. I needed to check my email.

Back to my RV. I rode the raging beat of my heart, my breathing shallow, staying focused on actions and not panic. I grabbed my laptop and headed for the Activity Center and cable modem access. Boot up took forever, checking email longer. God, where do all these messages come from! What the hell am I looking for, anyway?

Then I saw it. The subject line read "Wallace". Just that.

Fear pumped through my veins and banded tight across my chest. When the message opened, I stared at the brutal photo slowly painting on my screen. Trent, cobra eyes fixed on the photographer, leaned awkwardly against a blank wall, hands bound to his feet with something, maybe rope, his face bloodied and hair matted.

"Oh, no. No. No." Pain pierced my heart. I began to black out. Please God, not a heart attack. Not now. Then I realized I needed to breathe. Breathe. Breathe. Slowly the world brightened around me but inside, all remained dark.

I never took my eyes off Trent's. I needed to draw that defiance in, suck his life force into mine to give me the strength to think.

Scrolling down, I made sure nothing else appeared. Some impulse—document, document, document—made me save the email to my hard drive, then I ripped out the jack, slammed the case shut and raced back home. There I slid the laptop onto the couch and sat beside it, curling into a thinking ball. What the hell was going on?

Elbows on my thighs, hands together with the steeple pressed against my lips, I rocked back and forth, staring at the floor and breaking the recent events down into logical bits.

Trent had been taken for a reason. Maybe to get the rig, maybe to get me. Or both. They could get me without the rig pretty easily. But for them to take the rig out of the park themselves would raise questions, big questions. So they probably wanted the rig. Me, I'm gravy. I'm just the driver. A tool.

Or was I? I was also a witness, wasn't I. A glimmer of the whole sequence of events arose and sickened me. I slammed that door shut. I couldn't go there. I couldn't function if I went too far down that path.

But I knew exactly where to start looking for the reason why.

I grabbed the keys, dug out a big flashlight and started searching the storage bins in the undercarriage. Nothing jumped out at me. I went through the one I'd caught Uncle Charlie rummaging in, then around the entire rig, moving boxes and articles. By the time I returned to the starting bin, I was thoroughly depressed. I'd been so sure.

Time to reconsider. If he'd put something inside one of my boxes, finding it could take more hours than I had tonight, even with help. I took one more look around, climbing as far inside the bin as I could wiggle, shining the light around.

The storage bin continued under the rig to the other side. The bin opening from the other side had different pipes and things blocking part of the open space. I didn't have that much junk in this area. Camp chairs, a grill, a table. Ropes and things in a crate. Boxes in the unit on the other side, almost brushing the ceiling of the bin.

The ceiling.

Half-laying in the bin I could see this side had a lower ceiling than its mate. There was about a two-inch dropped grid of four rectangular panels, about a foot wide each, less than two feet long, maybe twenty, twenty-two inches.

I angled the light and couldn't see that any other bins had a similar grid on the ceiling. I went around the undercarriage again, checking each bin. No other grids. This time when I returned, I poked at the grid. Stiff, but resilient, like a treated paper cover. I pried at the edges, felt a give. Pried harder. The corner came loose in my hand, tearing a seam toward the center. Through the gap, the familiar green of money almost glowed in the light. I saw enough of the face to recognize Ben Franklin.

Ben Franklin. Hundred dollar bills. My hands picked and tore at the covering, but I already knew. When the two-inch packet of bills fell into my hand, I fanned the bundle. All one hundred dollar bills. I picked at the covering for the next bundle. Andrew Jackson. Fifties.

Casino money? What else could it be? It looked like each grid contained two side-by-side rows. I used the loose stack to estimate the length. Four grid-panels, eight bundles long, two wide, two inches thick. A lot of money.

Hyperventilating again, I eased back into the fresh air. Sweat soaked my shirt, ran down my face, my neck. It was Charlie all long. Charlie the Sonofabitch had Trenton.

Trent's photo seared my mind. I couldn't control the rage anymore. It clawed its way free and spewed from a deep core of violence I hadn't known existed. First heat then ice rushed across my skin. My veins threatened to blow. I couldn't wait to get my hands on Uncle Charlie.

On Billy.

First, I needed the money safe. Safe and well documented. Snapping shots with my digital camera, the painful irony rained tears down my face. It'd all started with this damn camera, taking that shot of Uncle Charlie, crouched at this very storage bin. Had he been after the camera when he'd sent his goons to attack Gwen? Steal my purse?

I remember I'd tucked the camera into my Miss DD purse, the one he had eyed so carefully at the casino the next day, the one like Gwen's that had been searched. The wallet was a red herring all along. He had wanted the camera.

Working the tiny buttons to review past shots, for a moment I regretted taking the camera out of my bag before it'd been stolen. Some of Benson's desperate actions might have been prevented if he'd just found the damn thing.

Then I found the images from that day. There he was. A nasty snarl contorted my face. Here was my proof. My revenge. Oh, how bittersweet.

The shots were dark, but lighting could be adjusted. In retrospect, his defensive body language at being caught in the act seemed obvious. A few clicks on zoom revealed his facial expression. He looked guilty as hell. I had his ass nailed.

Now for the money. I dug out a pry bar. The packets came off easily once I discovered the double-sided sticky tape applied in even rows across each rectangle. I left the packets intact. I had no time, no need to tally them up.

I carried the money containers inside, took more shots, and scrambled under the dinette, leaning the containers against the wall beneath the table, well hidden from view. Adjusting the opened package, a small disk dropped onto the carpet. Bigger and fatter than a silver dollar, it was shiny, with faint markings. Crawling out into the brighter light, I saw enough to scare me spitless.

It looked like a tiny GPS tracking devices law enforcement agencies used. Crooks used them too, apparently. Back under the table, I carefully felt through the other packages, discovered three more transmitters, and extracted them through a small slit, capturing each one in digitized images before and after removal.

Bouncing the GPS devices in my hand, I thought through the implications. Benson no doubt had a receiver keyed for these transmitters, and he'd know when—or if—I took my rig out, and where I went.

God, the audacity of this man!

He must be skimming millions from the casino, maybe from several for all I knew, but how could he launder it in a city as sensitive to money crimes as Las Vegas? He couldn't.

So how could he get the money out of Sin City?

Airports detect large sums of money passing through security. Couriers become obvious and unreliable—unless the courier is unaware of what they're carrying.

"He uses mules," I said aloud, understanding a few more pieces. "That's what all the questions from Billy and what's-his-name, the studly mechanic, were about at the very beginning. How long would I be here, where was I going next—they were fishing for mules! They *are* part of the whole freaking scheme! Or...maybe not, they could just be passing on information unsuspecting...no, wait."

My mind worked furiously, almost in awe of Benson's bold plan. "The mechanic...John? Yeah, John practically bribed me to go to their shop in California, with free inspections and discounts! Someone there is in on the deal, he would remove the packages and away he'd go. By using transmitters, if I didn't show, they'd follow me and...and remove the packages, quietly I'm sure, somewhere along the road. I wouldn't have a clue. Man, that's slick. No wonder he's pissed at me!"

The innocent disks lay in my hand, telltale hooks sunk deep into my flesh. Trent's life could depend on the trip these babies took right before 9 p.m. tonight. How could I find where Trent was being held and still make that trip?

I walked a disk across the back of my hand from finger to finger, mentally running the options. The police were out. I wasn't stupid enough to think I could do anything better then armed professionals—if I could gain their cooperation and if they would respond in time, but how likely was that?

Then there were my friends, which given the situation narrowed to Erwin and Tremaine. I could use their help. I could turn the whole GPS problem over to them, and oh, by the way, bring Trent home on your way back. I'll wait right here all safe and sound and chewing my nails to the quick. Right.

I couldn't do it. Endangering them was bad enough, but they were take-charge men with good intentions toward the little woman. They'd try to take over, they'd argue about it, and then they'd sulk. With less than two hours to pull out a rabbit, I had no time for that shit.

By this time the GPS disks walked smartly across my hand, weaving in and out of my fingers. I still had the touch, but I needed a new level of magic for a rabbit trick. Trent or my life weren't simple props.

Props. Good golly, Miss Molly, I had all the game pieces! Well, except for Trent. I had Benson's identity, his money, his GPS devices, the photos of him and the anonymous one he sent—and he knew only about that last one!

He thought his GPS's were golden, but I could turn them against him. Oh, yes. He'd be there tonight, watching the signals move closer to him, the money and the dame falling right into his greedy hand. He'd sweat with the thrill of it. Then poof...no motorhome, no money, no dame.

What was he going to do? The devices aren't where they were supposed to be—with the money—and he is not going to do a damn thing until he finds out what's going on, now is he?

No way! That gave me the power for my magic show. Just like Las Vegas, it was all about illusion, sleight of hand, and making the other guy blink first.

The doorbell rang again in the recesses of the posh McMansion near Sunset Park. My finger headed toward the button for a third round when the door opened a modest crack.

"May I help you?" the middle-aged woman inquired. From her baggy shorts and rumpled tank top, she could have been Billy's mother or the maid. No, the mother. She had Billy's wide mouth.

I smiled. "I hope so. I'm Ms. Hannon, a friend of Billy's. I have some photos he wanted to see. Is he here?"

Please, please, please. It'd taken longer on the Net to get his address than I'd hoped. Not knowing which side of the family was "Benson" slowed things down. Sunday night didn't mean teenagers stayed home, but I prayed this one was home tonight, and more curious than cautious.

She eyed my long-sleeved black, button down shirt and black jeans. Even after dark, the temperature was almost a hundred, but she ignored the odd outfit and smiled. "Yes, he is."

That smile nailed the relationship. I wondered if people would see me as readily in Kaitlynn's smile, in the shape of her eyes. "Shall I give him the photos?"

"I'd like to give them to Billy myself, if I may. You might tell him I found some photos after we spoke yesterday and would like to share more of the story. It's regarding a mutual friend, you see."

I must have sounded convincing, as she opened the door wider. "Please come in. He's upstairs. I'll call him."

The home's foyer made a lovely statement about the family's taste and net worth. Modern and substantial. I studied the artwork, the tile, the textiles, until I heard the clatter of steps beyond the entrance and turned to meet Billy's angry and wary gaze as he stopped at the doorway.

"What are you doing here?"

"I'm sorry, Billy, but we have no time to spare. He's kidnapped my friend."

"You're lying!"

"No, I'm not." I took the printouts from my purse and showed him the one of Trent, cruelly bound and defiant. "I'm telling the truth. Please. I need you to come with me. Right now!" I shook the pages of photos.

Billy stared at Trent's image, making no move to look at the others, his face stricken, his voice thin with shock and anguish. "He wouldn't do that. He wouldn't."

I noticed we never had to refer to who "he" was. "Then prove it, Billy," I challenged the trembling boy. "Come with me. Prove it isn't him."

He raised his head, glanced down the hall. "My parents—"

"Tell them you're going out for a while. A couple of hours, that's all I'm asking."

Billy studied the three photos in the overhead lights of Shay's SUV once we were underway. The first with his uncle crouched at the storage bin, the second of the same bin with the exposed money and containers stuck on the ceiling, and the last one of Trent. Also the note demanding the motorhome, and perhaps me, as ransom.

"We only have fifty-two minutes," he said, calmer now that he'd set out on a mission to prove me wrong.

"It'll be tight," I said, punching for more speed. "We have to stop by my RV first."

"Why?"

I nodded toward the printouts. "I didn't take the time to print out the rest of the photos, but I found a GPS transmitter in each of those money containers. Whoever is at the drop will be tracking the movement, so I couldn't bring them with me. I've decided to send a message by pretending to go along with the ransom demand."

"What message?"

Picturing the greedy, scum-sucking bastard holding Trent, I bared my teeth. "That I've upped the ante."

He worked it out in silence, and when he spoke, his voice held an incredulous touch of awe. "You want...whoever to know *you* have the money?"

I darted around a cab blocking the fast lane and shot forward. "Think about it. He wants all the marbles. Well, he has Trent, he may even get me, but I've got what he really wants."

He threw me an anxious look. "What do you mean, he may get you?"

"That's not important. Tell me about your Uncle Charlie, Billy. Where he lives, if he has a girlfriend, a cabin, anywhere he might hold Trent." The silence dragged out and I thought I had lost him.

I glanced over.

He held Trent's photo almost against his nose.

"That won't be necessary," Billy said. "I know where he is."

Imitating the pace of a behemoth RV bus stretched the limits of my sanity. "We're going to be late," I moaned for the fourth time.

Billy's temper showed. "If you're sending a message, what difference does it make if we're a few minutes late?"

I sighed. "Yeah, you're right."

"Besides, if he's tracking us, he knows we're coming, and you're just a dumb tourist. How are you to know how long it takes to get there, anyway?"

"Okay, okay! Spare me the mouth!" I snarled, braking for another stoplight. "Look, I know you want to come with me, but I can't let you. I didn't say you were a dumb kid. I said you were too young to get more involved, that's all."

"He's my uncle. I have a right to be there."

Now he sounded like Kaitlynn at sixteen when she'd wanted to drop in unannounced, uninvited, on her dad in Chicago. We'd lived in San Francisco at the time. "He's my father," she'd said. "I have a right to see him! You weren't even here for my birthday!"

Do all teenagers have some version of that line memorized with the exact tone down pat?

"I know Billy, but I can't risk your getting hurt."

"He's my uncle," this time he sounded shocked. "He won't hurt me!"

Turning onto Bonanza, we headed up the hill toward the Temple spirals about three miles ahead. "I'm sure he wouldn't" —not sure of that at all— "but I know he has at least two other guys working for him. I can't take the chance you might get hurt. Accidentally or...whatever."

"So I won't go into the guesthouse with you. I'll help you scope out the place, and then distract Uncle Charlie at the main house. It's not that big a risk and it'd be safer for you and your friend Trent."

Canny little bastard. I sighed. I couldn't argue with his logic. As I recall, I'd sent Kaitlynn to her father, too, with prior and rather surprising approval of course. "Okay. But no funny stuff. No heroics. No questions. You're just out cruisin' in a friend's SUV and stopped in for a few minutes. Got that?"

Grinning ear to ear, Billy slouched down in the seat. "Sure. No prob."

We were almost there. Billy wasn't grinning now. I think he'd forgotten for a moment how serious the situation was, what the stakes were. Fantasy came easy to the TV generation. It was reality that sucked.

Recognizing the pattern of the Berber carpet and the molding behind Trent's back hadn't been pleasant for the sunny, doting young nephew. Trent's capturer had thought he would be safe, placing his prisoner against a blank wall, heartbreakingly reminiscent of the terrorist abductions and executions in the Middle East, a fact I'm sure he had played on.

He hadn't counted on a nephew remembering laying the carpet and cutting the baseboard with his handyman dad and uncle the summer before, and having the guts to confront the harsh reality of what it meant.

I turned down Temple Street. Six tall spirals jutted above the flat lines of the Temple roof, the large building dominating the area, silhouetted against the barren red peaks of Sunrise Mountain in the background. The Temple side of the street had few buildings, falling away to a panoramic view of Las Vegas lights below. I didn't spot the spotter watching for my arrival.

Instead, I pulled into the subdivision across the street, twisting around several turns and corners, looking for a likely place to dump the GPS transmitters. I counted on the fact the accuracy was general, not to the exact foot. That would require a bigger device than these small gadgets.

"See anything?" I asked Billy, anxious to get out of there and rescue Trent.

"Naw, nobody's looking. Why don't you just throw them into someone's yard?"

I thought it undiplomatic to mention the truth, that I wanted the police to recover them for evidence. "I want them harder to look for. Maybe buy some time. There. This will only take a minute."

Braking, I jammed the gearshift into park before we'd come to a full stop, the truck still bouncing as I slipped out, quietly closing the door behind me to kill the interior lights. The gutter I'd spotted was located between two lots in a cul-de-sac. Bushes and the SUV shielded me somewhat, but I hurried, worried about homeowners and whoever awaited my arrival.

"Darn," I murmured, crouching above the gutter safety grate. I'd had a wild idea about stashing the disks out of sight inside the gutter, but couldn't see how...wait, maybe there was a way.

I pulled a long hairpin from the French roll at the back of my head, bent it into an S curve, hung one end on a metal bar of the grate and pressed hard to bend the curve over the angular shape. Satisfied, I pulled it back up.

From the pocket of my night-stalker jeans I pulled out a palm-sized velvet bag closed tight with a pull-tie. I'd saved the pretty, dark blue bag from a jewelry purchase years ago, and tonight used it for something more important than the collection of foreign coins I had kept in it. Inside, a sealed plastic baggie protected the GPS disks.

I attached the loops on pull-tie ends to the lower curve of the hairpin, suspended the flattened curve back over the bar, and brushed street dirt around the top of the pin. Perfect.

Now to crash the lion's den and hope the mangy bastard wasn't home.

Charlie Benson lived in Summerlin, ten or twelve miles from the Temple. I took to city streets until we reached the Las Vegas Expressway and prayed Sunday night traffic would be light and the cops busy. We were blessed with both.

We reached the tree-shrouded neighborhood of five-acre estates in good time, drove slowly past Benson's, turned and drove past again.

"I don't see any cars. Think he's gone?" I asked Billy in a hushed voice, as if the man I hoped was absent could hear us in a car on the street in front of his house, a sprawling two-story Mediterranean villa behind a high, adobe-style gated fence, with a circular driveway and a desert landscaped front yard bigger than most house lots.

"Can't tell for sure. He usually parks his Acura NSX in the driveway for the neighbors to see, but it could be in the garage," Billy also spoke in an undertone, hunkering down so he could stare out my window. "He's got a four-car garage around the side, but they've got like five or six cars. My grandpa says he buys and sells them like trading stamps."

Billy giggled, a nervous, wild sound. "Whatever those are. My cousin, Annabelle, got an Alfa Romeo Spider this year, can you believe it? Spoiled brat. God, I hope she's not home. What if she's home?"

"One step at a time, Billy. That's all we can do. You said the guesthouse is in the back. Is there another way to get inside the walls?"

"Yeah," Billy seemed to brighten again. "The alley, where they pick up garbage and stuff. Most of the places have a parking area. I usually park back there anyway. Take the next right."

I did, thinking about the various security systems I'd used over the years. "Tell me about security. The front gate had a keypad pedestal. What about the back?"

"There's the alley. Should you kill your headlights? There're no streetlights, just some lights from back yards or something. You could use your parking lights."

"Good idea." I plunged us into near darkness and slowed way down. "Now about security...."

"Yeah, well, there's a drive-through gate back here, too, but you can only open it from inside or get buzzed in. The gardeners and such use that. But there's a regular gate for people, with a keypad in the wall."

"Does it ring an alarm or signal inside?"

"Naw, not with the right code. I guess if you're watching the main security panel, it blinks red while it's open, but the panel's back in the laundry room with all the other house tech controls."

That was nice. "About the codes. The exterior walls and the buildings are all secured with keypad access, right?"

"Sure. And Uncle Charlie is fanatical about arming them, too."

"Do they have separate codes?"

"Well, there's the master override code. See, at first all the family members had their own code, like for tracking things, but that caused too many false alarms, which aren't cheap. So now everybody just uses the master code."

Better and better. "So if the guesthouse code has been changed, say for guest access, if you enter the master override code, it would still work."

Billy's wonderful smile broke out. "Hey, that's right. We've got the power!" He did a little victory dance in his seat and then gestured ahead. "Park here. We're a couple houses down. Dr. Howard is only here during the winter, so everyone uses this space for extra parking."

I parked, killed the motor and sat in the dark, listening, fighting the terrible mix of fears that boiled just below the surface. "Okay. Here's the deal. We'll go in, see if we can spot anything at the guesthouse. If we have to talk, let's be very careful. We'll try the doors. What if we have to break in?"

"Hmmm. The doors are solid. There's a slider in the living room, but you can see that from the house. See the front door, too."

He frowned, slipping further into the crook mentality like a good TV junkie. "But there's a slider in the breakfast nook off the kitchen in back, with a little garden area against the back wall. Maybe we could bash the glass in there?"

His eyes twinkled, his grin irresistible. Bet he had been a handful as a kid, the eager, go-for-broke daredevil who got into one scrape after another.

Since my crook experience came from the same venue, his solution sounded likely to me, so I nodded, and went back to my summarization. "We'll try the back door only. If it's open, I'll go in alone to scout. No, don't argue. If it's not, you go on up to the main house as if everything was normal, seeing if your cousin wants a spin in your borrowed ride. If she's not there, get me fifteen minutes if you can. Either way, meet me back here."

Spotting the perfect place to wait—God willing, with Trent—I pointed. "I'll be in that recess between the garbage bin wall and the neighbor's fence."

I placed my hand on a slender shoulder. "Please do exactly what I say, Billy. Be back here, quietly, in less than half-an-hour, forty-five minutes tops. If I'm not here, wait for no more than fifteen minutes. No more. Then you're out of here. Period. No detours back, no delays, no heroics. Go to the police, ask for Detective McInnaw. Got that?"

With a sour face and grudging nod, he agreed.

Leaving the keys under the floor mat, I smiled at my young accomplice the best I could. "Okay. Let's do it."

Chapter 14

Billy stopped me in front of his uncle's back gate with an upraised hand. "Wait. Let's synchronize watches."

What, he thought we were on Mission Impossible? Who did he think he was, Peter Graves...I mean, Tom Cruise?

If he'd seen my face instead of his watch face, he'd have lost his enthusiasm. But I did owe this boy for his help. He deserved a little taste of heroics. "Sure."

He studied his hi-tech digital display. "Mark. Eight forty-seven," he read, and then looked up, waiting for me to finish the routine.

I estimated the time on the vague face of my numberless, black-faced Movado in the dim ally light. Close enough. "Mark."

Billy's code released the gate. The hinges were quiet as we went in, our steps on the cement path almost soundless in the dark cocoon of night. We went left to the unlit guesthouse, partially obscured by trees and shrubs.

The main house loomed up ahead, beyond more yard and a fenced pool area, light showing through several windows. Lush landscaping shielded the meandering path connecting the two houses and their separate yards, such a contrast to the Spartan desert look in the front. Pleasant as it looked, I appreciated its skulking attributes more.

We circled the guesthouse, carefully peering into windows and at the front from the protected corners. Nothing disturbed the feel of deserted peace. Except for the lighted windows, the main house appeared equally peaceful.

Back at the rear corner, I kept one eye on the sheer-curtained slider off the designer patio with its padded lawn furniture and potted geraniums and one eye toward the back of the main house. I gave my companion a small push. Billy didn't need to be a part of breaking into his uncle's property. "I'll take it from here, Billy. Go on now."

"Jeez. Why can't—"

"Go on!"

He turned away.

My hushed voice barely carried. "Thirty minutes."

Billy waved a hand over his shoulder and disappeared around a bend and into the dark.

The moment of truth. I suspected this wouldn't be as easy as it seemed. A good-sized rock lay in a cluster of decorative stones. Billy didn't need to see this part, either.

I stripped off my black t-shirt, wrapped it around my hands, gripped the rock and struck my blow. Whoa! Glass shattered in a rock-sized hole and tinkled to the ground, a shocking sound that left me frozen in terror.

I expected armed men to dash through the dark kitchen, leap from the shrubs, holler from the main house. Where are the neighbor's, for chrissake? I demanded silently, somehow indignant on behalf of property owners everywhere.

Using the shirt as a pad, I brushed aside the loose glass around the hole, reached through with my bare hand, released the lock and pulled open the sliding door. Stepping beyond the pile of glass, shards crunched underfoot and I froze again. Listened. Nothing disturbed the quiet inside the house except the faint beep of the alarm from the keypad by the back door.

Even expecting the security alarm, my heart thundered faster, my lungs bellowing in desperate, shallow pants. The ominous beep seemed more bomb-like than that stupid alarm clock had.

A few quick steps and Billy's master code turned off the beep. It worked, it worked! Hysterical laughter tickled the back of my throat and I pressed the hand gripping my shirt against my lips. Pain nipped my chin.

What the hell? I dabbed at my chin, saw a dark blotch of blood. Oops. Must be a glass shard. I thought safety glass didn't have cutting edges.

After a few vigorous shakes, I put the shirt back on. My skin tingled. I imagined my torso lacerated by hundreds of minuscule crystal knives and shuddered. Safety glass, safety glass, I told myself, and headed through the kitchen.

From Billy's description, I knew two small bedrooms and a bath were down the central hall located just beyond the archway dividing the kitchen and living room.

The few open steps beyond the archway exposed me to uncurtained windows facing the house. It seemed like a target zone. My mind knew without an inside light I was impossible to see, but my heart didn't get the message.

Once in the hall, I tried the closed door to the front bedroom, my hand vibrating on the knob. In the dim light, I saw nothing disturb the room. One down.

Pausing at the other bedroom door, I hesitated. What if Trent wasn't here? He could have been moved. Worse yet, he could be here and...I swallowed, too sick with fear to finish the thought. Turning the knob, I pushed the door open, standing back from the doorway. This room faced the back wall, the light more faint.

A form, a human form, lay dark against the bedspread.

Yes! I couldn't move. Forgetting to check the rest of the room, my feet broke the paralysis and rushed to the bedside. It was Trent, lying still and motionless as if asleep. Please God, let him be asleep!

I dropped to my knees. Tears blurred my vision. Silvery duct tape bound his wrists and ankles, a rope anchored his wrists to the headboard.

"Trent?" I croaked through a parched throat. He didn't move.

"Darling, wake up," I said louder and touched his chest.

Joy exploded like an opiate, wiping out all terror and fear as I felt him jump, saw his eyes flutter open.

"Are you all right?" I asked, cupping the side of his face and refraining from throwing myself on top of him.

"Lotsi?" His voice sounded weak, disoriented.

Dismayed, I began worrying about a concussion. Or drugs. Silly me, I'd counted on his being able to walk out. Might need Billy's help again after all.

"What...what are you doing here?"

"Came to collect you, of course. Just give me a minute." I dug into my pocket. Two things I'd brought with me. A small flashlight I daren't use now, and a knife. A nice, sharp pocketknife.

When he saw the blade open, his teeth flashed white in a credible smile. "Good girl."

The rope severed after sawing a few strokes. Trent's arms remained locked overhead. I waited a second for him to move, then realized his muscles were frozen in place. It took all my strength to get them lowered to his chest. I dreaded the pain of returning circulation, and spent a moment massaging his shoulders and forearms. When he groaned, I didn't know what to do. Continue massaging or leave him alone?

The need to hurry decided me, and I starting sawing at the tape binding his wrists. The sticky layers gummed up the blade, slowing the process. "Golly, they must have used half a roll of tape," I groused, fear rearing its head again as Trent's face reflected the intense pain he felt.

"I need to know, love. Are you injured beyond the head wound? Be truthful," I said as the first shake of his head about rolled his eyes back.

"Bruises. Nothing to...worry about."

Yes, I could see I had nothing to worry about. Men! Wrists freed, I started on the tape at his ankles. By now dull and sticky, the knife didn't cut, it hacked. We were running out of time. "Look, we need to get out of here, but if you can't walk, I can get help in about five minutes."

Voice reedy with pain, he said, "No, I'll make it. Who's here, Erwin?"

"Uh, no. Billy."

"The kid?"

An inner voice snickered at the inadvertent reference to the outlaw. A human mind sure has some quirky byways. "Yeah. He recognized where his uncle had you from the photo." One last tough fiber resisted the useless blade. I sawed and tugged, sawed and tugged, until it parted, his legs falling free.

Angry, Trent struggled to sit up. "The bastard sent that picture to you?"

Surprised he hadn't known, I helped him sit at the edge of the bed for a moment, watching as he canted to his right side. "Benson didn't tell you you're hostage for my RV?"

"Your RV?" Trent swayed and then steadied, his pale face beading with sweat. "Hell, he didn't even say his name was Benson. What's going on?"

"Later. Let's get out of here." Supporting as much of his weight as I could, we wavered at first and almost fell. Recovering, with each step we gathered speed.

Optimism filled me. Against all odds, I had found Trent— found him relatively unhurt—freed him, and we were on our way to safety.

Exiting the hallway, we headed toward the kitchen and the back door, my arm now more for comfort than support. I couldn't help teasing him. "We're going to have a long talk about who needs a bodyguard. Billy should be at our rendezvous—"

"There's been a change in plans," the man's sardonic comment came from behind us. Even before I swung around and saw him, I knew it belonged to Benson. Who else?

Light blazed as he flicked a wall switch. An arrogant smirk twisted his full lips as he enjoyed our shock. He and his men had waited back against the dark living room wall for us to emerge.

The man holding Billy was the truck driver who'd tried to run me down while I was on my Ninja. The boy stood at an awkward angle, one arm jacked up behind his back, his mouth gagged by the man's hand. Eyes eloquent with despair and horror, blood dribbled down his temple, stained a rough patch on his cheek.

Dark and muscular with a barrel chest, Truck Driver shared Billy's penchant for droopy drawers, but on him with his hard face and mean eyes it looked sinister, not youthful. I had no problem imagining him in a violent gang, sticking gun barrels down the baggy legs. He released Billy's mouth, but instead of speaking, Billy bowed his head to hide the tears slipping down his face.

"My nephew told me about your trick with my transmitters." His arrogance slipped. Rage ate his eyes. "I want my money, bitch."

The second henchman, wearing a Hawaiian shirt and slicked back hair, held a gun pointed at Trent and me and spoke in a whiney falsetto. "It's in the camper, boss. She'da tol' the kid, otherwise. I'll slip in tonight and get it. Tol' ya I'd get it before. We should waste 'em right here." He raised the gun as if to carry out his suggestion.

Trent erupted from under my arm as he went for Hawaiian Shirt.

"Don't shoot!" Benson shouted.

Hawaiian Shirt struck Trent a glancing head blow with the gun barrel as they crashed to the floor and rolled. Trent came up on top, one arm braced across the man's throat, the other wrestling for the gun.

The smaller man was fresh and uninjured. Viper mean. Teeth bared, he clawed at Trent's arm pressing his neck. Their jointly raised hands gripped the weapon, tendons raised into furrows, muscle's straining.

Trent's arm quivered, his strength ebbing before my eyes.

Frantic, I wished Hawaiian Shirt were on top. Then I could jump him or hit him or *something.*

First, I needed a weapon. A quick look around revealed nothing dramatic, like a baseball bat or a sword—jeezel bezel, what would I do with a freaking sword?—so I settled for the best thing I could see, piddling though it was. I grabbed the skinny plastic lamp off a side table. Threw another quick glance around.

At the back wall, Billy struggled against Truck Driver. Benson watched the men wrestling on the floor, letting his man battle for him. I edged in closer, hoping for a shot at Hawaiian Shirt's head.

Then Katie bar the door, the battles escalated before I could blink.

Trent's raised arm collapsed. Before Hawaiian Shirt could react, Trent jerked up his other arm and brought it back down on the man's throat. With more strength, he'd have killed the man right then. As it was, Hawaiian Shirt gurgled and went limp.

Beyond them, Truck Driver cursed and spun Billy around, wrenched his arm higher and shoved him hard into the wall. With a sharp cry, the young man slid down into a heap, cradling his arm.

Benson's disgusted complaint shocked me cold. "Christ, why do I pay these assholes." As Trent lunged to scoop up the gun, Benson stepped forward, taking up the battle at last.

I swung the lamp at him like Babe Ruth at bat, but as I'd feared, the acrylic deco base bounced off his back with no noticeable effect. Pathetic weapon. I needed a tool to suit the job. A sledgehammer would do.

Poor choice of images, I thought, as Benson's foot struck Trent's side. The blow lifted Trent off Hawaiian Shirt. He landed on his side and lay still, curled inward, gasping in pain. Benson picked up the gun with casual ease, sneered at me and aimed at Trent's head.

"I hid the money!" I screamed, hands painfully clenching the lamp. "I hid the money!"

The barrel didn't move. He asked in a calm voice, "You think that'll stop me from killing him? Or you, for that matter?"

Thoughts crawled through a frozen slush of fear. I prayed for inspiration. There had to be a reason for Benson to keep us alive. Think! Why would he need us to get the money? I had to buy more time. Throwing the lamp aside, I tried to sound scornful. "You think I'd tell Billy everything? Your nephew?"

Benson's head snapped around, the cold thrust of his shark-eyes piercing my veneer of bravado. Afraid I'd show my desperation if I looked away—looked at Billy—I watched those eyes.

I'd seen that look before. At company meetings, at meetings in his office or mine, sometimes in the hall, I'd see those narrowed eyes and cruel smile as my former CEO would throw out his taunts and verbal slams, by no means unique to me, when he thought his directives were being thwarted. In his god-like self-perception, the head of Franklin Industries believed that despite all evidence to the contrary, his mandates should create reality.

He'd thrown his power around as if he were above any moral standard of ethics. That he had a divine right to increasingly larger bonuses and options while the staff's proportionately minuscule bonuses decreased. While he upgraded and increased the airplane and limousine fleets for the exclusive convenience of upper management, employee's salaries were frozen and their benefits cut—although the employee insurance contributions increased.

Yet those not-uncommon business practices paled in the significance of the underlining standard the man set for the company, the real corporate mission statement his actions and attitude proclaimed. For where the captain steers, so the ship follows.

I'd wondered, when I was going through my travails with Franklin and the ensuing sex-discrimination action I'd brought against them, just how far up the ladder my bosses' decisions had gone. I hadn't been sure, even during the hearing when my bosses' had him on the phone as I fought to recoup the salary I should have been paid.

Now I knew. Staring into Benson's eyes, seeing that same cold, no-holds-barred look, I knew that the captain's course hadn't varied one iota because my CEO had made the call. His men had only carried out the details.

Well, I'd stood my ground and beaten those eyes against all odds then. I'll stand my ground and beat these deadlier eyes now. I just needed to calm down and figure out where ground was in this hellish freefall Trent and I were in as Benson exercised his self-perceived divine right to make his call regarding our lives.

Oh, Benson saw my desperation. Men like that always do. It's part of the thrill for them. But hey, who wouldn't be a little desperate, right?

Desperate but smart, looking for new ground on which to play the wild cards I'd thrown down in a last-minute bluff.

That's it, I thought. This is a new hand. You folded the last hand, but you're still in the game. Deal him the cards that'll convince him he needs you and Trent. That's your ground—he needs you. Now play to win.

Calmer, I stood on my new ground and finishing dealing the new cards. "I took someone a package. Don't bother finding out who, they're local, not even in the RV Park. I locked the money in a container and stashed the key. I

163

showed them the picture of Trent, so they'd know how serious this is."

I smirked, full of myself, as if I wanted him to know how clever I'd been. "I told them to hide the container somewhere safe, I don't even know where. If anyone but me, alone and in person, asks for it, they'll call the police. And I have to pick it up by nine tomorrow morning. Or they call the police."

Benson lowered the gun, turned, his face hard, and mean as he studied me. I had him hooked.

He looked at Truck Driver, gestured with the gun toward Hawaiian Shirt, pale and semi-conscious on the floor, shallow breaths wheezing between his mutters and moans. "Get him to a hospital. He fell, hit by a rock. Whatever."

Truck Driver started to move and then paused. "What about the kid?"

Benson looked down at Billy and my eyes followed. Propped against the wall, Billy's head and shoulders curled over his arm in an air of dejected pain. Dark splotches of drying blood stood out against his pallor, his face glistened with sweat.

Devoid of expression or inflection, Benson asked. "Did you break his arm?"

With their attention occupied, I crossed over and hunkered at Trent's side. He remained where he'd fallen, arms wrapped around his chest. His eyes followed me, intent, aware. When I placed my hand on his arm, his hand sneaked out and covered mine.

Was he seriously injured or laying low? My eyebrow asked. His hand pressed tighter and released as one eye blinked. Good.

"Naw," Truck Driver said with a disgusted snort in Billy's direction. "Wrenched some, but I didn't break it."

The cold promise that flashed in Benson's glare wiped all expression from Truck Driver's broody face and he jerked straight.

"Be grateful," Benson said. "He's still my nephew. Move it!" This time the gun's message was emphatic.

Truck Driver hitched up his sagging drawers and didn't hesitate removing his assigned burden.

From his superior position as the only standing person in the room, Benson ignored his nephew and concentrated a narrow-eyed stare at Trent and me. His words slapped out a sharp challenge. "These friends. What's to keep them from running off with my money themselves?"

Dabbing at the dried streaks of blood on Trent's moist face with my shirtsleeve, I paused and shot Benson a grim smile. "Insurance."

"Explain."

With a last swipe at Trent's face, I tried his trick with a winking eye, the one opposite Benson, and stood, folding back the stained sleeve. "I will, but I'd like to help Billy while we talk, if that's okay."

Benson glanced at Billy. His expression softened, touched by an affection and concern I never expected from the brutal and greedy man I'd seen thus far. Then he stiffened, shook his head. "Don't coddle the boy. He needs to toughen up. Explain your goddamn insurance."

Billy had peered up at me from under his brows while his uncle considered my request. With Benson's words, his head dropped down again. Ohhhh, my hatred for Benson grew. I could only imagine the bitter disillusionment the young man felt, beyond his pain and fear, but I could do nothing for him now.

Walking further into the living room, I sat on the arm of an overstuffed chair. "I had several hours to plan this, you know. That's a lot of money. A lot of incentive. So I protected myself from all sides, from you, my friends, and the cops."

When he looked incredulous, I smiled, relaxed but not too cocky. "Hey, I don't trust the cops any more than you do. So I built in overlapping controls. I printed out the photos— you know, of you in my storage bin, the money I found there, the transmitters, Trent's photo—with a quick summary of all that's happened. A few of the bills, just in case they're traceable. Oh, and the key from the container. All that went into an envelope addressed to my friend, LVPD Detective McInnaw."

I laughed. "But I overnighted it to a friend in Seattle with instructions that if I don't call to retrieve it before it arrives, it's to be sent immediately to McInnaw."

"Shit," he said, shoulders lowering just a bit.

Now to reel him in. "But wait, it gets better. I have teleconferencing, so I talked to my friend and the Detective's voice mail at the same time." I buffed my nails. "Of course, McInnaw will have kittens, but what can he do? I'll explain it away."

"Wait a minute," Benson's voice turned belligerent. "You sent an overnight package this evening, on a Sunday night?" His weight shifted, the gun coming up to underscore the consequences of his disbelief.

Oops. A lead weight of fear sunk to the pit of my stomach. Well, I thought, they always say it's the little things that mess up a good lie.

Guess they're right.

Chapter 15

Benson's cold eyes and threatening gun stared me in the face. What could I say now? Think! Think!

The elaborate lie I'd been constructing hung suspended in my mind, a spontaneous collection of actions I *could* have taken if only I'd been smart enough to prepare before being caught. If I had planned it, how would I do it? Oh, yes.

Shaking my head, I pursed my lips and tut-tutted. "Such suspicion. Ever hear of twenty-four-hour self-service shipping stations, Benson? You need to get out more."

I dropped the humor and speared his eyes. "So here's the deal. You have us. I have the money and the evidence on a remote deadman's switch. Tomorrow morning I pick up the money, which I exchange for Trent. You still have a long arm, I still have the overnight package, but remember I don't care where the money came from and I don't trust cops. Trent and I leave Las Vegas. I retrieve the package, turn the key over to you, and keep the paperwork in a blind location as long-term insurance. We don't interfere in your business, you don't interfere with us. Deal?"

Benson batted the gun against his leg as he thought it through. The waiting kicked my heartbeat up another notch, my senses on high alert. Everything registered, the bright light overhead, the gun's thud, the woven fabric of the chair beneath my hand. Thoughts clicked by at super speed, the better to see the holes in the brazen deal.

He'd see them too, of course, but I prayed he'd go along with the surface logic. His self-interest in getting the money back would encourage him, wouldn't it? The riskiest factor was the premise that he'd honor a negotiated deal. He'd only agree if he believed I believed he would.

In a pig's eye, I believed. To Benson, deals were expediencies and completely non-binding on his part. I had no illusions about his capacity for ruthlessness. I'd seen it in his eyes several times now. None of us was safe. He could pick up Trent, or Kaitlynn or Bianca, at any time. I would give him everything he wanted long before he exhausted his well of ruthlessness.

I looked at the man I believed capable of removing body parts with the calm assurance of a naive, trusting woman, and continued to wait.

With a final slap of the gun, Benson said, "All right. Looks like I got no choice." He stuck the gun in his belt. I stood, braced and tenser than ever.

Ignoring me, he walked over to Billy, who looked up at his uncle with fear and anxiety battling a stoic expression. "You ready to be sensible about this?" Benson asked as if discussing a childish tantrum over a toy.

Billy glanced my way. I gave a tiny nod. "Ah, sure," he said, lurching to his feet as his uncle gave his good arm a tug upward.

Trent struggled to rise, and I hurried to his assistance. "Don't let him separate us," he urged in a soft undertone, leaning on me.

"Not if I can help it," I breathed back, concerned at the way he stood hunched over, arm pressed against his chest, swaying. I sure as heck hoped he wasn't as bad off as he looked.

"So here's *my* deal," Benson said before I could ask Trent any questions. The way he used my words, the smirk on his face, made me very nervous. He hadn't liked being dictated to, and he wanted payback.

"I've got a safe room downstairs at the house." He shot Billy a look. "Good thing I got the wife and daughter outta town. You two are my guests. One of my guys'll meet you in the morning, follow you to your friends. Don't do nothing stupid and try to lose him. Wallace stays here. You get the money, give it to my associate, I'll let Wallace go."

Yes, of course you will.

My ex-husband used to say I was so stubborn I'd argue with the devil himself, so I puffed up like a blowfish and kept pushing back. "I get the money. Your guy calls, you release Trent. Since Trent's injured, Billy goes with him to help. I give your guy the money after Trent calls me from his motorhome."

A violent mix of emotions, primarily rage, roiled just beneath Benson's surface. His lips thinned, his face flushed then whitened, hands clenched at his sides a couple of times. I thought one twitched toward the gun, but it could have been my imagination.

Arguing with the devil certainly posed unusual risks.

A tremor ran through my body. I didn't know how much more of this I could take. Any second now, I'd explode into hysteria and fall blubbering to the floor. As he leaned against me, Trent's hand at my waist began to soothe in a comforting rub. The small, deliberate contact steadied me.

Benson's lips swished to one side several times and his stance relaxed. "That'll work. Let's go." This time he did take the gun in hand, to use as an almost-casual gesture of direction. The threat worked well.

Eyeing the way Trent moved—his painful grimace as he shuffled forward leaning heavily on me for support—Benson's face lightened and he relaxed even more.

"Billy, you stay with me. I'll make some calls." Benson sneered at Trent. "Move it, Mr. Toughguy! Ain't got all night."

He stepped back as we passed, keeping at least six or eight feet between us. Benson's caution reminded me the man was a professional security expert. I didn't know if that thought was intimidating or reassuring.

Trent managed a faster pace. I still wasn't sure how much he feigned his incapacitation, but within minutes, we entered through the back of the house and traversed down a wide hall to a staircase leading below.

Everything about the main house was grand. Grand rooms, grand hallways, grand art. Major decorating bucks for a grand display worthy of a TV appearance as a home of the rich and famous.

Once inside Benson's safe room, I looked beyond the surface. This room merited a shot as the grand guest suite for the wealthy paranoid. Bedroom/sitting area, large closet, scrumptious private bath. Windows barred with cheery decorative Mediterranean metalwork, extra-strength. Then I turned back, noticed the suite's solid-core door, heavy-duty locks, and recessed door sets inaccessible to tampering from either side. I knew with chilling insight this "safe room" was designed to keep someone in as much as someone out.

My gaze flicked to Benson, watching me from the doorway, an amused smirk twisting his lips as he said, "I trust you can entertain yourselves until morning." Then his whole demeanor changed, hardened. "My guy'll be here at eight sharp. Be ready, Ms. Hannon. I want this...misunderstanding resolved."

Nodding, I pasted on a smile, thinking how gentle the word "misunderstanding" sounded, how threatening its delivery. "So do I, Mr. Benson. So do I."

As the door began to swing shut, I looked at Billy, standing silent in the hall behind his uncle, and tried to convey, I don't know—thanks, encouragement, entreaty. Goodbye. His head dipped in acknowledgment. It was the best we could do.

Trent and I stood bracing one another until we heard the locks tumble into place. With a burst of motion he straightened and spun me around, wrapping me in a fierce hug.

Oh, God yes! Joy and relief swept through me. We were together, alive, and alone. And Trent wasn't as injured as he'd seemed.

Then he grabbed my shoulders and stepped back so he could glare down at me. "What the hell do you think you're doing, woman? You scared ten years off my life. I swear to God, I'm going to paddle your butt for a week when we get out of here!" Then he shook me. Shook me!

I knocked his hands loose. "I scared *you*! What do you think you did to me, moaning and shuffling around like a wounded duck? I thought you were really hurt!" I stomped away. Anger and tears warred inside. "Yell at me, will he?" I growled, focusing on the mad. "Of all the nerve...."

"Slow down, Stretch. I can't keep up." Despite the humor I heard in Trent's voice, when I turned I saw the tension and pain in his face, the stiff, cautious way he moved, and my anger melted.

He kept coming until his hands threaded into my hair, holding my head as his thumbs brushed the curve of my jaw. "I can't keep up," he said more seriously, eyes hot and burning into mine. "I'm still reeling, trying to figure out what's going on, how to keep you safe, how to help since you seem to have an edge. And I keep thinking, what if she gets hurt? I won't have it, do you hear me? I won't have you hurt!"

Before I could answer, his lips attacked mine, a quick and searing demand that changed to something deeper and more primal as his arms enfolded me again and he held on. "Now do you understand?" he asked in a soft, strained voice.

I swallowed, understanding the need to protect all too well, and the fear of not succeeding. "I do," I said, holding him tight against my heart. When he gasped and twitched, I jerked back. "You *are* hurt!"

Just like a man to yell at me when he's the one injured.

"It's nothing, maybe a cracked rib or two. I think. Come here." With a glint in his eye, he reached for me again.

"Oh, shut up. And quit that." I batted his hands aside and looked him over. "Boy, are you a mess. I'll see if I can find something to fix you up."

When I returned in a few minutes, he'd settled into a high-backed chair and propped his feet up on the ottoman, looking comfortable and at ease, except for the streaks of blood and various abrasions sprinkled over pale, clammy skin.

My heart stuttered and swelled in my chest. How could this man have come to mean so much to me so quickly? So much it stunned me, so quickly it staggered me. I'm a practical woman. Confident. Focused. At least I had been.

Had this need for Trenton Wallace sneaked through the emotional cracks created by my imploding career? Or was the need he assuaged sealed up inside me all along, freed now to come alive in the new life I'd had thrust upon me?

I felt on the brink of realizing something important, but the moment passed, lost in the slipstream of the recent events.

"You're in luck," I said, lifting the large metal case when his eyes flew open. "Industrial First-Aid Kit. Even has a couple of cold packs and Ace bandages. I'll have you cleaned up, iced down, and wrapped in no time. Can you loosen your shirt?"

"Ice sounds good," he said, unbuttoning his shirt. "And you can explain how you've managed to steal Benson's money and blackmail him to boot." Even with my help, he went through some painful-looking gyrations before getting untucked enough to reveal a red swollen area on his left side.

"Ouch. Bet that's going to bruise like crazy." I talked while I popped the cold pack, mixed the chemical components, wrapped it in a washcloth and placed it over his ribs. Then I went to work on his face.

He winched. "So after you found the money, you took it to someone?"

"Hold still. No, I told Benson I did. It's still under the table in my RV."

Trent grabbed my hand. "Jesus, Lotsi, you made that up? And the package you sent, you made that up, too?"

"Why are you pissed? He was going to shoot you! I had to think of something, a reason for him to keep us around. I just stacked the deck in our favor, that's all!"

The incredulous expression turned to an angry frown and his grip tightened until it hurt. "He would have turned on you like a rabid dog!"

"I'll need that hand again, love," I said softly, and when he released it, went back to swabbing the lacerations on his face with Betadine wipes. "I know it was risky. But I didn't have much choice, did I?"

He looked mulish enough to argue, but relented with a sigh. "No, I suppose not. What a fucking mess. Another ten years, I swear."

I finished coating the cuts with antibiotic cream and put on waterproof band-aids. "That's about all I can do for these. Let's get your ribs taped up properly."

Trent roused and glanced at the open kit. "Got any drugs in there?"

"Just some aspirin and Ibuprofen." I hesitated, and then drew a prescription bottle from my pocket. "I did find some Vicodin in the medicine cabinet, but the prescription is for a Mrs. Sally Wainwright. I don't know if you should use it."

Trent looked at me, blinked, and then started to laugh but the pain caught him up short. "God, Lotsi, I can't believe you. You take money from a crook, tamper with evidence, illegally break into a house, lie like a pro blackmailing a dangerous man, yet you stand there worried about me using someone else's prescription?" He held his elbow pressed against his side, staving off the pain caused by his suppressed guffaws.

Served him right. Idiot. "Well, that's different. I told you, I didn't have any choice. And someone else's drugs might...might hurt you." I gulped back a sob and turned away, embarrassed at the tears that caught me by surprise.

"Come here, sweetheart," Trent said, and the gentle softness spurred more tears. I shook my head. He pulled at my arm. "Come here."

When he had me settled against him, he rubbed the base of my spine with his good hand and nuzzled his face against my hair. "I'm sorry I offended you. I really can't keep up, you know. You're a fascinating woman, Lotsimina, and a joy to me. That's why I laughed. Okay?"

I nodded, sniffed. He went on more briskly. "And I've taken Vicodin before, so it's not a problem, but I have to tell you, I'd wrestle you for those pills right now. Am I going to have to get tough with you?"

"You run a weak bluff, Wallace. A three-year-old could whip you right now." I wiped my face as I pulled away and popped the lid, shaking out one small tablet. "But I'll think of a price to extract for the drugs."

Trent gulped the pill back without water, a skill I'd never learned. "Extortion now, is it?"

"Crime is habit forming, don't you know?"

"I think we'll have a talk about rehabilitation. Later. Right now, I need the facilities, and if the drug kicks in, I'd like a shower."

"A shower? What if...what if Benson comes back before morning?" I couldn't help the quiver in my voice as my eyes darted around our cozy prison and at the heavy door locking us inside. "Can we lock him out somehow?"

"We could. We could move the dresser in front of the door. A chair under the doorknob wouldn't slow them down much, but it'd make a racket." He smiled, as if unconcerned about making such choices. "The thing is, Benson needs your cooperation, at least until tomorrow morning, when you supposedly meet your friends to retrieve the money. He's not going to upset the applecart tonight. There's nothing for him to gain by doing so, and everything to lose."

I nodded, my mind agreeing completely but my emotions still quaking in fear underneath. God, are there any more terrifying words than "What if...?" I pushed the fear aside. "Well, in that case, a hot soak should help, and if you get the band-aids wet, there are plenty more. We can wrap the ribs when you're done. Can you manage okay?"

His instant grin and sexy invitation, which I turned down, reassured me. Yet a few minutes later, as the water started running I prowled the room, pausing at the bookcase, the paintings, the bed. It was barely ten o'clock. So much had happened, my world felt more than turned upside down, it felt destroyed.

I looked at my hand, my reflection in the mirror, and wondered why I looked the same. A little mussed, a little bright-eyed, but the same me on the outside. Inside, though...well, now, what was I to do with all these feelings dithering around, settling into the pit of my stomach?

My eyes came back to the bed, my thoughts to the man in the shower. I'd almost lost him before I'd had him. I didn't want to think about tomorrow yet, but one thing I knew. If this was my last night, I wanted—I needed—to share it with Trenton.

I knocked gently on the bathroom door, eased it open and stepped inside. He'd chosen the shower over the garden tub and steam billowed from the large stall. Through the glass block wall and the foggy door, I could see Trent's silhouette. It had been a long time since I'd seen and touched a naked man, and vice versa. My bold nerve started to fail until Trent's arms reached toward his head and he moaned.

That resolved my dilemma. I shut the door. "Sounds like you could use some help after all."

All movement and sound from him ceased. Then, "Are you offering just your help, Lotsimina?"

Licking dry lips, I gathered my courage. "No, not just my help."

The shower door inched open. "Then get in here."

My clothes joined his on the floor in record time. Trent stepped back from the spray, his eyes catching mine as I eased into the space in front of him, facing the water. His hands rested at my waist. I'd thought it would be awkward, but he hadn't ogled me, and his hands didn't grope. They rested there, connecting us, welcoming me, accepting me. Thank God.

I relaxed into his hold, the warmth from the water cascaded over my body, releasing knotted muscles. A world of tension flowed out on a deep sigh, and then Trent pivoted me so that the water heated my back and he heated my front. Jumping Jehoshaphat, fifteen years of sexual lightening stuck from head to toe.

Panic exploded. My heart thundered, my breath froze. Trent moved gently, hard wet male rubbing soft needy female. Every nerve in my body went into shock as the incredible sexual stimulation blew whatever electrical circuit breakers my body possessed and nerves flared into overload. A giant shudder struck, lungs inflated in a rusty wheeze.

Arms cradled around my hips, Trent's eyes roamed my face, taking in all my expressions, feeling all the reactions as my body responded to his slow, thrusting movements. A gentle tenderness touched the curve of his lips, smoldered in the depths of his eyes.

"I've thought of our first time together," he said, a husky rumble to his soft words. "I would start very slow, letting you adjust to me, adjust to yourself. I'd show you how wonderful you are, how wonderful we are together. We'd take all night...we'd take forever."

His hands slipped over the wet skin of my bottom, caressing, squeezing, dipping down lower, rocking me harder against him, still in a slow movement that matched the flex of his hips. "But Lotsimina, we don't have all night, and I'm afraid I'm going to shock the living hell out of you, because we aren't going to go slow."

My knees threatened to collapse as I opened my legs for his probing fingers. "I-I think I can keep up," I squeaked, feeling the strange sensation of bones melting into liquid heat.

His sexy, throaty laugh tingled through me at the same time my hands discovered his backside and began to roam. My lips sank to his chest and began to taste, a sound rising in my throat, half moan, half purr.

"I know you can," Trent whispered, but I'd lost track of the conversation.

After a time his voice penetrated the drugged haze in my mind. "Lotsimina. Stop, baby. Any more and I'll take you right here, only I can't trust my strength right now."

I blinked up at him. His hand cupped my face. "That's it, come all the way back to me." His lips brushed mine. When I lifted my lips for more, his tongue licked slowly across them on the outside, coming back at the center to flick inside just enough to touch my tongue, tip to tip. Then he withdrew. I whimpered.

Pressing my head against his throat, he spoke softly near my ear. "Oh, the things I'm going to do to you once we're in bed, Lotsi-love. I don't know if I'll survive."

Feeling his heart hammer in rhythm with mine, I spoke with the same husky promise in my voice. "I'll do my best to see you don't."

Chapter 16

Trent's chuckle feathered across my ear and vibrated through my body as I pressed against him. "Let's go find that bed," he said.

Smiling, I drew back to savor this moment. He was so sweet. He'd wanted our first time together to go slow and easy. Silly man. I'd had all the slow I could take. I had a fifteen-year thirst to satisfy. I wanted to gulp, not sip. Maybe next time.

Then I noticed Trent's hair and frowned. His beautiful silver mane hung in wet, matted ringlets, a normally sexy foil around his handsome face, but right now, the red-tinted water seeping onto his chest slapped me back to reality.

"Let me wash the blood from your hair first," I said, brushing at the stained ends, frowning at the abrasions on his face.

His eyes flickered as if he'd also pushed reality aside in the heat of our loving. "All right. But hurry."

Some of the wounds under his hair began seeping fresh blood. Gentle as I was, the washing and rinsing must have hurt. After I'd finished his head, I paused. What should I do now?

Reaching and twisting surly caused him pain, but could I wash him...everywhere? I wanted this man as my lover. I'd taken steps to make him my lover tonight, but truthfully, I wasn't ready for this kind of foreplay. I'd think of him as a patient.

That settled, I went on, washing him with more speed. Through the washcloth, I felt male curves dip in and out under my hand, so different from mine, strong and hard. The strokes slowed. Slowed some more. Became soapy caresses. No way could I touch Trent this way in anything but foreplay.

"Someday I'm going to do this again, and I'm going to take my time to enjoy all of you," I promised us both as I finished up. "But for now, go wrap yourself in a towel. I'll be right out."

"I can't return the favor?" He nodded at my soapy hands.

Shaking my head, I ignored the leap in my pulse and used the soap on myself. "The movements would hurt you, and I'd feel guilty. Go. And let me dry your hair."

His expression turned thunderous. "A little pain won't stop me tonight, Lotsi. Don't even get started."

"And later I won't want you to stop, but this I can do myself. Quicker, too. See, I'm almost done."

Maybe he took that as an invitation, because he stayed, watching my every move and every move got slower and slower and I had to rinse carefully, too. When I shut the water off, we stood looking at one another, both so hot I'm surprised the water didn't instantly evaporate from our bodies.

Trent pushed the door open, and waited for me to exit. I headed for the towels, intending to dry him and take care of his head wounds immediately.

I twisted my hair in a towel and came back with two more. His hands clasped mine over the thick bath sheets. "Let me do this. Please."

Trent waited for my nod, and then laid one towel aside, opening the other to cover his hands. With muffs of softest cotton, he stroked over my face, down my neck and shoulders, drying each arm and hand and moving on, cupping my breasts through the warm cloth, his eyes following his hands, rubbing softly around each hardened nipple, then down over my stomach and hips as he knelt in front of me, stroking down each leg, taking each foot in one hand and drying it, then continuing up between my legs, softly, thoroughly. God. My body created more liquid down there than the shower, and the towel soaked up my juices as I made room between my thighs for him to blot every nook and cranny. Watching him watch his work didn't help the problem.

When I moaned, he looked up and gave a devastating grin of need and satisfaction. My knees loosened. Moving behind me, he went up the backs of my legs, my buttocks, smoothing cotton over the dip of my back, and up each side to my shoulders, where he placed a slow sucking kiss at the base of my neck.

Then he stood before me, both of us breathing ragged and shallow. Color flushed his face. His eyes blazed. I reveled in his response to me, my whole body pulsing with desperate need.

He reached for the other towel. "Let me," I whispered, and lifted my hands. They trembled. Had I ever trembled for a man? If I had, I couldn't remember.

"No," Trent's soft voice rumbled across my bare skin. "I want you in bed. Just stand there, let me see you. All of you."

Trent dried himself, his eyes roaming over my body from head to foot at will. I felt no self-consciousness, only acceptance. And heat. Especially when his voice roughed with a sensual burr, hot and sexy. "One day very soon my hands and then my lips and my tongue are going to touch you everywhere my hands just traveled. Everywhere."

I nearly collapsed. "Trenton," was all I could say, trying to chastise him and ending up pleading.

"Don't move."

"What?"

His slashing grin should have warned me. "I need to do something, and you need to do exactly as I say. Don't move. Understand?"

I wet my lips, not understanding the incredible excitement that blazed in me at his implacable tone, but willing to do anything he wanted. "Yes," I whispered.

Before I could blink, he knelt again and without touching me anywhere else, laved the tip of my breast with his tongue. Gasping in shock, I felt a shaft of sexual heat lance from his mouth to my womb and trickle down my thigh. Shudders rocked through me as his tongue flicked back and forth, switching from one breast to another, biting, sucking, then licking again.

I clenched my hands to keep from grabbing him. His name ripped out of me as a cry for mercy, a demand for more, and he came to his feet in a rush. Holding his hand out for mine, he growled, "Come to bed."

"Your head—"

"Come to bed."

I took his hand and had just enough presence of mind to grab the last dry towel on the way out. He started to slip his arm around my waist as we walked to the bed and winced.

Realty just wouldn't let us forget.

"I'm going to tape your ribs. Don't argue. You'll be more comfortable. And you'll be a better lover."

That snapped his mouth shut but he still scowled. I carefully refrained from smiling.

He sat on the edge of the bed as I rummaged through the first-aid kit for the Ace bandages. Trent had to hold the bandage at each side of his chest so I could scramble behind and pass it around his back. The first wrap was done before his lips twitched.

"Smartass," he muttered.

"Whatever works."

Stretching out the elastic bandage and passing it around to his front, my face neared his. Seeing the twinkle in his eyes, I let the smile I'd been fighting show, and leaned in to brush a soft kiss over his lips. "This'll be over in a moment."

"I liked the moment we were having before this," he grumbled, holding the second bandage in place for me to grab on the other side.

Aligning the next layer, I said, "I have an idea about that," and sent the elastic strip around again. "How do your ribs feel?"

"Much better. I can breathe more easily, too." He held the last section ready. "What's your idea?"

I used the metal clips to secure the end, scrambled around to his side and stood, facing the still moment of decision. Part of me felt intimidated by the door that kept us in but couldn't keep our enemy out, by the uncertainty of our safety tomorrow. By the uncertainly of having sex after all these years. A greater part wanted this man. Wanted him now, despite the risks, or perhaps because of them. Nothing short of someone storming through that door was going to keep me from having him.

Ignoring his question, I let my actions speak. "All done. Stand just a second, will you?"

He quirked his eyebrow and complied as I turned the bedside lamp down to the base globe, enough to see but without glaring brightness. Then I stripped back the covers and tossed them over as far as I could, which on a King bed, didn't reach far, but left us plenty of room. Scooping up the towel I'd brought, I spread it across the pillows and waved my hand. "Come. Lie down."

Sweet man. He laid down on the bed for me, anticipation teasing his lips in a sexy curve. I looked at his smile, his face, his eyes, his hair spread on the white towel. Did he know how much I loved him?

"What's your idea, Lotsi-love?" He all but purred.

"You need to do exactly as I say. Don't move. Understand?"

"Lotsimina!" Gone were all signs of softness.

Crossing my arms under my breasts inadvertently drew his eyes, so I pushed my arms up a little more. "Understand?"

His Adam's apple jumped as he swallowed. He nodded.

I'd placed one knee on the bed and leaned forward onto my hands when he spoke with a frantic edge to his voice, tearing his eyes away from my chest. "Three, no, two minutes."

Pausing, I frowned at him. "Two minutes! You had—"

"Take it or leave it." His eyes dropped to my chest again. "On second thought...." He started to reach for me.

"I'll take it!" I flowed over him like morning fog, straddling his hips with my knees, keeping my weight off his chest with my arms. As I lowered to take his lips, the fine hairs on his chest above the bandages nestled around my nipples, sending exquisite shivers coursing through me.

"That's so...wonderful," I whispered. Throwing back my head, I held that position, sliding the hard nubs back and forth across his upper chest. Gone were all thoughts of Benson, of our prison. Of the door. All my focus centered on the feel of Trent beneath me. My legs stretching open around him, his hard shaft pressing between the slick swollen folds of my cleft, my swaying breasts raking across his flesh—all of me seemed stimulated to a point of madness.

I wanted more.

Seeking his mouth once more, I took his lips, sucking and licking until his tongue coaxed mine to delve deep inside. I savored his taste, his hunger. The intoxicating scent of sex and Trenton Wallace.

"More," I murmured.

Dragging my lips down his neck, I tasted as I went. Feeling the wild pulse at his throat beat under my tongue, I lingered, licking again and again, my heart drumming in time with every quiver under me. I heard him chant my name, and my body responded to the need in his voice. Balancing on my knees, I rocked my hips at the same beat my name left his lips, spreading my feminine moisture against his shaft where we touched. Some part of my mind registered his fists buried in the sheet, his muscles steeled beneath me, and marveled.

Then I dismounted and took my mouth south, down past the bandage where I picked up his taste again, the feel of flesh under my lips. My hands led the way, one caressing the soft tip of his erection, the other running down the hard length to cup his testicles below. I lips followed close behind.

"Two minutes," Trent's voice grated like a rusty hinge and I sailed through the air and landed on my back.

"No!" I tried to squirm but I was pinned beneath a heavy body.

"Yes!" he said, taking control of my world with a single word.

I cried out as his fingers thrust deep and took me over the edge. "More," he growled, and pushed my legs wider and took me with his mouth, lapping and sucking until I erupted again. The second climax still quaked through me when he surged inside, buried himself deep in one long, shattering thrust. He waited then, brushing the sweat from my brow, the tears from my face.

"Look at me, my Lotsimina. Look at me," he repeated softly, until my eyes could open and focus on his precious face, soft in the dim light.

"Are you okay?" His concern made me realize I was sobbing, so overwhelmed with sensation and emotion I had lost myself completely. I nodded. "You sure?" and he moved enough for me to know he waited for a real answer with the thinnest of control.

"I-I think I've died and gone to heaven. How else can this be so wonderful?"

That soft, sexy Trent-smile touched his face and faded into one of fierce passion as he pulled almost out and thrust back again and again until I strained against his pace, trying to find what I'd waited fifteen years to have only with him.

"Please. Please," I begged shamelessly, using my voice, my body.

This time his hand reached between us, his fingers sliding through my moisture, pressing against my clitoris as he pumped harder and harder. I burst apart, melting from the inside out, and as I shattered, he buried himself deep and the music of his release brought me to tears again.

Solo sex had never been this great.

Trent's weight eased down on me. He kissed my temple and started to withdraw. I held onto him and whispered, "Don't go. Stay inside."

"I'm too heavy."

"Just for a little while."

The sweetness grew and took me away. How long I slept, I don't know but I woke with Trent's arms wrapped around me and his body spooned to my back. Light still spilled from the bedside lamp base, a gentle glow to the strange surroundings.

Strange, too, being with a man. Being with Trent. I loved the feel of him against me, the way his hand curved under my neck and cupped my breast, the earthy scent of sex that still lingered in the air.

Yet reality intruded as the night ticked away. Tomorrow—this morning—Benson's plans for us probably didn't include letting us both go on our merry way. We had to do something about that before eight o'clock, when his henchman came to collect me.

Various options began drifting through my mind as I turned to look at the man beside me. My lover. All thoughts fled as I watched Trent come awake. Bristly faced, scrapped, bruises beginning to darken his skin, he looked delicious and rumpled, with steely ringlets tumbling over his face and drifting across the pillow. How could the man look so sexy in his condition?

His eyes blinked open and focused on me propped on my elbow looking down at him. "Hi, beautiful. Are you all right?"

Rough and low, the vibrations of his voice rasp against my skin, stimulating nerve endings and sending a hum through my body. I laughed, surprised at the husky sound. "Hey, you're the one who's been battered and bruised! I've just been...been—"

What? Destroyed and remade? Overwhelmed? I felt physically and emotionally sore and used in ways I'd never experienced before, and it pleased me in a wonderful and exciting way. I wanted to ask him if he had this effect on every woman he made love to, but I couldn't. He did with me, and that's all I cared about.

Trent grinned, his hand moving up my thigh and over the hill of my hip to rest cupped at the low dip at my waist. Rubbing slightly back and forth, his raspy burr whispered, "You've just been what, sweet baby?" He started to move closer but winched and stilled.

Reality again. Whatever I'd just been, if I wanted it to happen again, I'd better care about getting us out of here, but his pain bothered me and I unwisely asked one question. "How did you manage all that with your sore ribs?"

"All that, huh?" Satisfaction oozed from his voice.

Wishing I hadn't popped such a foolish question, I compensated. "Don't get cocky."

"Are you wondering what we'll do when I'm 100%?"

I hadn't until he mentioned it, dammit. "Boy, what an ego!"

"So you weren't going to tell me you'd just been thoroughly satisfied?"

"What? Of course I—no, you're right. Maybe next time will be better, when you're 100%. Oh, well."

Trent choked off his laugh. "Ouch. Who'd of thought laughing would be harder than sex? No, don't say anything. I'm devastated by your last remark already."

"Oh, shut up. You know you were...were magic. I've never—you know I've—oh, forget it."

Trent moved me onto the pillow and tipped my head back, forcing me to meet his eyes. I expected triumph, pride, something like that. I'd confessed my inadequacies when it came to sex, and he had to know he'd taken me beyond all previous experience.

What I saw was tenderness. Compassion. Something almost...humble. "Lotsi, you have to understand something. Usually a man gets an orgasm with a woman and he thinks, hey, I'm great, everything's fine. Sometimes a man realizes his woman needs something more than that, and maybe he'll do that for her."

"Like you did for me?"

"No, baby. This was all in you." His thumb brushed over my bottom lip and his soft smile turned my heart over. "I'm amazed how few men realize this, but I do. You see, a man's woman has all his magic inside her, and he has to release it in her before either of them can feel it."

"In *her*?" What did he mean? *He* had the magic!

"Yes, love. You have my magic inside you. I recognized it the first time we met. You did too, didn't you?" His hand cupped my face. "Didn't you feel something special awaken inside you, that first evening?"

My mouth was dry, the word hard to release. "Yes."

He nodded. "I know because it calls to me. It's my responsibility to release it in you, and when you respond to it, we both feel the results. And we both felt the magic, didn't we?"

"Yes, but...." This almost made sense, but he was driving me crazy!

"And before you ask, no, I haven't found this magic with anyone since my wife died. I've had sex, just like most men.

187

And no, the magic isn't the same. Only you carry this magic. Let's see. Oh, yes. Only I can release this magic in you, because it's my magic." Looking pleased with himself, he brushed his lips over mine. "My magic." Then he kissed me, as if sealing a claim. "Any questions?"

Goodness, he had me confused. "Not now. Well, just one. How-how do you know what will release this magic?" This was a silly game, right? So why was my heart thumping?

He smiled and tucked my hair behind my ear. "Aw, Lotsi-love, I'll always know. It's my magic. You can hide it, run from it, fight it, use it yourself—but with no one else—but it's my magic. And I want and need it very, very badly." His lips brushed mine again and he whispered, "I'll always know."

This time his kiss took my breath away, took me away. It *was* magic. I wanted so very much to believe his magic lived inside me. Just for him.

When he brought me back, he said, "Now for your question about the ribs. I was able to make magic love with you because I am a very careful and determined man, who could use another pain pill. Think it's time?"

Yes, I thought it was time. "Have to find my watch to see. But one thing's for sure. It's time to get out of here."

Chapter 17

I fumbled with the bedside lamp to turn on the three-way light while I tried to remember where my watch was. Probably with my clothes heaped on the bathroom floor, I decided, trusting I hadn't showered with it on. I'd been a little preoccupied at the time.

"What are you grinning about?" Trent asked in the suspicious way of a wary male.

Blinking at the low but brighter wattage, I could see him more clearly now, and what a sight. Stretched out on the white sheets, toned and tanned—and oh my, yes, that tan went everywhere—marred with red patches, cuts, bruises just going black and purple dotting face and body, hair a mess I'd hate to comb, and a strip of elastic circling his chest. Such a mess. He wasn't young, either. He showed his years. Still, I'd never seen a sexier man.

"Hmmm, just wondering where my watch was...and remembering our shower."

Funny thing about nudity. My ex-husband and I had avoided open nudity even after years of marriage. Yet once I'd opened that shower door and saw the honest lust and sexy appreciation in Trent's eyes, being nude with him didn't bother me. Maybe I was more pragmatic in my old age, but here I stood before him bare-assed naked in my timeworn body, relaxed, enjoying seeing him, and enjoying his seeing me.

My eyes traveled back up to meet his eyes, and ran into a heated laser beam. He deliberately dropped his gaze to study me in turn as he half-purred in that sexy way I was learning all about. "Yeah, I remember that shower rather fondly, myself. Want to take another one?"

Incredible as it seemed, Trent's shaft swelled. Catching back a gulp, I realized my breasts tingled, and knew they'd hardened into crinkly points. "Ah, no."

Trent glanced down and grinned. "Liar." He started to shift off the bed.

I turned and walked away. "No way. Beside the fact if it wouldn't kill you, it probably would me, remember we're prisoners here, and if we aren't careful, we may not survive the experience."

"Damn." I heard him mutter, but choose to ignore it.

My watch had rolled aside from where I'd tossed it. Not as much time had passed as I'd feared. Just after one in the morning. We'd slept only a couple of hours.

I gathered up all the clothes, glanced longingly at the shower, and decided a two-minute wash wouldn't jeopardize our breakout. When I stepped out, Trent leaned his butt against the vanity beside his stack of folded clothes. "You cheated. You said no shower."

"Not one with you. With your magic doing what it does to us we'd still be—" I held my hand up to ward him off. "No!" I'd seen his head come up and his nostrils flare, and some instinct warned me how close he was to coming off that counter.

I grabbed a towel and wrapped it around me. "You've got five minutes. Don't get your elastic bandages wet." I took my stack of clothes and headed for the door. "I'll help with your shirt when you get out."

With my hand on the doorknob, I turned. "You can take a Vicodin now, if you want. And oh, by the way," I said staring at his lap, "did I tell you how much I love your tan?"

He was on his feet, growling "Lotsimina!" when I closed the door. Clasping the bundle to my pounding heart, I covered a wild grin with my hand. I'd never taunted a tiger before, and wasn't sure he'd stay safely behind the closed door, but I couldn't resist. How often did a woman of my years get a chance to tease a handsome, sexy, naked lover?

Maybe I should have retired years ago.

When Trent came out, he'd taken care of his own shirt, and from the look on his face, wouldn't appreciate any comments about it. Just as well.

I'd pulled back the curtains to examine the windows up close. None of the windows opened. The full-length metal grillwork was outside, and looked sturdy as hell, embedded into the woodwork, not attached by little screws.

"I don't see how we can exit from any of the windows," I said as Trent came up beside me. "And the door seemed formidable from what we saw last night. I-I'm beginning to freak here. Seriously."

"Just a minute," he said, and turned me by the shoulders, studying my face. "Yes, I see you are. Okay, before we get into that, I have one thing to say. I'm taking a rain check for two sexual favors of my choice."

I blinked several times. "What is this, a diversion?"

"So?" he said. "I'm still collecting on your sexually teasing comments about showers and tans. Looks might be free, might cost you...depends on the look. And circumstances. But you owe me for the sexual comments, and I'm telling you right now, I'll collect. That's fair, don't you think?"

"Fair? You're trying to be fair?" When he nodded, I was more confused than ever. Sure, the situation was crazy, although I agreed completely with Trent that Benson needed my cooperation and wouldn't disturb us until morning, but that didn't make our situation less crazy, or less scary. Maybe that's why I grasped at Trent's blatant diversion. Feeling sexy is more fun than feeling scared, even if it's temporary.

Yet his casual sex talk startled me. Did people talk about such things nowadays, as if we were collecting coupons? How about two-for-one deals on racy comments? What was the going rate for looks, anyway? Was there a scale for clothed and unclothed looks? "Why are you doing this?"

His hands rubbed across my shoulders. "Because I'm preparing my magic in you. You've never understood the magic before. Now you need to feel it, understand it as I release it in you."

He looked so serious, in a tender, affectionate way, that I had to remind myself he was teasing. Wasn't he teasing? "This is magic, like...earlier?"

For an answer, he kept his eyes on mine, swooped down with his hands and fingered the hard points on my breasts. "My magic," he said, soft and possessive, "in you." How had he known? I swear he hadn't looked. Still didn't look.

My knees almost buckled. All the time I struggled to catch my breath, his fingers circled and played with each nipple as he watched my eyes go blind and flutter closed.

"Trenton," was all I could say, and my legs gave way. He caught me tight against him, and I felt his heart hammering, his breath rushing in and out as a body quake shook him and I knew he was as affected as I. Before I could burrow in and go for gold he spoke.

"You see, Lotsi? I release my magic in you, and we both share it. Potent magic." He drew back and tipped my head up, sending me a rueful look. "I haven't adjusted to how potent. I didn't mean to collect—actually, that was a demonstration, I'll still collect my sexual favors from you later."

While his chatter distracted me, his hands soothed up and down my arms, my back, easing me down from...from his demo?

"Oh, I think that counted as collecting a sexual favor," I said, settling my hands at his waist and moving back. "And a really hot sexual favor considering it was for a couple of pretty weak sexual innuendos. Maybe I should get a sexual favor back, like a refund for overpayment."

Trent threw back his head and laughed. He tilted his torso to one side and pressed an elbow against his ribs, but he kept gasping out the laughs until he ran down enough to talk. "Sweet baby, we will discuss that one later. Now tell me why you think we have to get out of here before morning."

He turned back to the window I'd been examining before he brought up his promise about collecting sexual favors. I reeled from the change of topic, but when my mind caught up I almost exploded. "Why? I thought that was obvious. I have no friends who I left Benson's money with, I have no blackmail packet mailed off somewhere safe, I left no voice mail for an unfriendly cop. I leave here with his henchman in the morning, and we're screwed. History. Kaput."

He watched me pace in front of him, taking in my waving hands, my rising voice, and the teasing glow on his face darkened. His diversion hadn't lasted long for either of us.

I lamented the loss, but a brew of frustration and panic started to bubble too close to the surface to play games. "Hell, I'd be glad to give Benson the money. I was serious about that. I don't give a damn about his ripping off a few measly million from the casino. It's not worth your life, or mine. And I could make up that blackmail packet in ten minutes. I have those pictures, that's why I thought of it."

Whirling around, I planted my feet in front of Trent. "But don't you see, Benson won't stay blackmailed. He won't allow that risk to hang over his head. All he has to do is threaten any one I love, you, or Kaitlynn or Bianca...hell, how could I allow *anyone* to be tortured or maimed or killed when I could turn over proof of something I don't even care about to prevent it?"

I ran both hands deep into my hair, grabbed the roots and held on. "He could threaten anyone...."

Trent took a wrist in each hand and pulled my hands down, clasped them in his. "Let's take this one step at a time. You think Benson would resort to torturing, maiming or killing someone to get this supposed blackmail packet?"

"Yes, I do. I've seen his eyes, seen his actions. So have you, what do you think?"

Trent hesitated. "It's possible."

"Yeah, like it's possible the House wins in Vegas. But the possibility is enough. If Benson had someone, I couldn't risk his doing it, could I?"

"No." Trent's thumbs ran up and down the outside of my hands. "You couldn't. And you invented this blackmail packet because you can't trust him after you give him the money tomorrow...I mean this morning?"

"He'd still have you, wouldn't he? I couldn't think of a way to get you out. I couldn't...." Tears flooded my eyes and I blinked them back.

He squeezed my hands. "Shhh. You've done an amazing job, in every way. Don't beat yourself up now. So this was your lever to pry me loose after he has the money in his hot little hand, even though you'd be free and clear."

I looked at him, not understanding his point.

Lifting my hands, Trent kissed each one in turn. "How many times shall I thank you for coming to my rescue? Dreaming up this scheme, breaking into the house, hell, for meeting me that night at the pool gate?"

How could he lump all those things together? Did he mean to imply I rescued him when I met him? How...intriguing.

"So," he continued as if he hadn't just turned me inside out, "you're afraid your fast shuffle with Mr. Benson will come to an end when you leave here in the morning."

I nodded. "I'm sure of it."

"Well, since I've already decided on the sexual favors I'm going to collect, we'd better take care of that little problem." A gentle squeeze to my hands and he released me to begin prowling around the room, studying everything, the shelf contents, the furniture, under the bed.

Caught up wondering what sexual favors he intended to collect, I stood watching him for a moment. With a jolt, I refocused. Replaying the conversation, I locked my arms over my chest and waited until he pulled his head out from underneath the bed. "You've got our little problem all figured out?"

He glanced at me and examined the headboard, tapping across the fabric, peering at the frame. "In concept, not detail."

"Care to share?"

Abandoning the bed, he headed for the closet. "Sure. Since we can't get out, we'll have to disable Benson's henchman. We get past him, get out, and we're gone."

The empty closet hadn't taken long, one long glance and he'd shut the door, and stood looking around the room again, intent on finding...something.

"And while you're working out the details, I'm supposed to be occupied with what...thinking about sexual favors?"

Trent whipped his head around, stared at me a moment then walked toward me, a smile building in his dark eyes. "Have you been thinking about sexual favors?"

I lifted my chin and toughened my stance. "Of course not. Besides, that's not the point."

"Oh, but it is," he said, stopping in front of me, mesmerizing me with the intensity of his gaze. "I want you thinking about sexual favors, Lotsimina. Think of it as magical foreplay, my own special fairy dust."

He cupped my face, lifted it, brushed his lips against mine each time he paused. "And when I've prepared you exactly enough, I'll tell you the sexual favor I choose, and you'll give it to me." Then he took me into a kiss where I would have given him anything. Anything at all.

When we surfaced, Trent rested his head against mine. "Benson has a lot to answer for. Using you, scaring you, hurting you." His voice lowered until it growled. "And taking magic-time from us."

Then he straightened and looked around the room. "Okay. Now for the details of my plan. I can't take out our henchman in a close fight, unarmed and, ah, less than 100%. So I'm looking for a weapon, or something we can make into a weapon I can use from a short distance, say four or five feet. Think poke, bash, or stab."

Think yuck! I readjusted my thoughts and considered his plan. "How about throw, or bombard?"

Trent flashed a devilish grin and headed for the bathroom. "That would work, but striking a target is more accurate than throwing at a target. It's a compromise between effectiveness and a safe distance."

Skill, too, I thought. I was lousy at throwing accurately, but I could bash really good. Came from years of hanging the rugs outside and bashing them with a broom. I pictured Truck Driver, Benson's probable henchman. Remembered him shouting across the parking lot, his pursuit as I fled on my motorcycle. Besides, he'd manhandled Billy, a young boy half his age and size.

Oh, yeah, I could bash with a vengeance.

I found Trent burrowed under the sink, lifting containers and scanning labels. "What if there is more than one guy?" I asked, addressing his backside.

Incomprehensible mutters answered, and then he backed out of the cabinet and rose holding two bottles of household cleaners. "We could make a nice irritant by mixing these. Blind a guy for awhile, certainly get his attention off us." He set them on the countertop. "Let's keep these in reserve. Now what did you say?"

"What if there is more than one guy?"

"I was a good Boy Scout, I'll be prepared, but this should be pretty straightforward. We know the given time, we know there is one point of entry, and we know Benson intends to send at least one man."

"Truck Driver."

"Excuse me?" He rummaged through the drawers in quick secession.

"That's what I call him. He was driving the truck that chased me the other night when I was on my motorcycle."

Trent froze in place. Something about the way he straightened and turned put me on alert. The cold fire in his narrowed eyes nailed me on the spot. This was the Trent who had attacked a man and nearly killed him. I'd forgotten this part of him. Not a wise thing to do, I decided.

"You didn't mention that before," he said. I didn't mistake the quiet tone as anything soft.

"No."

"Why not?"

I had to moisten my mouth to speak. "I-I didn't think it was important."

Hands clenched at his sides, the hinge of Trent's jaw bunched and twitched. "He tried to kill you. That's not important?"

My hand rose toward him. "Trent?" I knew he was reacting on my behalf, but why? Nothing had changed. Did he think the man would be more dangerous to us this morning because he had attacked me before?

"Don't touch me!" Trent snapped, tension cording his muscles, straining his face.

Shock struck my heart first, a shaft of pain that stole my breath. He was several feet beyond my arm's reach, but the emotional distance just became several miles. My hand fell and pressed between my breasts, as if it could relieve the pain inside.

Blinking furiously, I spun and headed for the door.

Chapter 18

I ignored Trent's blunt curse. The pain of his rejection struck deep to the core of all my insecurities about my sexuality, my self-esteem, my self-confidence in relationships. I knew I never should have weakened my "no men, no pain" philosophy. First slip in fifteen years and look what happens. You have sex and get screwed.

Never again, I vowed. I'm too old to put up with this shit.

As I reached for the half-open bathroom door Trent's arm shot over my shoulder and slammed it shut. Staring at the white panel inches from my nose, I listened to the harsh breathing behind me and waited.

"Lotsi, turn to me. Please." Responding to the plea, I turned to face him. His eyes reflected the pain in the voice, his tense face. "I'm sorry. I didn't mean that the way it sounded. I was trying *not* to hurt you, and I hurt you anyway."

His hands lifted, then fell. "Look, I wanted to kill that sonofabitch. I still do. If I'd known then he was the one...I swear to God I'd have taken him down instead of the other guy."

Then Trent paused and cocked his eyebrow at me and asked in a completely different threatening tone, "Did the other guy do anything—"

"No! No, never saw him before. I called him Hawaiian Shirt, because of his...shirt." I was beginning to catch the drift here, and was fascinated and horrified at the same time. I'd never had a protector before. Didn't need one now, either.

Trent nodded, and seemed to relax, regrouping while he ran his fingers through his hair in a distracted way, until he encountered a sore spot and winced.

Reminded of wounds already taken, I decided to help things along. "So you were upset about Truck Driver—"

"Upset, hell!"

"So you weren't upset?" I taunted him, cocking my eyebrow right back at him.

Before I could blink he grabbed my forearms and pressed me against the door, two inches off the floor. "Do you call this being upset?"

I looked through his narrowed eyes into a cauldron of passion—hot, turbulent, angry passion—and nodded.

"Do you think I don't know how terrified you were that night? The third time on a bike and you're racing, *racing* down a goddamned freeway to save your life?" He lifted me a couple more inches off the floor until we were eye-to-eye. "Do you think I might be a little *upset* about that?"

"Trenton?"

His lips dove toward mine, devouring my words, my mouth, my thoughts as he lowered me to the floor. His emotional thunderstorm broke over me, washing over my skin with his kiss, flashing down my body with his hands, flooding my senses with his raging need. My shirt parted and his hungry mouth followed in a frenzy to reach my breasts, sucking first one lace covered nipple and then the other while he attacked the rest of my clothes.

Back against the door, I reached for his shirt, but he would have none of it. "You. I want you," he said, still driven by his fury, and he returned to my aching, feverish breasts.

"Hurry," I said, "oh, hurry. More." He ducked down and removed my shoes, stripped off my slacks and panties. Shirt gone, he leaned back to remove my bra and stared at my bare flesh, quivering with each inhalation.

"Please," I whispered.

"Look at you, Lotsimina. Feel my magic in you. Can you comprehend how I might be *upset* if someone hurt you? You *are* my magic!" A primitive and fierce energy filled him, and he reached to my breast, watched my lips part and erratic pants shake me as he played there. "Say it again, Lotsimina."

I could barely speak with my mouth so dry. "Please."

Then he stood and stripped, watching me watch him. His sexuality, his body, his entire being drew every cell in me to him. Nothing else existed but him.

Kneeling before me again, he lifted a breast to his mouth, bathed it with his tongue, circling, flicking the hard point while pinching the other, teasing and tormenting me—but not enough.

"Trenton!" My hands held me upright, pressing against the door. I raised one and punched him on the shoulder.

He grunted and began to suck, drawing me deep into his mouth. The fire in me burst into a storm of sensation. I arched harder into the pleasure he gave, breaking into small moaning cries.

As I began to climax, Trent's hands widened my stance. I started to slide downward and he pinned me to the door with one hand pressing my hipbone as the other darted between my legs, slicked over heated flesh and plunged inside. The sounds I made peaked as he continued to thrust deep and hard. I felt my inner flesh convulse around his fingers, ripple through me.

Lost in orgasm, I heard Trent speak but his words had no meaning. He pulled me away from the door and lowered me until I rested on my knees. Then he knelt at my back and pressed my shoulders forward. Confused, I looked back at him.

Face flushed and strained, his lips curved. "That's right, baby, I want you this way. Spread your knees. Stay with me now, Lotsimina. Stay with me."

His hands showed me where he wanted, held me the way he wanted, and when he entered me, I began to climax again and didn't stop until he'd pumped out his release and we lay cradled together on the bathroom floor, his arms a safe haven from the storm I'd just survived.

Trent's fingers combed through my hair in soothing caresses as intermittent quakes rocked me. "I'm sorry I hurt you. I thought...I was in such a rage, I thought I'd be too rough. Do you understand?"

"But you said for me not to touch you." I drew back and turned enough to look at him. "I don't understand."

He brushed back the loose hair sticking to my face. "Call it a testosterone thing, if you like. I'd held my reactions back the other night, but tonight...we'd just made love, for God's sake, and you casually say this jerk's attacking you wasn't important? First of all, I wanted to kill the bastard, and second, I thought you must have missed something about our making love."

"Missed what?" I sat up, reached for the nearest clothes and started sorting.

He shrugged, watching me, wary, intense. Waiting for my reaction. "You should have known you're mine. And I protect what's mine."

Whoa! A statement like that sure got my heart going pitter pat but was I ready to accept it as fact? Accept the implications? I'd have to think about that later. I pulled on my panties. "And the no touching?"

Trent stood and started dressing. "I knew if you touched me then, I'd take you in a rage. And I won't allow anyone to hurt you, Lotsi, especially not me."

"So you were protecting me from yourself, just like you want to protect me from Truck Driver?"

"Getting a little too rough during sex is hardly 'just like' trying to kill you."

"You're right. I apologize. My point is I don't feel comfortable being protected. It can be too much like suffocation."

His fingers paused while he tied his shoelaces, but he kept his voice calm. "I don't think I suffocate anyone, but keep me posted if I do."

"Fair enough." I concentrated on buttoning my shirt. "Just for the record, do you think you were 'a little too rough'?"

"You mean just now, when we made love?"

"Yes."

Silence. I could feel him watch me. His voice sounded cautious, neutral. "Do you think I was too rough?"

I tucked my hands in my pockets and studied the bottles he'd left on the counter. "Well, now that you mention it...."

He stepped into my line of sight. A rush of uncertain excitement filled me, and I ducked my head, looking at him through the veil of my lashes. A smile played at the corners of his mouth. "You do not think I was too rough, Lotsimina. You liked everything I did to you."

I couldn't keep the smile from peeking out. "Oh? And where do you get off telling me what I like or don't like?"

His hands moved to grip my hips, holding me in place. "I keep telling you. It's my magic."

No verbal answer occurred to me. The shiver running through my body seemed to say it all. His lips curved even more and brushed mine. "Now let's find a weapon and get ready for company."

A half hour later, we'd gone through every drawer, cabinet and shelf, examined every piece of furniture and every knickknack and decoration. Twice.

Our pathetic stockpile of potential weapons rested on the bedroom carpet. The household cleaners and a couple of bottles we'd empty later to hold a possibly blinding irritant, a long-stemmed metal candle holder, a metal picture frame with points at the top corners, a plant stand—maybe we could use the legs?— a couple of heavy vases, a statue of an organ grinder's monkey about a foot high that from its weight must be nearly solid clay, and four hand-sized throwables that could knockout Godzilla.

I stood staring down at the pile, dispirited. "Not much to stage a breakout with." I'd hoped for something impressive, something to even the odds. How could two unarmed people, the strongest one injured, prevail against one or more of Benson's armed goons?

Tears pricked the backs of my eyes. I hadn't intended to endanger Trent. I hadn't intended to endanger Gwen, either, but she was dead because some dumb thief mistook her for me. If only he had gotten the right one...I bit down on the inside of my cheek. That's crazy-making, I lectured myself. You are not responsible for Gwen's death or for endangering Trent. Benson is.

Yet logic didn't wipe out the guilt I felt. I hated myself for getting us locked in this room, for not being able to talk Benson into letting us go. Last night I'd thought we could get away in the morning. Now I couldn't see anything to make that hope a reality. Chilled, my hands gripped opposite elbows, squeezing tight.

Trent stepped closer. His warm hand cupped my shoulder and slid down my goosebumps and around to rest at my hip. I drew in his magic, comforted and warmed by his touch.

"There's more here than you think," he said, calm and reasonable. "I could disable one man with the monkey, blind another with the chemicals and take out a third with the paper weight on the fly in about the time it takes to tell you about it."

My head jerked up at the flat certainty in his tone. I looked up into his eyes and realized he meant exactly what he said. "You've, ah, done this kind of thing before?"

He studied my expression, and his eyes began to twinkle. "Just what kind of terrible past are you imagining, Lotsi? Street gang? Crook? Mercenary? Tell me. Don't go shy on me now."

"You're being silly. I never thought anything of the kind." I flounced away to part the curtain and stare out of the nearest window. Dawn pressed upon us as if it were in minutes, not hours. "I thought maybe martial arts, self-defense, that kind of thing." I turned back. "Besides, I thought you wanted something to give you a safe distance."

Trent nodded. "That would be nice, but it's not an absolute requirement. Surprise is a great equalizer. I'll be fast and I'll take them down hard. What I don't want is an extended fight. However, your guess is close. I've had plenty of training...in the Marines."

I frowned. "Marines?"

Shaking his head, he stalked over, twitched the curtain closed, hooked an arm around me and drew me away from the window. "There you go again, deflating my ego. What, you think because I don't have tattoos and wear a buzz cut I can't be a jarhead?"

Since that's exactly what I'd thought, I felt my face heat. "No, I...well, okay, it crossed my mind, but you haven't mentioned it before now."

"It was a lifetime ago. Except for some martial arts practice, I've put the military behind me."

Not as much as you think! I almost laughed, realizing this explained some of his...machismo. What a pretentious, sexist word, but sometimes it described a male strength that simply existed. I have to admit, right now I didn't mind one bit.

I looped my arms around Trent's waist and pressed closer. He welcomed me with a hug, wrapping his scent, his strength, his warmth around me. With all my heart I wanted to hold back reality, make this moment last forever. My heavy eyelids rose to half-mast. Over his shoulder, I saw the pile of collected items we hoped to transform into weapons.

I blinked. God, could it be that simple?

Trent's lips searched out the curve of my ear and began to nibble and suck. My bones started to melt, my breath gone right when I needed to speak.

"Curtain rods," I blurted, wispy and weak. His tongue swirled and...lord, he could patent that tongue and retire. Again. Erotic flames flickered and rose.

Fight it, fight it! "Trenton, pay attention."

"I am. I will." He probed deeper.

"Ah...oh God." I grabbed his hand as it found my breast and set to work. "No...listen to me. Look at the curtain rods. That feels so...Trenton! The curtain rods!"

His mouth stopped its hot wet journey down my neck. "What the hell are you talking about?"

Heart racing, I struggled to focus. "The metal curtain rods. They pull apart. Tie the monkey on one end—"

Trent moved and left me swaying, my flesh chilling without his warmth. Well, hell, he didn't have to stop *that* fast! I snapped out of the sexual lethargy scrambling my brain when I saw Trent wince as he reached to take down the rods.

"Here, I'll do that part," I insisted and detached the gold tasseled rope tiebacks, thinking they'd come in handy, and stripped the curtains from the rods. Long, thick metal rods. Trent threw the rolls of adhesive tape he'd collected from the first-aid kit onto the floor, and we commenced our project.

By the time we finished attaching the monkey to the five-foot rod, the end result looked less than elegant but with the leverage of Trent's long reach and good arm he had one wicked weapon.

He took an easy practice swing, a nasty evil look of satisfaction on his face. A warrior's look. I wouldn't want to be on the receiving end of that look.

"Oh, yeah. That'll pack one hell of a punch. I'll call it my slugger," he said, and grinned.

I shuddered. Then I braced for a fight. "I want a slugger, too. I can use the vase."

Now why wasn't I surprised when Trent frowned and started out in a placating tone. "Lotsi—"

"Look, there's no way I'm letting you face one or more of Benson's men alone. I am not hiding. And I'm not going unarmed, either."

"Dammit, Lotsi, I don't want you hurt!" He roared at me, every part of his body tightened in angry denial, his eyes flashing with male dominance.

My, oh my, what a turn on. I wanted to eat him up. My chin jutted out and my shoulders squared off. "Well, I don't want you hurt either, so get over it. We have one shot at surprising these guys. I can help. Two threats are more surprise than one."

Right then I felt like a tiger. I remember an incident when Kaitlynn was about twelve and we were vacationing in Mazatlan. She had wandered away from where I was looking for trinkets at a street vendors stand. My mother-radar picked up on her voice, some note of distress as she'd faced the unwelcome attention of an older man. I think I teleported between them and lit into him like a banshee. Nothing is more primitive or more vicious than a mother protecting her young. Unless it's a woman protecting her lover.

I began to understand Trent's protective attitude more. Which made me even less tolerant of his offended male pride when he snarled and sneered at me. "Christ, woman, what the hell do you think you can do against one of Benson's men? He'd swat you like a fly."

I stepped closer, right into his face. "Look, bud, I may not be Rambo, but I sure as hell can whack someone hard enough with that vase to ring his bell!" I poked him in the chest with the point of my red-painted fingernail. "You, by God, need me! For a diversion if nothing else." Poke. "And you know it. We're in this together, Trenton Wallace." Poke. "Together."

He grabbed my hand and almost crushed it. We stared each other down. My blood sizzled with fierce determination. Trent looked just as agitated. Then he sighed, his face softened, and he pressed my hand to his chest and rubbed where my fingernail had marked his flesh.

"Shit," he said with a wealth of resignation, even acceptance.

My heart filled with a sweet pain. "I love you."

His eyes dilated, but never wavered. "Yeah, I get that." He buried one hand in my hair to cup the back of my head, the other circled my hips and drew me against his lower body. I hadn't realized he sported a hard-on until its length pressed between us.

"I love you, too, my Lotsimina," he whispered.

Heartbreaking soft. Tender. A gentle brand of lips to lips, soul to soul. Then he tucked my head into the cradle of his neck, where my cheek rested near the pulse in his throat. Home.

So help me God, there wasn't a man alive who could keep me from coming back right here. This was my spot. Mine.

The absolute possessiveness of that feeling rattled me. Where it came from and what it meant for the future were questions I had no time for. Tonight time was running out.

I eased away, drinking up the look softening the face of this handsome, wonderful man. For me. I still couldn't believe it. "We need to finish this up, get some rest."

"Yeah."

By the time we finished my slugger, concocted the homemade mace and selected a few sharp items as our backup weapons, we were both dragging ass. I could see the pain in Trent's squint and the whitened lines around his mouth. Bruised or cracked, his ribs hurt more as the night wore on.

Despite our exhaustion, I wished we didn't have to wait another five hours. Five hours for the stiffness and pain to settle into Trent's muscles. Getting up a couple hours early should help, but how much? Would he be capable of swinging the slugger with enough force to count? Able to throw the paperweight and hand-sized glass ashtrays he had laid aside to pocket?

God forbid he injure himself more when he tried.

My mind wouldn't shut up as I straightened the bed from our previous tumbles. All in all, I worried a heck of a lot more about Trent than I did about myself. I needed to give it a rest, give my body a rest.

Sitting on the edge of the bed, I studied the alarm clock. *What is with all these buttons, anyway? You could pilot a space shuttle with fewer buttons!*

Trent came out of the bathroom. I growled at the "set alarm" option panel. "I hate these damned fancy things. Why can't people use a plain old alarm clock anymore?"

"I'll take care of the clock, love. You go do your thing. Just don't take long, okay?"

My breath froze when I looked up. He tossed his shirt on the nightstand, held out his hand. A sprinkling of silky hair dusted his chest, broken by the band of elastic encasing his ribs. His jeans fit well. Comfortable for him, an eyeful for me. They displayed his trim waist and engorged manhood.

My, oh my, that man was seriously built.

He drew me to my feet. Then he cupped my jaw, ran his thumb over my bottom lip, and lifted my chin. "Okay?"

I blinked a few times as I met his eyes. Saw that devil smile. He was a sex popsicle and he knew I wanted a lick. Lick, hell, I wanted to suck him down.

"Okay," I managed. Ghirardelli eyes mesmerized. I couldn't move while he touched me.

"Go," Trent's voice lowered into a quiet rumble, "before I keep you here." He turned me loose and stepped back.

Our eyes feasted on one another until I could turn in a daze toward the bathroom. Yet as I went about my ablutions, I realized my thoughts had become fixated on Trent's boxers.

I rinsed out the purloined toothpaste and stared into the eyes in the mirror above the sink. What was I doing here, obsessing about boxers? Fast-forwarded impressions began to fracture my mind, sending my thoughts into a disjointed jumble. I struggled to find a sense of perspective, but my world image remained shattered. How could it not be?

Less than two weeks ago, my biggest grievance concerned an unethical employer, my greatest desire to repair a troubled relationship with my daughter. I remember thinking that first day when my Rexall nearly caught fire from the seized bearing, that my troubles weren't over. But this went beyond Murphy's Law run amok, beyond diabolical. This was obscene.

Now my best friend was dead, her murderer held me captive, and I might join her in a few hours. I was about to sleep for the first time with my new lover. A mind-boggling, heart-pounding lover with whom I'd recently had life-altering sex. Several times.

Sleep, as in set the alarm, climb between the sheets and fall asleep with a man for the first time in fifteen years.

So now, a night that began with a kidnapping, brutal violence, blackmail and dire threats ended with a flinched toothbrush, a quick scrub, and a nervous stomach from worrying about *underwear!*

How pathetic is that?

Get your head on straight, girl. You've got jury-rigged weapons you're going to use on a human being in mere hours stashed beside the bed and you're worried about whether you should leave your panties on and if Trent will be wearing boxers?

That sounded so stupid, but wait. What if Benson's men came even earlier than Trent suspected and we were caught naked? Maybe going to bed at all was a bad idea. What if the alarm didn't go off? Now that I thought about it, Trent and I had had sex, but we hadn't actually gotten...well, undressed. I mean, getting naked in the heat is not the same as casually disrobing. Or casually lying skin to skin. Naked.

I continued to look at my naked reflection, someone else's toothbrush in my hand, until I faced the truth and sighed. My mouth turned down. I guess my mind couldn't focus anymore on the big things going on, so it'd focused on something petty and small.

Underwear.

In truth, underwear represented a trainload of inner fears, so much more familiar than all the new fears. I wasn't a young woman anymore. However much I'd like to present the body of my youth to Trent as a gift, he would get the real me, without the fire of passion clouding his mind.

His younger mind.

My fear wondered how I could possibly hold this beautiful man's interest for more than a wild night of sex or for a few more convenient nights while we shared a campground.

I discounted Trent's playful words about magic and his sexually charged possessiveness. After all, his passionate nature had years of experience pleasing a woman, saying the right words, making the right moves, honing the right feelings.

Not that I thought him insincere or phony. Quite the contrary. I thought him very real, open, easy with himself and with women, but...why me? All my failures and bleak warnings about relationships rose in a lethal wave of self-doubt.

Tears stung my eyes. I hated this. I hated the ugliness within me that tarnished the feelings growing between Trent and me. I hated the ugliness outside us that forced us into this awkward, scary, dangerous situation, and cheated us out of what should have been be a wonderful, loving, night together.

Damn them to hell!

A ball of rage burst into incandescent fury. I threw back my head, body rigid, and silently snarled a wordless scream. The scream faded as the air emptied from my lungs. My body relaxed. The fury fizzled and snuffed out.

I threw down the toothbrush. Enough of this pity party. Regardless of how we got here, or why, we were together this night. Those bastards would not ruin everything. Not when it came to my personal feelings, my personal choices. I'd choose being with Trent anywhere, anytime, any way I could have him.

I wrapped a towel around me, folded my clothes—including my underwear—and carried them with me. As I opened the bathroom door, I decided I hoped Trent slept nude. I wanted to feel all of him. With all of me. No barriers. No doubts. Just us.

Chapter 19

The muted light from the bedside night globe illuminated my way, a beacon leading to Trent. Poor baby. Battered and bruised, he had fallen asleep, covers pushed down near his waist. I smiled. The boxers were still in question.

I stacked my clothes on my side of the bed. What a concept. My side of the bed. We were both hostage in a stranger's bed, but nature is a powerful force. Where Trent slept, I had a proper place beside him.

The towel dropped to the floor and I reached for the covers. Oops, the light. I'd rather walk around the bed to turn it out than wake him by reaching across his body. I didn't make a sound, barefoot on the carpet. I swear. Bending down, I reached for the switch.

"Now that's a beautiful sight to see."

The shattered quiet startled me, but his words, the soft gravelly sound, vibrated over my skin, rough suede over silk, leaving goosebumps in its wake. Impossible as it seemed, heat flared again.

His eyes gleamed in the light, dark pools of seduction that trapped and lured me. "Leave the light on," he whispered and lifted the covers.

My God. Everything he said and did was an aphrodisiac! My skin flushed a rush of heat from my breasts to my face.

Still tender from our previous lovemaking, my breasts swelled and the nipples puckered into aching tips. I melted all the way to my sex, cream coating my channel, outer lips so full I almost parted my legs. I needed him so much I could die.

Climbing onto the bed, I paused. "Your ribs...we can't—"

"Shhh. Yes, we can. We will."

"But—"

"Come here, Lotsi. I need you. I need you."

No boxers. Just hard man. I trembled, adjusting to his heat, his flesh against mine. Lips met. His tongue licked and teased its way inside. I needed this kiss. Hungry, devouring.

How could I be so desperate for more sex? How could he? Maybe he was on to something with his talk about magic. I wiggled and pressed closer. When he moved to cover me, I felt his spasm of pain.

Oh, no. Can't have that. I broke the kiss. "Let me," I whispered against his lips, my hand on his shoulder gently urging him back. I climbed on top and took us for the ride of my life.

Music wormed into my consciousness. Movement stirred. What the....? My eyes snapped opened, registered the strange room, the strange sensation behind me.

Mmm. Trent. I smiled and relaxed into a sleepy lassitude, enjoying the arm beneath my neck, the warm hard body spooned around my backside, stirring against the cheeks of my butt. Hello!

Oh, the possibilities that flared through my mind. My body. Ever ready to respond without mental direction, my hips pressed back into the lovely intruder pressing at my gate, when a niggling thought of reality rose and I came wide awake.

Shifting aside onto my back, I turned and saw Trent watching me. The arm he'd kept cradled between us to protect his injured ribs moved, his hand lying on the soft curve of my abdomen between jutting hipbones, little finger spread slightly to burrow into the dark pubic thatch. Just resting there.

Was that good or bad? My eyes darted down to his shoulder, his ribs, back to his eyes. Jeez, I couldn't believe we'd acted like a couple of randy teenagers last night instead of sane, mature adults! We had no business making love with Trent's cracked ribs. He needed rest, not sexaerobics!

Hadn't I tried to spare him the last time? But he'd gotten carried away there at the end and even taped, his ribs could separate and—

Trent's lips twitched. "I'm okay, sweetheart. A little stiff and sore, but it'll loosen up. Don't worry. I'll be ready." Then he let out that killer grin of his, circled his palm over my skin. "Thing is, we'd better get moving, or I'll be ready for something else."

"Too late. I already felt just how ready for something else you are." Relieved he seemed okay, I couldn't resist teasing, just a little. I loved his soft chuckle, the way his eyes crinkled and danced.

"Oh, no doubt of that, love, but we'll have to save it for another morning. Besides," he said, turning serious, "you must be pretty sore. I didn't take very good care of you last night, and I'm sorry for that. And with these damn ribs, I didn't do a very good job of making love to you, either. I'll make it up to you. I promise."

Was he crazy? Mentally I sputtered in disbelief. I'd had the hottest sex of my life and the guy *apologizes*? Was he fishing or what? No, I felt his sincerity. The man didn't need compliments, he was too busy beating himself up with regrets and I was not going to stand for it.

"Are you crazy?" I pushed up on my elbow and looked down into his startled face. "Maybe we were foolish to risk injuring you even more, but don't you dare regret the...ah...the way we made love. All you have to do is touch me and I go up in flames." My smile went a little flat and wobbly. "It's...it's your magic."

Trent didn't smile, but his face relaxed. "Yeah. It's my magic. In you. And I don't regret one moment we've had together, Lotsimina. Not one."

"I'm glad." I'll have no regrets either, I promised myself. No matter what happened. A tear slipped loose despite my furious blinking.

He brushed the wet line from my cheek. "Aw, love, I wish we had more time, but we have work to do before Benson's men get here. It's almost over."

Yeah, that's what I was afraid of.

Pre-dawn light filtered through the window as Trent eased out of bed and snagged his clothes, clutching them tight against his wounded side, loose ends dangling in a haphazard veil as he frowned down at me still modestly snuggled beneath the covers. White slashed across his chest, dark splotches blooming on either side, a modern art display of pain and mayhem on a physical canvas. His free hand finger-combed hair back from a haggard face. For a man usually so handsome and easy-going, he looked like hell.

"Benson's going to send two guys, not one," he said. Last night he'd hesitated in saying how many he thought would come, probably to spare me, but we had both agreed they would try to catch us in bed by coming before the appointed time of eight o'clock.

He didn't hesitate this morning. "I'm sure of it. Maybe three. We need to draw them inside the room, so your illusion with our bodies is critical."

"But no pressure, right?" I snorted. "I understand, Trent. My illusion will look very real."

He nodded, glanced at the pile of curtain material by the denuded window. "I'll tack up the curtain when I get out of the shower," he said with a preoccupied air, and marched off to the bathroom.

215

Well, if one could call a crumpled lurch *marching*. He'd claimed he was "stiff and sore," but he looked "seriously injured," despite the determined lurch. Then my attention shifted to the rest of the rear view. No veils there. I smiled, not even embarrassed. I have always been one to stop and smell the roses whenever possible.

The spell broke when the door closed. "Wow," I whispered, then scrambled out of bed, yanked on my wrinkled black pants and shirt and left my underclothes on the nightstand. As I arranged all the non-essential bedding and spare towels under the bedspread, my thoughts returned to worrying about Trent's health. I'd also been a champion worrier.

Soon my worries turned to the all-important doubles. In good light—hell, in almost any light—the fake hair draped over the stuffed white towel would never pass scrutiny. I couldn't find anything to emulate Trent's mix of stone grey and dark locks, so I didn't try. I stepped back, scratching the back of my head through the tussled brown of my shoulder-length hair. My straight hair.

Even a man wouldn't take the black curls on the towel-stuffed double for mine.

Discouraged, I sighed, and rested both hands on my hips. Cocked my head. Shrugged. I went over to the door and looked back. Arms crossed over my chest, I tried to imagine the dim light once the curtains were tacked up. From this perspective, the forms looked more believable, one on its side obscuring the head area, the other—me—face down, hair showing.

Hmmm. I went back, rearranged a few things. Back at the door, I studied the bed again and nodded. The hair billowed more, the curve of a butt suggested a rather nice backside.

I checked the whole scene, and hurried around clearing the leftover bits and pieces from our various projects. The bathroom door opened while I rearranged the pile of curtains, getting the two heavy panels ready to hang.

A wave of anxiety washed over me. I wanted...needed to help, but my best weapon was a strong contract, not a strong arm. Arranging convincing doubles to lure in the bad guys seemed more realistic than bashing someone with a cobbled-together slugger. Had I done a convincing enough job?

Trent strolled into the bedroom, dressed and looking more like his usual self. Whatever he'd done in the hot shower seemed to help. He moved easier, smoother. The chilled knot of fear lodged in my stomach eased. Now if only the doubles passed muster....

Trent's glance turned from me to the bed. He stopped and studied the doubles. He licked his lips, his cheeks bunching and eyebrows twitching like he was fighting back a laugh.

"What?" I let the curtain drop and fastened one hand at my waist. I hadn't expected amusement. Criticism, yes. A load of more orders, yes. A last-ditch argument to make me hide in the bathroom, yes. But not amusement.

All he said was a mellow, "Nice butt."

Then he dismissed the bed and its shrouded bodies and the expected orders poured out. "Go take a quick shower. I'll put up the curtains. Look alive, woman, we don't have much time."

I stared at the bed, the butt in question in full view. I hadn't realized I'd placed the stuffed forms exactly where we'd slept. They looked so...intimate. Personal. My face heated.

Stiffening my spine and planting hands at both hips, I demanded, "What's wrong with my—her—its butt?"

Drilling him with narrowed eyes, my chin lifted higher and higher as he came closer, his deadpan face laughing at me until he stopped just short of my toes.

Trent's hand smoothed down the seat of my pants. "Not a damn thing," his soft rumble assured me. "Go take your shower." Then he reached for the material on the floor.

I blinked a few times. Shut my mouth. Oh, that man made me stark raving crazy! I shook my bead clear. "Ah...not so fast. You'll need help with those curtains. Believe me."

"Lotsi, you don't have time to shower and—"

"I'll shower when we get home." I repositioned the vanity chair I had brought over earlier.

"I don't need any help. I can—"

"You can't hold these heavy curtains up over your head with cracked—"

"They aren't cracked!"

"With sore ribs." I dumped the box of stickpins with the little colored plastic heads we'd found into my shirt pocket.

"They're curtains, for chrissake, not a goddamned—"

"Even if you can hold a panel up one-handed and tack it down with the other, you can't hold it up long enough to get to the end." I grabbed the metal-edged picture frame/ hammer and stepped onto the chair. "Soon as you had to let go, the pins would pull out and you'd have to start over." Reached for the end he held.

Trent eyed the dainty spindle-legged chair, shut up, and handed me the curtain.

Smart man.

The dim light certainly helped the illusion of bodies buried under the covers, I noted as I headed for the shower. I had no intention of skipping one completely. A quick cool rinse sounded fine. However, maybe....

"Do you think the butt's too big? I could take out some—"

Trent choked and cleared his throat. My suspicious eyes whipped around, but only spotted a bland look on his face. He looked erotically masculine as he toted the frilly vanity chair back across the room. "We don't have time for modifications. Don't worry about it."

Yeah, right. He hated the butt. He probably hated my butt....

"Lotsi-love," he purred in a sexy rumble as I reached the door. "Didn't you forget something?"

I looked back. He nodded toward the nightstand. Shit. My underwear. I stomped over to get the little scrapes of satin and lace and headed back to the bathroom.

"Don't forget your sh—"

I quietly but emphatically slammed the door. As if I'd go barefoot!

Grrrrrowl!

We stood pressed against the wall on the hinged side of the door. Waiting. My clothes stuck in various places. I'd been very quick with the towel. I finger-combed my damp hair for about the fifth time. I hadn't washed it, but the ends were wet, the rest misted by the two-minute shower and tangled in disarray. Combing helped calm the flutterbys in my stomach. Bianca pronounces it that way.

I think Kaitlynn did, too. Oh, my God. What if I never saw my granddaughter or my daughter again? The butterflies turned into triceratops, or maybe I mean ptrea...pteranodon or whatever. Even Bianca can say ptrea...pteranodons! How can she say ptr...that word, and not butterflies?

But hey, better pteranodons than Truck Driver!

"Calm down." Trent's words floated on the air, a wisp of sound not a whisper, not regular speech. "Breathe."

How did he know? He wasn't even looking at me. The minutes had ticked by while he stood there, still as granite, focused on the door. How can he stand it?!

So I breathed. In. Out. In. Out. Like a meditation. I focused straight ahead, looking through the bed. In. Out.

I imitated Trent's wispy voice. "Do you think I have a big butt?"

My peripheral vision caught his shaking shoulders. I turned my head. He still focused on the door.

"Quiet, Lotsi-love."

The slight sound of the tumbling lock stopped my heart. The slow turning of the knob brought it thundering back. We were right. They had come early. I swallowed, eyes stuck on the door, metal shaving on a magnet. I'd never believed in the concepts "air thick with tension" or "testosterone level" before. I felt it now: a physical awareness, a change in atmosphere that triggered something in my body.

My nipples tingled. Every inch of skin tingled, vibrated as my awareness of surrounding energies kicked into overdrive. I now understood another couple of concepts.

Adrenaline rush.

Then as the door wafted open in a slow arc, fight...or flight.

Sweat trickled down my forehead, the small of my back, slicked the curtain-rod weapon under the whitened grip of my hand.

The door came to rest about three-quarters open. Trent had placed us away from the swing. He said there was about a fifty-fifty chance they'd slam it open to nail a lurker or go for a silent entry. Coming early predisposed them to a silent entry. Looked like he was right.

The open door hid us for another critical step or two.

Thank God, the special recessed security hinges eliminated the open crack of a normal door, the better to hide behind. I'd never have thought of it. Gotta love a well-spent military tax dollar.

Finally, finally! Two men stepped inside, neither with the broad chest or baggy fashion style of Truck Driver. Their gaze fixed on the bed. They moved beyond the door on silent feet, one gesturing—*ohmygod, they really did have guns!*—

to the other and their direction split, one headed toward what he thought was me, moving about six feet in front of my position against the wall, the other headed around the foot of the bed toward Trent's side.

Trent had warned me about the slightest movement. About staring too hard, breathing too hard. I kept my focus indirect, tracking the one headed toward my side of the bed.

My teeth ground and clenched. That one was mine.

Why was Trent waiting? I didn't want to sprint across the entire freaking room to reach my target!

Then movement stirred in the hall and coalesced into form. Truck Driver stepped through the doorway, partly obscured by the door, leading with a gun fisted in his right hand.

Trent struck like a snake.

I heard the explosion of the door striking Truck Driver. In a rush of hyperawareness, my head ratcheted between the two men in front, and Trent's action at the door. Like a video playing in my brain, movements appeared in slow motion, sounds distorted and enhanced at the same time.

The gun spun away as Trent released the door he'd slammed into the silent intruder. Thrown back and to the side, Truck Driver crashed to the floor, his face contorted and frantic, bellowing in pain or anger or fear. Or all three.

Trent had already surged forward, seeking his next target. His long metal pole moved through its deadly arch, swinging by my position. For one endless second, I saw the clay monkey bound to the pole like a pagan sacrifice in a jaunty red hat and vest, with a seemingly maniacal grin frozen on his furry little face.

In front of us, both men reacted, heads snapping around and then their bodies moved, guns swiveling toward the door. Toward Trent.

I screamed "Nooooo!" in my mind—maybe aloud, I don't know—as my body lunged forward. How much time had passed? Two, maybe three seconds? Not much. Until then, they hadn't reacted to me, only to the noise, the violent assault to their comrade at the door.

Now some part of me saw them halt and jerk my way, their attention divided, their timing thrown off. That part crowed, "Yes! Here I am!" As detraction, I was a great success.

But the human mind processes information incredibly fast, and before I'd completed a single step, both men had identified the two threats coming at them, Trent and myself, analyzed the risks, and jerked back toward Trent.

Go figure.

A terrible sound indicated Trent connected with his own target in a solid hit. My focus never wavered. I had momentum, I had advantage, and I had a raging intent to destroy.

I struck my target with every ounce of power I possessed. The head of my weapon, the vase, traveled in an upward-swinging arch. The blow thudded against the top of the man's shoulder, glanced over and struck his head. The impact staggered me, numbed my hand and forearm. I saw...I saw blood spew from his head. The man stumbled. Fell. My ears didn't hear anymore. It took a few heartbeats to realize his gun had discharged. Somewhere my mind processed a memory, and I knew the bullet struck the floor.

By then I reeled with shock, a sick realization churning in my gut. Trent moved about the room, dealing efficiently with first one then another of Benson's men. I don't recall much. I remember his rising, turning towards me, and saying, "Lotsi? Are you all right?"

That's when my memory fades out.

Chapter 20

"Lotsi, answer me!"

The voice comforted me, despite the rough tone, but I couldn't make the words connect with any meaning.

"Dammit, you're beginning to scare me. I swear to God, I'm going to paddle your butt for sure."

Physical sensations registered. The arms holding me, the floor beneath me. Where...why? More sensations. Oh, no. My stomach churned something fierce. Muddled and thick, my mind fought for control. Don't get sick! Don't get sick!

"God, I can't take this...Lotsi!"

The panicked torment in Trent's voice pulled me out of the fog. I started to sit up. "What...ohhhhh." Bad move. Pain lanced through my temple.

"Thank God! Don't move. Are you hurt? Tell me where you hurt! Lotsi! Where do you hurt?"

"Head."

"Okay. Okay." Trent's fingers groped through my hair. "Maybe I missed...were you hit? I thought you'd been shot but I couldn't find a wound. Maybe—"

"Temple."

"Temple. Okay." His probing stopped. He tilted my head away from his chest and swept back a fall of hair. "Yeah. There's a swelling here, all right. Skin's broken a little." He supported my head with one large hand, smoothed around the pain with the other, then ran his fingers directly over the area.

"Ouch!"

Trent's voice dropped into a soft tone. "I'm sorry, baby. I needed to check. You'll have a bruise, but the bone's okay." His breath bathed away the pain, lips anointed his benediction.

My eyes opened. His face filled my field of vision. Darkened by stubble, battered features sharpened by concern and pain, he looked disreputable, even dissolute. Precious. I smiled, and watched his face soften and relax.

"We need to get out of here," he said. "Before Benson shows up, or sends someone else."

Oh, my goodness. How could I have forgotten? I wanted to jump up, take Trent's hand and run like the dickens. Instead, I stalled at the first move like an arthritic tortoise and groaned.

"Not so fast," Trent said quite unnecessarily, and helped me to stand. His eyes darted over me as he held onto my arm until he saw I was steady. "Okay, let's go."

I hesitated, looking down at the man I'd struck. "Did I...kill him?" Nausea rolled again.

"No, they're all alive. That one," he nodded toward the one he'd hit with the monkey, "might have a problem. We'll call it in later. Come on."

I started to shake a few minutes after we left the alley in the SUV. The normal world seemed surreal. Alien. How could everyone—everything—simply go on as usual? Didn't they know...no, of course not. *I* was the alien. My arms wrapped around my torso, hands rubbing bare skin to fight the chill.

Monitoring the mirrors as he worked through traffic, Trent glanced over a couple times, fiddled with the heater. "When I was in the Marines, we'd come back from our missions and decompress. That's a nice word. Decompress. We'd been under pressure all right, sometimes intense pressure, especially the wet work. Everyone had their own way of dealing with the emotional and physical aftermath."

He had my attention. My stomach still made its presence known and I still shivered, but I knew he was trying to help by sharing his experience...and maybe I'd learn something important about him in the process.

The morning traffic thickened when we hit a larger intersection. Stopped at the light, Trent turned and studied me with that thorough way of his, taking in the whole body but reaching deeper at the same time.

"It's more than coming off adrenaline," he said as he faced me. "That's the shakes, the nausea and chills. Sometimes there's a sexual reaction. The men worked it off with sex or exercise. Or they got drunk. Then there's the other part. More from the emotional fallout. That's the disorientation, sometimes shock. Or guilt. They can go into withdrawal, depression. Sometimes they suffer alienation, and other long-term effects."

"You mean post-traumatic stress disorder."

"Yeah. But what people don't realize is post-trauma begins about five minutes after the action stops. It can become a disorder when smaller events accumulate over time or when one event is highly traumatic."

"How did you...how did the men deal with the stress?"

Please don't tell me you used sex! I hated the thought of Trent acquiring his intimate skills that way.

"I did what most of the men did, I tried it all. The smart ones, maybe that's the lucky ones, stayed away from booze and bankrupt sex. I like to think I was both." He threw me a sharp glance and shrugged. "I turned to my friends. I didn't realize it at first, but they got me through the difficult times. Relationships, friendships. They're support anchors. A bridge to sanity, sometimes all you've got."

I nodded, and then my chin wobbled and my eyes burned. Blinking, I turned aside to watch the traffic. "Yes, I know what you mean."

How long does grief sneak up on you like this, I wondered. Support anchor. Yes, Gwen had been that. Even while she...she'd faced her own death from cancer, she'd been my bridge to sanity. God knows, I prayed I gave something back to her, but she'd helped me so much. Every day, her example of strength and hope and courage had shown me—shown all of us—how to find our own.

Now with her senseless, vicious, *mistaken* death, we'd lost our...no no no, don't go there. Live strong, Lotsi. Live strong.

I envisioned the yellow wristband we'd all worn for those awful months and realized that's what Trent meant, that he'd turned from his away from drink and mindless sex to his strengths in relationships, in connecting to others to cope with those terrible missions.

Thinking of his going through other traumatic experiences like this one sickened me. I don't know what divers would have done in the military, something dangerous and clandestine I suppose, but I had a new appreciation of people working on-the-edge jobs like firefighters, rescue and trauma care.

That Trent had emerged emotionally intact, with a strong and loving personality, seemed miraculous.

How many such missions had he gone through? A vivid image of the monkey, swinging in slow motion, the sound and feel of the impact when my own vase struck human flesh, brought a surge of bile to my throat. I swallowed. Did he have similar memories?

I had to ask. "I know you can't tell me any details about your...missions, but I wondered...."

Trent flicked on the turn signal as we approached the first gas station/mini-mart we had seen. "Yes?"

"Did you have many of those traumatic diving missions?"

He swung into the lot and looked for the pay telephone. "What traumatic diving missions?"

"The missions you referred to. I know you did a lot of diving, but I hope not many traumatic—"

"Where did you get diving?"

"From you, of course! You were just talking about the wet missions you went on! If they were Top Secret just say so, you don't have to—"

I stopped when Trent began laughing as he finished parking and grabbed the hand I waved about. Indignant, I jerked back. He held tight. "Lotsi-love, I was a Marine, not a Navy SEAL. The only diving I've done is strictly recreational. And any Top Secret work I did in the military has long been declassified."

He raised my hand to his lips and pressed a soft kiss against it, all humor gone, his eyes filled with regret. "I'm sorry, love. Wet work is a terrible euphemism for the bloody work of killing people. I shouldn't have used it. It's mainly for assassin or execution-type work, and I never did any of that."

I bit my lips and swallowed. "Thank God. Being a Marine was hard enough." I looked away. He'd survived the Marines. He might not survive me. "I'm sorry I got you involved—"

"Stop right there." He squeezed my hand, cutting me off. My eyes met his. "I told you. It's done. It wasn't your fault. No more apologizing about that. You hear?"

Nodding, I swiped at my face.

"It's harder for you, sweetheart. Not because I was military. Many people have traumatic experiences and intense jobs. But it's worse the first time, for everyone. Hell, the first ten or twenty times. You learn to deal with it."

Yeah. I'm sure they did. Live strong. I offered a damp smile. "I-I don't think I want to learn," I whispered.

Leaning closer he squeezed my hand again, soft and tender, and whispered back, "I don't want you to."

Straightening, he eased us back on track. "I've got to make that call."

While Trent talked to Detective McInnaw, I tried to reconcile the shaky state of my emotions. I didn't like feeling vulnerable. Fragile. I thought of myself as a strong person. I am a strong person. So why the emotional overreactions?

Oh, I understood what Trent had said about reactions, but there seemed more at work here. Was it from being the ball in the ping-pong match my life had become?

Really, how could I not be a basket case? The stress levels I'd brought into this situation were high enough, but then add Gwen's death, and this...affair with Trent and....and everything else going on. Rationally, I knew I should give myself a break, but I couldn't calm the emotional storm.

By the time Trent hung up the phone, my body vibrated with tension, my mind buzzed in chaotic mush. He climbed back into the SUV, his grin sardonic. "That went well. I talked to McInnaw, he growled, I explained some facts, and then he got mean."

"Good Lord. He didn't...." I panicked, thinking...I don't know what I was thinking.

Trent laughed, a deep sunburst of humor. "Easy now." His voice soothed, gentled my nerve endings. He pushed back the steering wheel, reached over and released my seatbelt.

I jumped like a startled cat. "What—"

"Come here. I've wanted this since we woke up." He lifted me over the console and juggled me until my legs straddled his lap, steering wheel poking me in the back, the console pinching my leg. Instinctively, I adjusted my position, feeling awkward and juvenile but needing to be close to him more than anything as mundane as comfort or propriety.

There wasn't much space but we didn't take much. His heat fed me. I might have been embarrassed by the whimper

I made, the trembling in my body, except I needed his body contact for my sanity.

Trent's big hands held me tighter. One cupped my head, one my lower back, and he pressed me against him as if he could absorb me into his body. God, I wanted that. I wanted to become part of him, sink into him.

"Shhh. Shhhh." I heard his soft murmurs, like the other times I'd lost control, and something inside me rebelled.

"I don't want to fall apart. Don't let me fall apart," my hoarse voice whispered.

He nuzzled into my hair, and for a moment his hands pressed almost painfully tight. "Okay," he whispered, his moist breath warming my ear. "Just let me hold you."

My muscles relaxed, the tremors stopped. Warmth flowed from his hands, his body. My lips touched his hair, his skin as I spoke. "This is...is nice magic, too." Yes, indeedy. Everything he did to me was magic.

I could feel Trent's lips curve against my temple, then purse into a soft kiss. "Yeah. I know." His hands eased, began to roam more freely. "I told McInnaw we were going to have breakfast before coming in. He didn't like it, but there you go."

His hands slid around my waist, sneaked inside my shirt, and came around front, laying me back enough so he could look into my eyes as he captured my breasts. Played upon their tips. Oh, yes please. Without thought, my back arched, seeking more of his touch.

Those wicked fingers bore down harder, twisting their captive flesh. A teasing gleam fired up his eyes, played around his lips. "Do you remember when I told you I'd collect on those sexual favors, Lotsi-love? Have you been thinking about it like I told you to?"

"Sexual favors? I...well, there hasn't exactly been time."

"There is now."

"But shouldn't we...we talk about our interview with McInnaw?" My hips rolled against his, hungry for the erection growing there. "Get our story straight?"

"We've got nothing to hide from the cops. Except the sex."

A few comments formed but I couldn't concentrate on anything but his tormenting fingers, and the wonder-wonderful feelings...I moaned. A tiny shudder quaked through my body.

His voice went lower, smoky. "No need to talk about our sex life with anyone but each other. I want you thinking about me collecting sexual favors, not about McInnaw."

"Ahhhhh." Fluid heat melted from me, soaked my panties.

Trent's lips sucked down my sounds, eating at my mouth, devouring all I had to offer. His hands left my breasts, pulled my upper body against him, then streaked to my hips, grasping them in a firm hold, rocking me against his marvelous erection, and then he stopped.

"No, Trenton! I-I need more!"

"Shhhh," His breath moistened my jaw, my throat. "It's all right, sweet baby. You'll get what you need."

Trent held my shoulders, moved me until the wheel bit into my back. I frowned, pinched by the awkward position and close quarters.

Brushing back the flyaway hair from my face, he gave me a gentle, incredibly sexy smile. "We're going to have our time together, love." His fingers stroked my bottom lip. "Soon."

Magic. Pure Magic. "Promise?"

"Oh, yeah. I promise."

He lifted me again, settled me into my seat, pulled my seat belt down and snapped it tight. I couldn't believe the strength that took, the power he had to maneuver me around in the confined space.

Before I had a chance to recover, he'd buckled up and started the SUV. "So for the rest of the day, I want you to think about those sexual favors you owe me. And my promise to collect them. Understand?"

Oh, I understood.

Then his voice quieted, forcing me to lean closer as he told me in sensual detail all the wicked things he could do to me. Make me do to him. Oh, it was awful. A relentless beast, he showed no mercy for my protests, my heated face, or my frantic looks around.

Sure beat passing travel time playing games with license plate numbers.

McInnaw nodded at our escort as we approached but never took the cold glare of his black eyes off Trent. "What the hell do think you're doing, Wallace, jacking with the police?"

"I don't know what you mean."

"Oh, don't you? A smart government consultant like you?"

"Ex-government consultant. Cut the crap, McInnaw. You know damn well that has nothing to do with any of this. Did you bring in Benson? Were those men still there?"

"I'm the one asking questions here. What were you doing in Benson's house?"

"I told you. I was an uninvited guest."

"Bullshit. Why were you there?"

The strange undertones puzzled me, but this pissing contest between the two men had gone on long enough. "Because he got involved with me," I said.

McInnaw startled when I spoke and drilled me with his frigid glare.

"Lotsi, I told you it's not your fault. "Trent stepped closer and put his hand on my waist.

I saw McInnaw take in Trent's action and his gentle tone. The detective raised a brow, eyes full of speculation. I turned to face Trent, my hand falling to his bicep, inadvertently forming half an embrace.

"No, Trent. This is not about feeling guilty. Benson took you to get to me. That's a fact."

Trent didn't like it, but had to accept it.

The little rat in McInnaw's brain was spinning its cage so fast I almost saw the smoke, and then he snarled, "Wallace, wait in the interview room over there. Ms. Hannon, come with me."

In minutes, I began telling the entire story. McInnaw rapped out some flat, brusque questions clarifying certain points, but the longer I spoke, the more his air of cold indifference cracked.

First, his fingers spasmed, then warmed to a few staccato patters, and finally thumped an angry rhythm on the bare table. His lips twitched in accompaniment, puckering, and then sucking in and out.

At last, his fist banged and he thundered, "Did you report a possible kidnapping? Did you report a cache of presumed stolen money or a crucial lead in a murder case? Oh, no! Not you! You compromise evidence and go haring off to the rescue like some middle-aged Nancy Drew! What's with you people? I should charge you with obstruction!"

Oh, that was too much. My face jutted out across the table about the same distance as his, my cold, even tone a counterpoint to his roar.

"Try it, Detective McInnaw. We might as well both get a charge out of it. I don't know about 'you people,' but I will tell you what's with *this* middle-aged Nancy Drew."

My finger jammed toward his chest but he was too far away to drill. "Listen to yourself. 'Possible kidnapping.' Trent was a murder suspect to you. You think I'd trust you to lift a finger to help him? 'Presumed stolen money.'" I snorted, contemptuous. "That's about what I expected. You'd have spent days trying to prove it was mine. And then there's the 'murder case.' Gwen isn't a case to me, she was my best friend. I did what I thought was best, Detective. You want to charge me, then charge me. But don't mess with me."

Anger causes tears, I assured myself as one slipped down my cheek. Anger.

I sat back, crossed my arms tight and turned my face away from McInnaw's offensive bluster and the dark yawning surveillance window.

A riff of thumps beat the table. Stopped. Thumped again. "All right, Ms. Hannon. Let's hear the rest of your story."

McInnaw stayed calm until I finished, asked several questions, and then pondered his fingers as they thumped a few more times. He shook his head and looked up.

"If your story about Benson checks out—now don't get your dander up—you're lucky to be alive. You and Wallace both. The men were gone when we got there, but based on your account, it looks like they left everything except their weapons. We're still processing the crime scene. Benson hasn't been located yet. We'll have to impound your RV, but with him loose, we'll provide you with protection."

Police protection! Did that mean...what did that mean? "I need to fly to Seattle for Gwen's funeral." That was non-negotiable.

"No problem. We'll have someone with you while you're in Las Vegas." He rose. "Wait here. We'll have more questions shortly."

"Detective McInnaw?"

McInnaw turned from the door, lifted a brow.

"What about Billy? Is he all right?"

"We'll look into that, Ms. Hannon. There was no one in the house or on the grounds." He opened the door.

"Detective," I called out, unable to keep the fear at bay. He lifted that brow again. "Does the...the protection mean...." I couldn't say it.

One side of McInnaw's lips quirked up. I almost missed it. "That you're in danger? Until we locate Benson, I won't take a chance. What...think I'm going to mess with Nancy Drew?"

Chapter 21

Five hours. Three different interrogators, six visits of fifteen to thirty minutes each and two bathroom trips. That's a lot of time sitting on a hard chair, in a tiny bare room with a glass wall I couldn't look out of and never knew who looked in. Gave me the creeps. At least they could have fed me.

"This is what we get for being good citizens? I would've made bail already if I'd been arrested!" I'd snarled at the last person. "Tell McInnaw he can forget the damn protection, I'm leaving."

I'd even tried using Trent's diversionary tactic, thinking about sexual favors, but that dammed glass wall killed any interest I could scare up.

The cop talked me into waiting five more minutes and the clock was ticking. I paced and watched the ticks. At five minutes, I headed for the door. I would have kicked it open, but McInnaw beat me to it.

"Ms. Hannon." He smiled, with lots of teeth, his voice almost civil. "I hear you're getting impatient. Sorry it took so long to arrange for your protection."

Oh, sure you are! That's why you're being so "nice" when I want to take your head off! I ground my teeth and didn't say a word.

When McInnaw didn't get a rise, he settled down to his normal crusty self and waved to the man behind him. "This is Sergeant Abernathy. He'll accompany you as long as needed, or while you're in Las Vegas."

My goodness, he was young, almost Billy's age. I could easily see the two of them, synchronizing watches and skulking in the hedges. I almost rolled my eyes. I needed protection, not another young man's battered face on my conscious.

Abernathy and I exchanged greetings and shook hands. I tried to look at the upside. The young officer, who looked mid-twenties at most, had an attractive, clean-shaven face, hair short and standing on end. He wore loose-fitting blue jeans and an overlarge, short-sleeved checkered shirt over a white t-shirt that bunched at his hips below the shirt. His feet sported some fancy brand of sneakers.

I sighed and bestowed a polite smile. At least he could pass for a tourist instead of a cop.

McInnaw ignored or didn't notice my tepid acceptance. "I understand you'll be staying with Wallace," he said with an edge of...what, smarm? Cynicism? This was news to me, but darned if I'd let McInnaw know that. "We were finished with Wallace a couple of hours ago, but he insisted on staying. Sergeant Abernathy will transport you to Wallace's and bunk there. You'll work out your schedule with him."

Before I could rail at him, McInnaw cut me off with a curt nod and left me staring at the fresh-faced kid. Abernathy offered a hesitant smile. "Ma'am," he said and gestured toward the door.

Oh, this was great. I sure as heck didn't need a couple of macho men making decisions for me, jerking my strings like puppeteers. I wasn't sure if Trent thought I needed a babysitter or a lover, seemed to me he was a little confused about the difference. Either way, now I had a chaperon. Arrrgh! Couldn't something for once be smooth and straightforward?

I couldn't even snarl at the kid. How could I jump on someone who'd "ma'amed" me with such gentle courtesy? Oh, but someone would pay. I hit the hall with a kick in my stride and fire in my blood, seeking the first target that came to mind. Man, was he toast.

Trent sat on a hall bench near the front of the building. He looked tired and infinitely patient, body hunched forward, elbows balanced on his spread legs, staring down at the empty cup clasped in his hands. He heard the brisk snap of heels and raised his head.

"Lotsi!" He surged to his feet.

Ignoring the wash of emotions flowing across his face, I grasped his arm. "Wait here a moment," I said to the shadow at my back, and then spoke to Trent, as sweet and even as I could manage. "Could I speak with you for a minute?"

I pushed on his arm, crowded him down the hall a ways.

Thoughts flashed in his eyes. Oh, he knew what was coming all right. I saw the guilt. "Funny thing happened. Seems McInnaw thinks I'm staying at your place."

"Now Lotsi. You know they've impounded your RV and—"

"Maybe I want to stay with Charlotte."

"Her place is too small, even without the bodyguard. Roxie is staying with her now, anyway. And Shay's got his daughters with him." His arms wrapped around my waist, reeled me in against his body.

Eyes locked with his, my hands thumped against his chest, keeping us separated a few inches. "There's Erwin and Tremaine. I could stay with them. Or Albert. He's all alone if Roxie's at Charlotte's."

He pulled me tighter. "Aw, come on. That's reaching too far, don't you think? Admit it. You want to stay with me. I told you I had plans for you tonight."

"Yeah, like that's going to happen. See my shadow back there? No sex games around the children." My lips drew back as his descended.

Trent hesitated. His eyes flicked to Abernathy, back to mine. "Shit. Are you serious?" He sounded incredulous but his head raised and his arms relaxed, releasing me from the hard press. Damn.

"You betcha. We're not exactly quiet when we're...ah, busy." I blushed. Hey, we were in a police station, for goodness sake.

"Busy?" He moved closer. "Maybe we could dial it down...."

"Uh huh." I pushed back a step.

His teasing look faded. "It doesn't matter, Lotsi. We can wait for the rest, but I want you in my bed. I want to hold you tonight. Just hold you."

I gave him my best narrow-eyed, you're-on-notice look. Strong men had quailed in their Guccis at that look. "No funny stuff."

Trent nodded. "No funny stuff."

Yet as we finished our business and headed back to the park, I couldn't help thinking that the moratorium on funny stuff wasn't going to save me from heartache. Four days. I had to leave in four days, even if I had to leave my RV in police custody and fly out.

Even without a chaperone, how could I fit all the funny stuff we both wanted into just four days? God help me if we tried, because how was I going to live with the pain coming my way when I left Trent behind after a mere four blissful days?

Fifteen years of celibacy looked pretty damn good after all.

By the time day rolled into night, engaging in sex games was the furthest thing from my mind. Everything except sleep was far from my mind.

The usual crowd showed up at Trent's to hear our tale and stuck around to theorize and rehash the details. Erwin paced the fourteen-foot length of Trent's living room in about four steps, alternately mumbling or exploding with vows to pound Benson and his goons. Seeing Trent wince at a movement, Erwin grumbled and paced faster. If I faltered or blinked, teary-eyed, he planted his feet and erupted. Twice I had my ribs crushed in a comforting hug when I sidled past him to the kitchen.

Tremaine caught me rubbing my side and smiled, an angelic light touching his stunning good looks. A curly spiral of coal-black hair dangled over his cocoa forehead. His dark eyes didn't miss a lick the entire evening, but he said little.

Charlotte fluttered like a startled hen, her eyes round, her hands flying in confusion, flapping from her lap to her face or stalling in mid-air. "Oh, my. Oh, my," she muttered repeatedly.

If Charlotte was a hen, Roxie was a banty rooster, blustering and charging around until she'd collided with Erwin a couple of times. Then she settled on the couch next to Trent and me and confined herself to twitches and vicious little tirades regarding various body parts of our attackers. Ouch.

After a while, Roxie and Tremaine rummaged around Trent's kitchen and prepared a round of eats. Roxie flitted some more and then came to roost near Albert, the closest I'd seen her approach him since their blowup at the last week's so-long-ago dance.

Maybe they'd reconcile tonight. I hoped so. Someone needed to get lucky. I meant more than sex. I wanted their hearts to be lighter, to have someone lift the heavy weight of stress and angst permeating our group.

Then Shay came by with the girls. He confirmed the coroner had released Gwen's body. We'd be flying her home tomorrow. That seemed to signal the end of the evening, and it didn't take long for everyone to leave.

Through it all, my police bodyguard remained perched on the sidelines in the driver's seat, quiet and observant, a fresh opening bud among our collection of faded blooms. I wondered where Benson was, and if the bud would grow thorns to protect us both should Benson try to pluck me.

Trent made Abernathy comfortable up front while I took first dibs on the bathroom. Too exhausted to worry any more about things beyond my control, I went through an abbreviated nightly routine. My sluggish mind and body needed sleep but I couldn't forget this was Trent's bed, and that I was where I wanted to be.

We'd agreed no funny stuff, but honestly, neither of us was in any condition to play around. Trent was on painkillers. We were both running on reserves. I suppose my borrowed nightie—an oversized t-shirt—gave exactly the right message. I wasn't there for sex, I was there for comfort.

The click of the door announced Trent's approach. In the dim light shining through the privacy shades I saw him linger at the bedside.

Who did he see, burrowed under the covers? Even at my best, I was no fantasy fuck, just a woman old enough to accept her limitations, young enough to yearn for her dreams. One of those dreams stood there, waiting. Returning Trent's invitation from the night before, I lifted the covers and welcomed my lover.

The shock of being body-to-body with a lover, my lover, my warm, completely naked lover, still overwhelmed me. Our exploring hands shared light, gentle caresses. Each stroke relaxed tight muscles, released inner tensions. Old wounds. Oh, dear. My heart pounded and I swallowed back my tears.

Trent's hands glided up and down my back. I squirmed a little closer into the curve of his throat, held on a little tighter. "Thank you," I breathed against the warmth of his skin.

"What for?"

"For being here."

His hand stilled. Then he speared through my hair and eased my head back to look in my eyes. As close as we were, the dimness hid little. "You're in my bed."

"Yes. But you're in my body space. It'd be...it'd be empty if you weren't here. So, thank you."

He just looked at me, his hand gently tracing points on my face, combing oh so slowly through my hair. A soft curve rested on his lips. After several minutes, he spoke, his voice gentle, incredibly sexy. I think he could bring me off with his voice alone.

"It's amazing how you redefine my world with just a few words. Do you know that? From the moment I met you, you keep turning me inside out. Rearranging my view."

"Is that a good thing?"

"Oh, yeah. That's a good thing." His lips lingered at my forehead. I got the impression he was as languid as I was, unable to perform the gymnastics needed to mate lips. "There's just one thing."

Still basking in the glow of his surprising comment, floating closer to oblivion, I responded on a thread of sound. "What's that?"

His hands slithered down and pulled up the cotton nightie. "This has to go. I want to hold you. Only you."

That sounded good. Too good. A woman could lose herself in an answer like that. With a little cooperation, the shirt went up and over my head.

I lay stiff, waiting. Felt him sigh, his breath tickle the loose hair at my face pillowed on his chest. "That's better. G'night, love." The muscles under me relaxed.

"Night."

Trent's hands soothed a slow path as far down as he could reach, from my neck, over my back and rear, to where his fingers tucked into my inner thighs. Then back up he drifted, slowly. Leisurely. A jaunt of sensual pleasure, a journey of intimacy.

My body responded, muscles unknotting once more, tension releasing until I felt like butter melting on toast.

Mmmmm. Male toast.

My defenses were non-existent. Tonight that didn't seem like a bad thing. Tomorrow I'd worry about defenses. The next couple of days were for Gwen. By the time I returned to Las Vegas, I'd have only two days left with Trent.

Tonight, I'd simply enjoy being served on warm toast.

Chapter 22

"The banners are a great touch, Evangeline. Really. Gwen would be thrilled," I assured the caller. Mentally I crossed my fingers. I think Gwen would approve...her streak of silliness astounded me sometimes, but would Shay, or her daughters? My gut churned, ripe with acid, muscles tense with another worry knot.

By now, my whole body felt macraméd with worry knots.

A borrowed cell phone planted deep in the crotch of my shoulder and neck, I juggled a carryon and purse as I rushed down a crowded McCarran Airport corridor toward the lines at security. Now that Gwen's body was flying home, funeral plans ran amuck. Having Lady Tacky, the Duchess of Ever Camp, handle arrangements for the Dazzling Darlings was a scary proposition.

I pictured Lady Tacky in all her glory—ruby rouge spots, eyes darkly lined and shadowed with purple, her ample frame bedecked in full regalia and every piece of Red Hot bling she could find. Only her heart exceeded her imagination.

Judging from her tone of voice, however, the new plans someone had come up with taxed even Evangeline's imagination. I scrambled to catch up. "They want to do what? My goodness. Oh, my goodness. Yes, well. I see. Look, maybe I can talk to their Queen Mum...yes, good idea. Tell her...tell her to hold off until I get there, okay?"

Saints preserve us. I hoped to God I could head that one off once I arrived in Seattle.

"Dammit, Lotsi, we've got to talk," Trent growled from behind my shoulder. I dodged around a bottleneck, a small group of stiff Japanese executives in suits stopped dead in their tracks by a toddler wobbling across their path. Laughing and seemingly unaware of the inconvenience, parents in shorts and flip-flops ran to retrieve their adventuresome offspring.

Finding a clear space, I glanced back at Trent. Oh, dear. His glorious hair hung in snarls, his eyes frustrated. Frown lines appeared etched in his face. Not the usual chirpy, sexy face I'd grown accustomed to.

Well, I'd known last night I needed to build defenses. Being busy seemed to work just fine. My entire morning had been filled with calls and hurried arrangements, last-minute trips between motorhomes, and then the frantic rush to the airport. Every time he started to talk about us, my cell rang. His patience now worn thin, he appeared close to losing it. I didn't blame him, but honestly, what could I say to him?

I ended the call to Evangeline. As soon as I pocketed the cell, Trent grabbed my hand and slowed our pace, just a few steps ahead of my police shadow. "Slow down, Stretch," he said, "Give me one goddamned minute."

With the security checkpoint in sight, we both knew there wasn't time to stop and chat. The line doubled back on itself several times, and I didn't have long until boarding.

"Trent—"

"No, Lotsi, listen to me. I know this trip is important to you. I know your whole life is a mess right now. But we're important, too, Lotsi. You and me. And by God, you're not blowing us off."

His hand gripped mine harder and he yanked me to a stop, crowded me into the wall. His whole body pressed against mine, his lips swooped down and took my mouth, searing me with a burning kiss of angry demand.

His moist breath heated my skin as the rough edge of his voice growled into my ear. "You get your ass back here to me, lady. We have some plans to make before you leave again. Do you understand me?"

"Ah...plans?" I managed to say through the lump in my throat. He couldn't mean....

Trent drew back and shook me by the shoulders. "Yes, plans."

How could one word be so intimate? So terrifying? With a flick of my eyes toward Abernathy standing nearby studying the crowd, I clamped down on my surging emotions until my heart hurt. Where were my damn defenses now? "Ah, er, plans."

He seemed to understand my response. Good. That made one of us. With a tiny lift at the edge of his lips, he stole a gentler, quick kiss and said, "Go."

As Abernathy and I stepped into the security line, Trent's voice reached me with his last words. "And Lotsi, on the flight back, think about those *favors* I'm going to collect."

There was no mistaking his meaning. My face flamed. Beside me, Abernathy chuckled. I cut him off with a killing look. I aimed the same look back at Trent. Separated by fellow travelers, he stood with his hands braced on his hips, grinning at me, unrepentant.

Now really, how could I defend against that?

Chapter 23

The small cathedral was packed. No one anticipated this many people. Shay gazed around the church nave and turned to me in the pew behind. He had a half dazed, half-awed expression on his face, and his voice was hushed. "Where did they all come from?"

I smiled and shrugged, feeling awed myself. "I know Gwen deserved this, but she'd be more surprised than anyone."

Shay's smile flattened with emotion, his eyes bright and glistening with unshed tears. "Yeah," was all he said.

No, nothing could end or hide the pain, but there was a tremendous pride, too, a humble thankfulness for the recognition of his wife.

Family, friends, social and business acquaintances— Gwen had touched so many people in her life. Some of her doctors and nurses came, teachers from the kids' schools, distant friends old and new. Then there were the Hot Ladies.

Wearing extravagant red hats and purple dresses resplendent with bling and long, dangling boas, thirty-eight Dazzling Darlings mingled splashes of wild color among the sober hues of other mourners in the pews.

At the narthex doors, two honor guards stood holding the huge Dazzling Darlings banners at attention throughout the service. Gwen and I made them, although I did the grunt work, she provided the vision and skill. We did them for the Las Vegas national convention, carried by the same honor guards.

Standing on ten-foot poles, the banners were two feet wide and four feet long, lusciously gaudy with gold tassels framing a purple silk background. Miss DD—it took us days to enlarge the template from Gwen's small original design on her bags—dominated the foreground, a resplendent red and gold giant stylized face and shoulder outline of a sexy female with an impudent flowing feathered headdress. Our chapter name anchored the bottom.

The Dazzling Darlings had proudly come to honor their Queen Mum with full regalia and loving hearts.

After the service, the family received condolences and a general milling around took place until the caravan formed up for the trek to the cemetery. The lull allowed me to double check arrangements and calm overwrought nerves as I fielded comments and questions from fellow mourners. Very soon, I was the only Hot Lady in sight.

I stayed with Shay and the girls as they moved toward the limousines, anxious to catch their expression when they exited the church. I wasn't disappointed.

A growing hush fell upon the spill of mourners.

Spread before us was a near-blinding double line of solemn women standing at attention, a tunnel of red and purple stretching from church step to curbside. At the end, the bright DD banners marked the lead limo.

Shay paused, silent but eloquent as he fought for composure. His daughter Kim held his arm, and I heard her gasp and then choke off a giggle. Michelle walked with me. She leaned close, and whispered, "Oh, Lotsi. I bet Mom just loves this. Thank you."

"I bet she does, too, honey. She always loved a good show, didn't she?"

Michelle's chin wobbled, her laugh wavered, but she hung tough. "Yeah, she sure did."

Emotions grew so huge my chest ached as we piled into the limo, and Shay laughed and shared his daughters' pleasure and pain at our chapter's simple show of respect. So many Hot Ladies understand loss. That's one reason we also understand fun.

The procession moved out under police escort, each vehicle receiving a flag. There must have been over a hundred in all. Pairs of motorcycle cops played leapfrog from intersection to intersection, blocking traffic to let the long line of vehicles with little flags on the front fenders pass unimpeded.

Then the line of women began as we neared the cemetery, marked by their own chapter flags. At first, I thought there'd been some mistake, that the chapter Queens had misunderstood my instructions and started forming their honor lines too soon. Then I realized they hadn't misunderstood. They had multiplied by several orders of magnitude.

Instead of the additional thirty or forty women I had expected, we passed more and more red- and purple-garbed women. Chapter banners waved in the breeze, marking specific groups, most of which I didn't recognize.

Some of the women wore purple t-shirts and red beanies, some wore fancy gowns and ornate hats, most wore something in between. Some were Pink Ladies, and wore pink hats and lavender outfits. Some women waved and hollered, some stood solemn and silent. All were there to honor Gwen.

God, my heart about burst. Everyone in the car chortled, jabbered, and slowly fell silent. There wasn't a dry eye in the limo.

They just kept coming. Both side of the streets. Single file and in clumps, some sitting or leaning on a walker and—bless their hearts—some in wheelchairs. By the time we'd passed close to four hundred Hot Ladies, I realized they also brought honor to themselves, to women everywhere, to the heartfelt connections we felt for each other.

Finally, the familiar DD banners and our own chapter ladies greeted us inside the cemetery gates, and there surrounded by her family and friends, I watched as Gwen Faye Evans was carried to her grave and laid to rest.

Gentle words, those. Laid to rest. My mind tumbled in an emotional whirlwind. One moment I prayed she'd found peace in her long rest, the next I saw her lying in a pool of blood and rage howled and battered at my control.

What now, Gwen? Do we...do we just leave you here and go on? This is so wrong. You shouldn't be down there, resting! You should be up here with us, living!

"Ashes to ashes, dust to dust," the priest intoned and sprinkled the casket.

Let her go, I told myself. Accept what is.

But I couldn't. She isn't all here.

What!?

Where did that come from? I could sense it now, as if part of her spirit was stuck elsewhere. She couldn't find peace until...until the missing pieces around her murder were known, until the persons involved were revealed and dealt with.

My mind whirled and stopped. Okay, okay, so maybe it wasn't Gwen who wouldn't find peace, maybe it was me. I don't know.

However, I do know that even in death, life is complicated.

Gwen's killer still walked this earth. Benson still awaited me in Las Vegas.

And my plane left in three hours

Chapter 24

"What, no watchdog?" I asked Trent as we swung into the flow of disembarking passengers. I needed to calm my pulse, quiet the feverish rush of being locked in his arms again. Dangerous territory, that. My defenses seemed to be off to a poor start.

In a couple of strides, he snagged the carryon from my shoulder, grabbed my hand and reined me in to a slower pace. "No watchdog. McInnaw says he needed Abernathy for another case, and couldn't spare anyone else for awhile."

"Does that mean they've found Benson?"

"No. Means they're shorthanded."

"Have they found Billy?"

"Yeah. Benson had him taken to a cabin that night. He showed up yesterday. Didn't have a clue were his uncle is."

"What about John, the mechanic? Was he part of Benson's scheme?" I crossed mental fingers. I'd told McInnaw about his suspicious questions that first day asking my destination, urging me to use their sister shop near San Francisco, but I hoped the sexy mechanic was innocent. Call me shallow, but I'd hate to have lusted after a crook.

"Doesn't look like it. The company has a bonus program for referrals. Seems to be the only financial gain involved."

"Oh, good."

I noticed Trent's frown. His soft welcoming look had hardened, tension and worry settling over his face, in his eyes, and I knew it was because of me. Worrying about protecting me from Benson, worrying about our relationship. If we had a relationship. My recent troubles and conflicted feelings seemed to have dumped a load on this wonderful man and suddenly, I'd had enough.

There wasn't anything I could do about Benson, but I refused to let my fear of some future pain cause both Trent and myself pain now. He deserved better, and so did I. I wanted the best possible two days we could create together. Knowing Trent, I just needed to nudge him in the right direction.

Flashing him a grin, I pressed my body against his as we walked. "Forget Benson. He has bigger problems than us now, anyway. And I'm glad Abernathy's gone. Having a chaperone sucked, don't you think?"

Trent resisted, a mulish clench to his jaw that seemed to say he wanted to worry some more. Since we were walking close, I used our clasped hands and rubbed the back of his hand against my thigh in slow, firm strokes. Gave him a sultry smile. He stayed stubborn. I rubbed higher, a grazing stroke across my mound and back. Raised one eyebrow.

His breath whooshed out. "God, you drive a hard bargain. All right, I'll let it go for now, but we will come back to this bodyguard issue."

We'd entered the airport casino area. Rows of slot machines blocked our exit in the best Nevada tradition where no potential player left a premise unfleeced. Trent pulled me in front of him, transferred his hand to my waist and guided me down a constricted passage where a small group gawked at an excited couple in front of a noisy flashing machine.

I glanced at the payout as we passed. Four hundred fifty bucks. Hey, not bad. People peeled off right and left to hit the slots.

Trent drew abreast hip to hip, his arm around my back and his hand curved low. Then he smiled and the sun came out, right there in the airport, right there in my heart. Thank you, God.

He leaned closer to my ear. "So, tell me sweetheart. Are you ready to pay up on the sexual favors you owe me?"

That was certainly in the right direction—my body responded with a hot rush of excitement. I must admit I'd already thought of the subject for a moment or two on the flight back. With his comment, I was so ready to pay up I was about to spontaneously combust, but still....

I choked back a quick agreement and put a strong note of suspicion to my voice. "Just exactly how many of these favors do I owe?"

His eyes. I loved his eyes, dark and alluring, full of sensual promise. His lips rose in a sexual dare. "More than you can repay in one night."

"Hey, I don't remember any deal like that!"

Trent laughed, a low sexy trek across my skin. My heart stuttered and kicked in double-time. "You owe me the sexual favors, so that makes me the scorekeeper. I choose what, when, where and how many. You got a problem with that?"

Now that was going too far! The way he drawled out his challenge set my feminine back up in a hurry. He chooses? He's the scorekeeper? I had a problem with that all right! I opened my mouth to blast him flat...and images began flashing through my mind. Oh.

My mouth closed. I ducked my head, hair swishing over the side of my face, and managed a hoarse reply. "I, ah, well, maybe not this one time."

Behind the veil of my hair, I smiled.

Driving down I-15 at night past the Strip is a close view of fairyland. I couldn't think of a single place on earth more filled with such fantasy on a grand scale. Giant castles, Arabian bazaars, miniature cityscapes, pyramids and ancient Gods, all in brilliant colors and blazing lights. From stately classic to extravagant modern, the incredible display demanded attention, yet the fantasy in the cab of the SUV eclipsed the exotic skyline.

My, oh my, what a devil Trent had become. His voice purred then demanded, his words arousing my body instead of his hands. He teased and tormented, making me do the most wicked things as we flew through the night, cocooned in our own erotic world beneath the dazzling Las Vegas glitter.

I thought my heart would explode in blissful delight.

Somewhere deep inside, I knew the sadness—and danger—hadn't gone away. None of that mattered right now. What mattered was the part of me that begged, take me away, take me away! I latched onto Trent's seductive spell with desperate abandon, sinking beneath his sexual power, responding to his voice until need burned in every cell, muscles quivered and shook, and pleading gasps and whimpers filled the cab.

By the time we arrived at Trent's RV, my knees were weak and shaky. Trent didn't seem to mind helping; in fact, he helped me right out of my clothes before we'd reached the bed, and then he stopped.

"Trent?" I asked, a soft breath of sound that barely disturbed the air in the dim quiet room. My hands kneaded his forearms, a pulsing rhythm mirroring the ragged beat of my heart, my lungs.

His eyes captured mine, dark pools dilated with lust. One of his hands lifted from my waist, brushed damp hair back from my forehead. "Lotsi-mine," he said, soft and quiet for such a deep voice. "I wanted to talk to you first, get things straight between us."

"Noooo—"

His fingers pressed back my protest, then softened into a caress, brushing back and forth across my lips. "But now...now I just want you."

The air in my lungs whooshed out against the pads of his fingertips. Dark eyes burning so hot they scorched a pathway inside, his voice lowered to a husky growl. "I want you."

All that intensity contrasted with the soft brush of his fingers moving over my jaw and cheek, circling my lips and brushing over them in mere wisps of touch, teasing the nerves in my skin and tightening the near-painful arousal pulsing through my body. He was killing me.

"Please," I begged.

His hand never paused. "What do you want, Lotsimina?"

"More." I didn't want to talk, I wanted his fingers, I wanted his thick length inside me, I wanted..."More."

"Yeah. I want more, too," he whispered. Then he stepped back and dropped his hands.

"Aaahhh!" Shocked, I swayed toward him, toward those hands.

He threw back the covers. "Lie down for me, Lotsimina."

Blinking, I struggled to breath.

"Now."

Still focused on those hands I needed on me, I saw them tremble and clench at his side. He stood rigid, waiting. That small sign relieved me. I wasn't alone in the sexual freefall I'd plunged into by giving myself over to him so completely in the SUV. Just thinking about it made my body sizzle and cream slide down my inner thigh as my sex spasmed.

I climbed on the bed and stretched out, the crisp sheet cool and fragrant beneath me. Then with a simple movement of his hands, Trent stole all my senses.

Reaching for his belt buckle, he slowly worked it loose, his eyes never leaving my body. He seemed hyperaware of every ragged breath I took, every hungry movement that rippled through me. The restless movements of my arms, my legs. The quiver of my breasts as I trembled, watching him strip bare his powerful, sleek body. He slipped the belt from the loops in his jeans, tossed it to the dresser behind him. My eyes stayed focused on the front of his jeans, bulging with his erection. A huge, luscious erection.

Trent's hands returned to his jeans. One flicked loose the snap. *Do it, do it!* I held my breath. The other hand rubbed over the centerpiece of my attention. *Oh my god.*

I glanced up. His narrowed eyes blazed, transfixed by my blatant reactions.

"Don't tease, Trenton. I-I need you." The time for titillation, for false modesty or hesitation was long past. I felt reduction to my elemental parts, to the core of my feminine being, and I wanted my man.

"You'll have me, sweet baby, but I won't rush. Wait for it, Lotsimina." He lowered the zipper a few inches, relieving the pressure on his swollen flesh.

Dry mouthed, I licked my lips. "I don't want to wait, Trenton." That breathy voice wouldn't convince a big strong man like Trenton Wallace. No way. So I sweetened the deal by opening my legs, lifting one knee and letting it fall to the bed. Upping the ante.

He studied the offering. A sexy smile gleamed in the faded light. "Oh, yeah. Show me what you feel. But I want one more favor from you, baby. Think you can pay up one more time?" Low and seductive, his slow voice poured inside me, erasing my objections, destroying my small resistance. His hands kept moving, unbuttoning his shirt, pulling it free.

"Answer me, Lotsimina." The shirt fluttered to the floor. Trent still wore an elastic binding around his ribcage.

I stared, seeing the vivid bruising, remembering...Oh, God. The monkey face, swinging in an arch, the sound as it hit. Guns exploding. The crunch when my vase/weapon struck flesh, the vibration up my arms—

"Lotsi!" My whole body jarred at Trent's sharp voice, as if I'd snapped back into my body. Kneeling on the bedside, he hovered over me. I blinked into his eyes, confused and lost. "Stay with me, sweetheart. Stay with me. Are you okay? Lotsi? Are you with me now?"

How had he known? I nodded, and realized I was trembling, not with passion, but with fear. I wanted...I needed Trent's voice to center me, settle me down.

His voice firmed. "Okay. Listen up. I'm not playing now, I'm taking."

Thank God. Thank God. "Hurry," I whispered.

Trent stood and made quick work of his jeans and shorts. He stretched out beside me, barely touching, locking onto my gaze. His hand stroked over my cheek, threaded back into my hair, gripped my head and then his lips sought mine, his tongue lapping and stroking before burrowing deep.

I couldn't catch my breath. A sound came from my throat, a broken cry that morphed into a moan as his kiss deepened. My hands ranged over his flesh everywhere I could reach, stroking, fingers flexing deep into muscle.

Trent tunneled his arms around me, holding me tight, tighter, and tighter still. Nothing gave me relief from the painful need in my breasts, between my legs. My body clenched and bowed upward, undulating against him, lost to all reason.

With an explosion of air, Trent broke the kiss and whispered against my lips. "Shhhhh, easy now, baby. Shhhhh." The strokes of his hands calmed, soothed.

Only then did I hear the keening sounds I'd been making, recalled the echoes of crying moans. Gasping in short rushes, I fought for breath, slowly coming down from the precipice I'd reached.

"Lie back, now. Lie back." He pushed me onto my back, smiling into my eyes as he brushed the sweat from my forehead back into my hair. "Let's try this one more time. My way, Lotsimina."

His fingers returned to feathering across my face, my lips, my eyebrows. I'd been so close! "Why?" I whispered, tears leaking down my temples. "Why are you doing this to me?"

The soft light hid little as close as we were. I saw the tenderness in his face and eyes, the gentle curve of his lips. "Because we'd last about five minutes going at it like we were. I want more than that, Lotsi-love. I think you do too. I know you will, once I've had my way with you."

Ah, man. His words thrilled me again, right down to that secret place that craved his having his way with me. Still, I pouted at him. Frowned for good measure.

He shook his head. "I told you. I'm not playing. I'm taking." He didn't allow for any response, he simply began. First, he adjusted the pillow more comfortable underneath my head. Then he shifted until he sat tailor-fashion beside me, about hip level.

"What are you doing?" I asked, thinking this was a fine time for things to get confusing. If this was his way, I liked my way better.

"Quiet. No talking unless I ask you a question or you have a serious problem. Got that? And close your eyes. I want you to feel. Just lay still, and feel. Do you understand?"

"Of course I understand, but why—"

"No, Lotsimina. Just relax, close your eyes, no talking. Do you understand?"

"Yes."

He looked at me. I looked at him. His eyebrow twitched up.

"What?"

He waited.

"Okay, okay. I get it. Golly, I thought we were doing fine until—"

"Lotsi."

I squeezed my eyes shut and let out a huge dramatic sigh. Funny thing. By the time my lungs emptied, every muscle began to release. Felt pretty good. I'd slept on the plane, but it had to be after eleven, maybe closer to midnight. Serve Mr. He-man right if I fell asleep.

Then he touched me. Just a slow skim of his fingertips, starting from my right collarbone across my shoulder and down my arm to the ends of my fingers. Again. Then down the left side, same pattern.

Tension drained out with each pass. Inch by inch. A tropical smell teased my senses, some vanilla-coconut blend, sensual, exotic. The RV was warm, a slight movement of air a gentle breath over my bare flesh. Trent's fingers became my focus, my center.

Both hands cupped my entire face. His fingertips rested at my hairline, palms brushed my nose, my chin. After a pause, pressure shifted to those magic fingertips. They stroked over my forehead, eyes, and cheeks, crested my chin and smoothed down my throat.

At the juncture of my collarbones, his hands shifted to span my upper chest, laying palm to fingertip. Another pause and his hands glided slowly down my chest, grazing over my breasts with their hardened tips, down my ribcage and lower abdomen where they paused again, just brushing the silky hair of my mound. Then they split, running down each thigh, angling just a bit to cup my lower legs, my ankles, and up the rise of my foot past my toes.

The smooth, gentle passes barely touched my skin, yet released muscle after muscle and tension flowed away.

I lost awareness of Trent, except for his hands. His magic hands. I became a reservoir, a cozy warm reservoir of amorphous consciousness. He slid one hand under my right calf, cupped my heel and lifted, pulling my leg open, bending the knee until my calf pressed against his chest. Both hands surrounded my foot in a warm cocoon.

Mmmmm. Cool air bathed my open crotch. I bet Trent was getting quite a view. My eyes slitted open. Oh, my. The sight of him fluttered through my heart. Trent's eyes were closed. His whole body cradled my raised leg and foot, his cheek resting on the back of his top hand as he enclosed my foot, his moist breath warming my skin. Bliss emanated from his face, his position, his demeanor.

He raised his head enough to watch his upper hand begin to move. His fingers caressed my toes. One tip penetrated the space next to my big toe before his hand slid under my foot and his palm cupped the bottom of the arch perfectly. Paused. He bent to place a long, soft kiss on the top of my instep. He moved on, over the heel, the calf, under my knee and on up my thigh, stopping at the apex with a little dip into the crease at my trunk.

His eyes followed the stroke up my entire leg, lingering on the folds of my sex. Maybe he heard the break in my breathing. His gaze flicked up. When he saw the lazy slits of my eyes—oops, I wasn't supposed to look—he smiled, just a little lift at the corners, and went on with his business.

This time when his palm nestled in the bottom curve of my arch, he rocked his hand back and forth. "This place. Feel how it fits my hand? So sexy, so perfect."

No, his voice was perfect, but the feel of his hand there— I had to admit, it was sexy. How could my foot be sexy?

My breathing picked up, blood surging through every tingling cell. A small rasping moan slipped from my throat, a wisp of air arising from the heat caused by his hand, a mere hint of the wildfire I sensed on the horizon, moving out upon the hills and valleys of my body.

Trent held my heel, fitting the soft flesh of my Achilles into the vee of his palm and thumb, stroking back and forth. My breasts swelled and ached. "Feel this? You're made for my hands."

"Mmmmm," I agreed, as my sex melted and leaked, trickling down sensitive flesh, an arousing feeling itself.

He stroked higher, embracing my calf, mating hand to muscle. Air shuddered into my starved lungs.

"And here," his moist warmth bathed my knee, his tongue licking a trail beside his hand. I keened, low and thready. "Here you're even softer, your taste richer. And your response—your body calls to me now in every way. Feel it, Lotsimina. Just feel it."

God, how could I not? I started to say something, but he shifted his hand until his fingers reached the underside of my thigh, his thumb spanning the upper curve, and he slowly moved higher.

"Ooohhhhh."

When he dipped into the crease, his fingers brushed wider, combing through the trimmed thatch of my pubic hair. The lips of my pussy swelled and parted, my clit pulsed and throbbed in aching hunger.

Sweat beaded my skin, trickled down my forehead, the backs of my bent legs. I could scent my own sex, dripping down my buttocks. The heat of a flush coursed over my skin, rushing from my toes, over my torso, up my face. I'd never last another circuit.

He spread my legs further this time, bending here, moving there, keeping one leg tucked into his body while he stretched his hands out to caress the other. He moved faster. Yes! Yes!

My body trembled with need, ready to explode—but I lay as still as possible, feeling. Always feeling. God help me. Feeling, as he neared my painfully aroused clit. I knew I'd shatter. I knew it.

Trent's hand slid from my thigh to cover the entirety of my pussy, the heel of his hand pressing tight against my clit, his fingertips dipping into my soft, wet slit. I convulsed. Exploded. Then imploded. Shuddering and thrashing, mind lost as sensations racketing around my body.

Before the quaking ended, Trent's shoulders forced my thighs wide, his fingers spread the tender swollen lips and his tongue licked from end to end. Another climax rose. As he lapped and sucked, it went on and on, wave after wave of quivering bliss. Dimly I heard other sounds joining mine, the wet sounds of sex with a hungry man driving me higher until I crested again, higher, harder, then fell.

His body heaved and he came over me, pressing me deep into the bedding. "Now, Trenton," I whispered, throat raw and bone dry. "Damn you, do it now."

"Yes," he growled, eyes wild and half-blind. His fingers gripped my head, pulling at my hair. Then he struck with a devouring kiss. I tasted myself on his lips, his tongue. He sucked in my incoherent noises.

I bowed up, slamming into his body, demanding he fill me. He answered, clenching his buttocks and ramming deep, then deeper still, until his sac slapped against my buttocks on each stroke. He filled me so full, so deep, I thought I'd die but first I needed more. More of his body shafting me, withdrawing and thrusting again. My hands clutched his backside, reinforcing the steady rhythm as he hammered me toward another peak. Withdrawing. Thrusting. Withdrawing. Thrusting.

My hands slid up his slippery back. Between our bodies, our combined sweat provided an even wetter surface, but the wettest...I swear, if it wasn't so exciting, I'd be embarrassed. Forget personal lubricants. I had Trent.

Shifting to his knees, Trent straightened my legs against his chest, leaned forward and pressed until I rolled up, my own knees nearly touching my ears. What...what was he doing?

Ahhh, reaching deeper, that's what. Deeper and harder than ever. I lost all awareness but for his body pounding into mine. He hit a new place inside and thrust again. Again. Oh, god...I couldn't...I couldn't...but I did.

My clit pulsed. Spasms rippled around Trent's hard, thick pole, reaching deep into my channel. He slammed deep once more and ground his hips. His whole body stiffened, arched back. I felt him jerk, jerk again, pumping his cum into me. My whole body convulsed and then shook as heat flashed through me. A cry broke loose and surfaced, a sliver of sound starting low and keening to a crescendo, dying out on a stuttering moan.

Another first.

Trent released my legs and sank down, turning me with him to our sides, locking us together as our chests heaved and our hearts thundered. His touch feathered my back as the quakes eased, until neither of us moved and I lay in a wondrous stupor.

The next morning I cooked a hardy breakfast for us, and told him about the funeral while we ate. Trent smiled at my teary eyes when I got to the part about the Red Hot Ladies honoring Gwen, and how it had affected us all.

He held my hand until I finished my tale. "What an amazing tribute, sweetheart. You must be very proud of them all."

"I am, and thankful, too. It was truly an amazing sight. I'll never forget it."

Then he got down to business. "Now then. I have two things to say. The first is a short version of the talk I've wanted for some time. I want to join you in Napa Valley."

Oh, no. I'd been afraid of something like this. I didn't want any token promises. "You don't have to—"

His fingers gripped mine, hard. "Christ, Lotsi. I know I don't have to." He eased his punishing grip, but his eyes still flashed with anger, and maybe pain. "What, do you think this is over? That we're done?"

I shook my head. He wouldn't release my hand, not unless I got a lot more adamant than I wanted to at this point. I didn't want a fight. Not over this.

Trent shook my hand, warning me. "We're not done, not by a long shot. Get that straight right now. We're just beginning, Lotsi. It's just that...well, shit, I can't believe the timing."

He released my hand to run it through his hair, a study in frustration.

Uh huh. Lay it on me. "What do you mean?"

"That's the other thing. The reason why this is a short version. Look, I have a client who needs me right now. I've been putting him off, but I have to go back East for a week or ten days." He glanced at his watch. "In fact, I've got to sign some papers at a lawyer's office downtown. I'll be back shortly. We'll talk more then. Okay?"

His glare, especially with that half-hidden glint of pleading, of suppressed need, didn't allow for any disagreement. I couldn't have offered any. A lump blocked my throat. "Okay."

Well, that was that.

It's not that I don't believe him, I told myself after he'd left. I do. It's just that I know how good intentions worked. Rather, didn't work. I'd leave, he'd leave. We'd move on. He'd forget about me, and my heart would be broken.

God. I had to get away.

Chapter 25

I checked in with Erwin first. I really did. I'd have asked him to take me, if he'd been home. Neither he nor Tremaine answered my knock at their door. Their truck sat in front. Perhaps they were on a walk.

Well, that wasn't going to stop me. My darling Ninja was at Trent's, collected from the empty spot after the police impounded my RV. Yes, that's exactly what I needed, an exhilarating, liberating, motorcycle ride in the fresh air.

Then maybe I'd go to the store. Trent needed some groceries. I could fix something special for us for our last dinner together. Last dinner. How pathetic that sounded.

Blinking furiously, I got my keys and backpack. For a minute, I lamented the loss of my wide-brimmed red hat with the flowers and trailing ribbon. Just as well it was locked away in the RV somewhere. This way I could go as fast as I wanted. I could fly away on my wild beast and forget my troubles, forget...just forget.

So I did. I wobbled a bit at first, caught the right balance and picked up speed. I flew down Boulder and kept going. The lights were with me. The wind blew my hair, flapped my shirt, and wiggled the heavy denim of my long blue jeans as it blew up the legs. It tickled. I laughed aloud, and went faster.

Oh, yes. I needed this.

After about a half hour, I turned back and slowed down, refreshed and relaxed, problems at bay. As I neared the park, I looked around, getting my bearings. I didn't recognize the cross street, but the next one looked familiar. I turned, and eventually spotted the street I wanted, and doubled back to find the mall with the grocery store.

I turned into the mall entrance. Recipes filled my thoughts. I decided on something simple but elegant. Chicken picatta. I'd slice the chicken breasts thin, make a lemon butter sauce and add capers. Some fresh basil, mushrooms. I liked to make my own pasta, but I might find some decent packaged pasta in the cooler section—

Why I looked in the little rear-view mirror, I don't know. I hadn't gotten into that habit yet, just now mastering the basics. Something caught my eye.

Bearing down on me was a huge pickup. The hair rose on the back of my neck. Jeez, the creep wasn't slowing at all. In fact—

I couldn't see clearly in the mirror, and threw a quick glance back.

Oh my god! It was Benson! Shit shit shit!

The change in position when I'd looked back threw the bike off center. When I raunched down on the accelerator grip it wobbled more, then straightened out as I picked up speed.

Benson stayed right behind me.

I turned sharp at the first corner, a parking lane leading to the supermarket entrance. Benson didn't make the corner, but I heard the squeal of brakes. Another quick glance back. He'd finished backing up and beginning his swing into the long aisle behind me. I'd never outrun him to the end.

What the hell could I do now?

Fear tasted metallic in the back of my throat. I raced down the lane in a panic. I had to calm the furious roar of my heart, calm my mind. I couldn't think like this. I had no time. No time.

The lane ended at the entrance of the store, directly in front of a series of double swinging glass doors. I had to slow for the turn. The back of my neck tingled: Benson, crawling up my back. A swift look over my shoulder.

Rage twisted Benson's face into a monster's mask, inhuman and evil. He was so close. Too close for me to slow down. I'd known I couldn't outrun him. Somehow, I knew what I had to do. If I'd thought about it, no way could I have done it. I just did it.

I threw one leg over the bench, like dismounting a horse, and laid the bike down, climbing on top of the moving chassis to ride it out as best as I could. Screeching metal under me shocked the nerve center in my brain. Sparks flew behind the skidding bike in a rooster tail. The world rushed by in slow motion. Somewhere in my head a voice cried out. The doors! The doors! I tucked into a ball, protecting my face.

Benson's truck hit the glass wall before I did, his greater momentum carrying him past me, striking the doors on my right. Safety glass and pieces of metal posts rained around me as I hit the doors in my path. The bike shuddered but barely slowed, swinging off abruptly at a new angle from the impact. Thrown off the bike, I rolled and rolled again until I fetched up against a solid wall to lie amidst the shattered glass, stunned and still.

I heard crashes, thuds, and more tinkling glass. Then shrill screams mingled with male voices shouting in the distance. Dreading the havoc and the possible injury to innocent bystanders, I turned and tried to push up with my arms. My head whirled. Pain came from somewhere, mostly my head. This was not good.

Glass crunched nearby. "You bitch! You ruined everything!"

Oh, no. Not again. Benson stood ten or so feet away, pointing a gun at me. Behind him I could see his truck, the door gaping and front fender crumpled against the large display case directly across from the entrance, radiator steaming. "Jesus, Benson, I never did a damn thing to you!"

"Like hell you didn't!" The man looked demented. Definitely scary, with blood running down his face and the whites of his eyes showing all around his pupils.

His mouth twisted, sneering. "Sticking your fucking nose where it don't belong. Taking goddamned pictures. Fuck! Nobody connects me to the money and the casino like that. Nobody! Then Jules whacks that lady—"

I gasped, fury and pain pushing me beyond reason. "How dare you blame me for Gwen's death!"

The gun exploded. Sound struck like a fist. I flinched and shook, prey staring down the barrel of death.

"Shut the fuck up!" Benson bellowed. Insanity blazed from his wild eyes, spittle ran down his chin.

Oh God, oh God. Whimpering inside, I frantically sought help. Beyond the immediate wreckage of the doors and the truck lay my motorcycle, littered with packages of toilet paper from the endcap where it'd come to rest. A few anxious faces peeked out here and there, but no heroes appeared likely. I couldn't blame them. I was on my own.

Benson's triad gathered steam. "She didn't even have the goddamned picture! And you! You could've fucking delivered the goods, but noooo. You had to blackmail me!" An incredulous expression rippled across his face.

"Blackmail me," he muttered as if stuck there, swiping at the blood running down his forehead. The gun dropped to his side as he looked at his red-smeared hand.

I spotted a length of broken metal frame near my waist.

Then the snarling mask of rage returned as Benson's insane eyes found me once more. "Should'da shot the both of you's that night. Now everything's gone to shit. Cops on my ass, a trigger's got me marked, my family's turned on me." The gun rose in his hand. "I'm ruined, you fucking bitch, and by God you're gonna pay!"

Hopeless, helpless, maybe so—but I couldn't just lie there, waiting for it. I lunged for the metal strip, trying to get my feet under me. The gun roared again, a bullet splatting against the floor where my head had been. One shot, two, three they blended into a seamless roll of thunder.

I came up swinging, the five-foot metal shaft locked in a death grip of deadly intent. At first I thought I'd connected, but I felt no impact. Benson staggered back several feet and wavered, a red stain blooming mid-chest, mouth working like a guppy as he stared beyond me. His arms fell noodle-loose, the gun clattering to the tile floor.

My eyes whipped around to the entrance. Standing between the broken slabs of glass stood Abernathy, my young, fresh-faced former guard standing in a police squat, double fisting his gun that still pointed at Benson.

He didn't look so tourist-like now, his face hard, his eyes cold, deadly. I gulped. Had I ever misjudged him!

Benson collapsed to the floor and never stirred again. "You all right, Ms. Hannon?" Abernathy asked, kicking aside Benson's gun and checking his...his body. I'd seen too damn many bodies lately.

I could barely hear Abernathy's question. "Yes, I'm fine. Just fine," I said and waited, propped upright by the wall and the metal strip, fading in and out as my hearing improved and the terror leached out of my system.

A few sirens screeched to a halt nearby. Uniformed people rolled in, took care of business. Then McInnaw appeared, flicking glances my way as he spoke to Abernathy. McInnaw sauntered over, his customary sneer a little less pronounced. "Ms. Hannon."

"Detective." My mind had started to function again, too. "So, you couldn't spare Abernathy, hmmm?"

His lips twitched. "Well, I believe I said I needed to reassign him."

"Yeah, right. Reassigned to a trap—with me as bait. A little risky, wasn't it?"

"Sergeant Abernathy is very good."

Yes, and if Benson had been less talk and more action, I'd be dead, but I couldn't work up enough indignation to fight over it. Besides, I was still standing. Barely. "He is. He saved my life. I owe him an apology. I seriously underestimated that young man."

McInnaw cleared his throat, pointedly glanced at my metal prop. "He's not the only one who's been underestimated. You, ah, seem to have an amazing capacity to surprise everyone."

My goodness, was that a compliment from Mr. Hardcore Cynic? I said something innocuous, growing more tired and depressed by the second, as if my subconscious recognized the danger was over, and my reserves were melting away.

I needed to rest. I needed to get on with my life. "Look, I need my home back. Are you done trashing my RV yet?"

A real smile tugged his lips wide for a quick flash of white against his leathery dark skin. Wow. Another stunning sign of humanity. "Oh, I don't think we'll keep it much longer, Ms. Hannon. I'll give the lab a call." He tipped his head in a genteel salute, and left.

Abernathy found me a place to sit in a quiet, cool office. As I waited to give my statement, I tried to regroup. I could understand the tired; who wouldn't be bone tired after all this? The depression, though, was more than the emotional letdown after a crisis. I'd had plenty of crises in my life.

This was heart-clenching depression, the kind that comes from love gone bad. I replayed Trent's words spoken only hours before, that he'd join me in Napa Valley, that we weren't ending a relationship, but just beginning one, and I wanted to believe. I really wanted to believe.

Want didn't seem to matter. I felt like the relationship was over, so how could I believe in a beginning?

I was so messed up!

Riding back to the park with Abernathy, I resolved to simply go with whatever happened. We still had these last few hours together. Perhaps later we'd have many more hours together. Maybe a lifetime of hours.

I wouldn't waste a single one.

Chapter 26

A sad little group gathered in the open space in front of my newly cleaned RV late the next afternoon. Well, they didn't look sad. The sad was in me.

Roxie rubbed against Albert with a satisfied gleam in her eye. "Albert says we're going to head for Niagara Falls. We spent our honeymoon there over fifty years ago. He says it's about time we had another one there. Isn't that sweet?" She all but purred and batted her eyes up at her bemused mate.

Albert didn't say anything. He so seldom did. He tightened the arm around her shoulders and looked relieved. Very relieved.

Charlotte smiled. "That sounds lovely," she said in her soft gracious manner that was always a balm to my troubled nerves. "Just don't get carried away and go over the falls in one of those container things."

Erwin's laugh boomed out, causing a few heads to turn at the exuberant sound. The park bustled, people out walking, parking, or like me, getting ready to leave.

"Do they still let you do that?" He asked. "Might try it myself."

"Oh, I'd love to see that," I teased him. "It would be my revenge for being carted around under your arm like a darned football."

If Erwin's black skin could have shown a blush, I'd bet he'd glow. He shuffled and threw Trent a rueful grin. "Well, I just caught the pass and ran with it."

"Humph! At least you didn't drop me," I allowed. After all, he and Trent thought they were rescuing me from a bomb. "But did you have to squish me while you were doing it?"

I saw his eyes dance and he started to speak, but I beat him to it. "And don't give me some line about how you thought it was a squeeze play."

Everyone joined in the laughter.

"She's got you there, old son," Tremaine teased his partner. Erwin sucked it up, grinning all the while.

I'll miss them. Many fulltimers have told me how they often met the same people in their travels. I hoped I'd see much more of these special friends. Leaving them was hard. Already I'd found a major downside to a transitory lifestyle.

A few spaces down and across from mine, a loud angry curse caught our attention, just before the breeze hit.

"Phew!" Erwin said, fanning a hand in front of his face. "What the hell is that?"

"Martha! Get out here!" Richard screamed for his wife and continued cursing at a steady pace. The air vent on top of the coach poured forth the vile sludge that flowed over the roof and down the side. "Martha!"

Tremaine's cultured drawl encompassed our group. "Looks like The Jerk still can't remember which lever dumps his tanks."

Martha hurried over to placate her vitriolic husband.

Leaving behind a neighbor like that was one upside to the transitory lifestyle.

"On that note...." I began, and we hurried up our goodbyes. Everyone dispersed, except Trent.

He caught my hand and drew us back from the street. I led him into my motorhome. I hated this moment. I never had gotten my defenses constructed and now I felt raw. A

271

long drive awaited me and Trent knew it, but even with the time constraint, this goodbye was hard.

Obviously, Trent felt the same way. He didn't hesitate. He wrapped his arms around me, holding me so we could touch and still talk. "Tell me, Lotsi. Is it that you don't believe I'll show up in Napa, or that you don't want me to show up? Be honest, love. I'm a big boy. I want the truth, not platitudes."

Emotions hit me from every direction. Desire, hope, joy, love, loneliness, grief, fear. Lots of fear. My heart beat on hummingbird wings and my chest tightened. I wanted to absorb him inside me. I wanted to run.

Mostly I wanted a crystal ball.

"I-I want you more than anything. I do. I want you so much it...it terrifies me. There'd be nothing...left if—" My voice ended on a thread, strained and hoarse. I swallowed. Scrambling for distance, I ordered my dry lips to smile. "But no pressure. I know sometimes things happen." I blinked rapidly. Looked away.

"Hey." Trent pulled me tighter against his chest. His hands soothed up and down my back and sides, his head pressed against mine. "So you don't think I'll show. Shhh. Be still. We'll deal with it. Not to worry. In fact, that's the problem. You worry too much. Stop worrying."

I choked on a laugh. "Yeah. I'll do that."

The lips at my forehead curved. "I'm serious." He drew back to catch my eyes, studying them for a long moment. "You know I love you?"

I dropped my gaze.

"Lotsi?"

"I know it feels like you love me," I whispered. "For now."

"Ahhhh." His hand tucked my hair behind an ear then lifted my chin. "I will meet you in Napa Valley as soon as I can, Lotsimina Hannon. You can trust me on that, but I guess you'll just have to learn that for yourself, won't you?"

Those dark Ghirardelli eyes were so serious, so full of patience and understanding. How could anyone doubt this man? His deep understanding of my buried fears eased a place inside, allowed me to accept that part of myself, too. I realized how much I had come to believe in him, to trust in him, and because I could believe in him, I could believe in us.

My hands cupped his face and I rose to meet his lips. I poured myself into the kiss. If I could, I would have inhaled his essence along with his taste, his scent.

He matched my hunger, our hands roaming freely, seeking to memorize for the last time the feel of that curve, this shape. I wanted to take more than memories of him with me. I wanted his body to brand me, and I sure as hell wanted to brand him. Mine!

Feeling his erection pressing against my hip, I adjusted, capturing it in the notch of my legs, rubbing it with my aching clit. What will I do without this delicious torment? Without Trent? God help me. As if to hold back the yawning emptiness, need exploded into wildfire, driving me to impale myself on him as I became lost in the raging hunger of my body.

Trent brought us back, his hands gentling, his voice soothing. "Lotsi-love. Easy now."

When I could focus, I realized Trent's shoulders leaned against the wall and my legs hooked around his waist. Heat radiated from our bodies, fine tremors echoed back and forth between us. I pressed my face into the crook of his neck and released my legs, leaning into him for support. I was totally wrecked.

"How'd that happen?" I managed, and felt his laugh shake my body. Yeah, very funny, I thought, but didn't move until he shifted and moved away.

So I tucked the sight of Trent away, deep inside me. Any time I want, I'll pull out that vision of his sexy smiling face, gently touched by years but deeply marked by his inner strength and good nature. I'll remember his silky gray locks, the feel of them in my hands, against my skin. Remember especially his body. That beautiful, talented body I crave more than chocolate.

Chocolate, like his eyes. I'll never get enough of his eyes, the way he turns that intensity on, opens a door and draws me in. Everything he is, everything I love, resides in those eyes.

Two weeks. I'd only known him two weeks. Now I'll be without him for two weeks. Both spans of time seem a lifetime. I'd survived one. Yet the burn left from the last few mindless moments against the wall makes me wonder if I'll survive the other. Guess I'll find out.

A few minutes later I pull out of the park and head south for I-15 to Bakersfield and on toward San Francisco, another odd GPS-chosen route instead of north through Reno. Thank goodness, this way is smooth freeway, because I can't concentrate on driving and have no interest in sightseeing.

The empty hole left by Gwen's death gapes like a wound. This is the first time I've been alone, and as the miles tick by, grief percolates and bubbles and drips down my face.

I tell Gwen how much I miss her. I feel a little silly, but I tell her about Benson—she already knows all this, right?—but I tell her how glad I am the bastard is on her side now; she can settle his hash for herself. Frankly, I figure he is happy he's dead because she can't kill him twice. Maybe she'll find a way.

We have a long talk about Trent. I swear I see her in the passenger seat, nodding her head and giving me advice. Good advice, too. She tells me to chill out and let our relationship grow. She tells me to trust him.

That's what I'm going to do. I'll be at Bianca's birthday tomorrow as I had promised. In the next few weeks, I'll begin to know my daughter and granddaughter like never before. Heck, even my son-in-law.

Trent will be there by then, and by God, I'll get to know him, too. Really know him. After all, I reason, I still have these superhormones to deal with. I grin, enjoying the tingling sensations from just thinking about those rambunctious darlings.

Since that feels like more, I think about the magic Trent says he has placed in me and how he had used it, which undoubtedly accounts for these other delicious sensations growing hotter by the second.

Yes, indeedy. On a roll here. Fast becoming my personal favorite, there's the oh-so-hot sexual favors. Don't I still owe him some? Surely, I owe him some. Maybe...yeah, that'll work. He owes me! Certain favors come to mind. My breasts ache. Blood throbs through my sex and moisture gathers. I wiggle on the oversized leather driver's seat.

Oh, boy. That's about enough of that, at least while I'm tooling down the road.

However, by now I am feeling much better, and waiting a week or two for Trent doesn't seem impossible, it seems exciting. I'll think of a whole list of favors he'll owe me. I can't wait to get started. That reminds me of a particular song that fits the moment. Maybe I still have it around. I dig in the CD box. Ah ha!

I check the tracks, then pop in the CD and skip forward to the one I want. In a few moments, I join the rusty-voiced cowboy in a rousing tune about being on the road, and I sing it loud and strong, my spirits lifting with each upbeat note until I feel exhilarated. Triumphant.

Sometimes life is not only good, it's fun. Red Hot Ladies know we aren't done with life's highways. We deal with what comes our way and go on, and we strive do it with a sense of style and just plain fun.

All my adversities take a backseat for the moment. I'm on a fun break. Goodness knows getting here hasn't been a picnic, but somehow that makes it more important, and more precious to enjoy the fun breaks when I can.

Gwen understood that years ago. That's why she wanted to take her Hot Ladies on the road with her. As easy as that, the lyrics and the insights combine and Gwen's dream becomes my own.

I even have the name. Crimson Cruisers.

Trent would be with me then. We'd meet annually at some nice RV Park, Hot Ladies and spouses and those just interested. We'd catch up with old friends and meet the new, have some games and events, celebrate life and fun—and being on the road again.

Would you like that, Gwen?

She smiles, gives a cool thumbs up and says, "You go girl!"

Oh, yeah. I slap in a new CD, jack up the sound and settle in for some serious cruising.